ACCLAIM FOR STEADMAN'S BLIND

WHAT READERS ARE SAYING...

"Just like *Nocturne In Ashes*, I found *Steadman's Blind* a one session page-turner and gave it five Amazon stars."
~ Ron Keeler, Read 4 Fun

"Ms. Chase's second novel is just as unputdownable as the first one was. I got lost in the book and the world the author created, transported to another place and time."
~ Gabi Rosetti (reader, Amazon.com)

"Author Joslyn Chase has now confirmed my first impressions of her being a formidable suspense writer bound to make readers sit up and take notice."
~ Manie Kilian (reader, Amazon.com)

"As always in her writing, the settings and action scenes are vividly portrayed and the relationships between the characters are seamless and authentic. Ms Chase has a talent for bringing characters to life."
~ ReadnGrow (Amazon.com)

GET YOUR NEXT JOSLYN CHASE BOOK FREE!

But catch up on your sleep now.
Once you start reading,
it'll be *No Rest* for you!

Get the book free when you join
the growing group of readers who've discovered
the thrill of Chase!

Get started now at joslynchase.com
OR
simply scan the QR code

STEADMAN'S BLIND

ALSO BY JOSLYN CHASE

STEADMAN'S BLIND

AN EXPLOSIVE ADVENTURE BRIMMING WITH PERIL AND SUSPENSE

JOSLYN CHASE

PARAQUEL PRESS

Steadman's Blind

Paraquel Press print edition October 2023, Paraquel Press ebook edition October 2023

Copyright © 2019 by Joslyn Chase

Published by Paraquel Press

All rights reserved.

https://paraquelpress.mailerpage.com/

ISBN: 978-1-952647-27-7 (paperback) 978-1-952647-26-0 (ebook)

Thank you.

CONTENTS

A NOTE FROM THE AUTHOR

THIS BOOK IS NOT a prequel, or a sequel. This story runs parallel to my thriller, *Nocturne In Ashes*, taking place in the same time period and setting, and sharing some of the same characters.

That's why I'm calling it a paraquel.

Each book can certainly be read as a stand-alone, but the two stories intertwine in a few spots, and if you've read one of them, I think you'll enjoy experiencing the crossover when you read the sister book.

Here's how one Amazon reviewer put it:

"Having read and thoroughly enjoyed *Nocturne in Ashes* by the same author, I really looked forward to reading this book, *Steadman's Blind*, as well.

Set in the same milieu as *Nocturne in Ashes and* having the eruption of Mount Rainier as a pivotal point in both books, I was rather curious as to how the author, Joslyn Chase, was going to prevent a huge overlap in the two mentioned thrillers.

I need not have worried.

Except for two chapters that simply touched on the events in *Nocturne in Ashes, Steadman's Blind* is a completely separate, standalone thriller and even more of a suspenseful, compelling read that just about thrilled me to bits.

The interaction between Chief Randall Steadman and Detective Cory Frost is especially insightful, leaving no doubt in my mind that I would love to read a whole lot more of these two characters in future."

To give you a better idea of how the two stories build on and relate to each other, consider this:

If you've already read the suspense-packed *Nocturne In Ashes*, you know that it took Chief Steadman and his partner, Detective Frost, three days to reach the scene of the crimes occurring in *Nocturne.*

When you read this book, you'll know why.

PROLOGUE

FIFTY-EIGHT MILES SOUTH OF Seattle, Mt. Rainier rises to meet the clouds. Reigning queen of the landscape, she symbolizes the pristine beauty of the Pacific Northwest, robed in emerald, and crowned with diamond-sparkling snow, the graceful sweep of her slopes soaring up to draw the eye and gladden the heart.

But the benevolent appearance of the mountain masks a deadly and volatile might.

Within the reach of that power, communities nestle. Secure in the belief that life today will continue as it did yesterday, and the day before, and for so many days before that, people build houses, elect officials, establish commerce, and do all manner of things to create a haven for themselves and their loved ones.

While deep below Rainier's surface, a river of molten rock pushes up against the stratified layers, fracturing the bed of stone into splinters and sending tremors through the mountain and surrounding areas.

For thousands of years, torrents of rain and melting snow have mixed with sulphuric acid, seeping into the rock, altering it into a crumbling clay-like substance, unstable and susceptible to landslides.

Fifty-six hundred years ago, Rainier's eastern flank blew sky high in the great Osceola mudslide, covering 212 square miles in a thick, acidic sludge, obliterating every living thing.

Now her western side is primed to go.

Early in the summer, the volcano woke like a fussy baby after a long nap, burping and bawling, grabbing everyone's attention, and mobilizing politicians, the media, and emergency response teams to prepare for a major catastrophe.

For months, regal Rainier has entertained her surrounding human subjects like an eccentric hostess at a cocktail party. Trembling, grumbling, puffing smoke—fierce and lively one moment, silent and sulking the next.

In her shadow, life continues. People sleep through the night, get up, and go to work. Families argue, play, walk the dog, and love each other.

Like the story of the boy who cried wolf, people find it easier and easier to ignore Rainier's dramatics as everyday life reclaims them.

Politicians give in to pressure from loggers and business owners losing revenue due to road closures.

Government agencies run out of money for maintaining watches and road blocks. Life in Seattle and surrounding communities returns to business as usual.

Only a handful of scientists and researchers remain vigilant and concerned.

They gauge the tremors beneath her, noticing how her shape is changing, like the burgeoning of a woman preparing to give birth. She is distending under the building pressure within, equalized only by the yards-thick layer of snowpack pressing down from without.

They worry that the icy shell is cracking, destabilized by the earthquakes and the heat of the magma as it travels up into the throat of the volcano.

They fear that a few degrees more, and the coat of snow will slide down the mountainside like butter off a hotcake, triggering an avalanche of unparalleled proportions.

They know what will happen next.

The enormous weight rolling off Rainier's western shoulder will allow the inexorable pressure of gas and hot stone to spurt forth, uncontained, blowing aside the weak, altered rock in a savage eruption with a power 7500 times greater than the atomic blast at Hiroshima.

A poisonous plume of ash and gas will rise into a hideously exaggerated mushroom cloud extending miles into the sky, where the negatively charged ash will clash violently with the positively charged gas to spawn a hellish network of lightning bolts and streaking balls of fire.

It will be the deadliest day in American history—ending lives, changing lives, reminding people how precious life is.

And how precarious.

Chapter 1

Chief Deputy Randall Steadman set his jaw and ground his teeth together. Fear wrestled against frustration somewhere behind his belt buckle, stirring up a queasy tightness in his gut.

For miles in front of him, traffic inched forward on streets crammed to capacity, allowing him to experience the full joys of a Portland rush hour, complete with rude hand gestures, honking horns, and blaring car stereos.

He itched to flip on the light bar and clear a path, but he wasn't behind the wheel of his service vehicle, and he was out of uniform and out of his jurisdiction. He'd made the three-hour drive south after a frantic phone call from his sister.

A phone call that left him cold.

Nan was a pretty put-together gal. Whatever happened down here in Oregon had spooked her good and that scared Steadman.

He'd relied on his big sister for most of his life, and now it was plain she was relying on him. For reasons that went deep—beyond standard sibling solidarity—he could not let her down.

The late summer sun beat down through the windshield of his car, canceling out the efforts of his air conditioner, and the engine temperature gauge was creeping higher than he liked to see.

He switched off the AC and powered down the windows, resigned to suffering through until traffic picked up again. According to the GPS, he only had two-and-a-half miles to go before he reached the hospital.

The hospital.

Nan hadn't told him why she'd chosen that as their meeting place and she hadn't left him time to ask, but Steadman knew it couldn't be good. He dreaded what he might find when he got there.

A sudden gust of diesel fumes from a truck up ahead permeated the air and Steadman felt like he might suffocate—from the smell, from the heat, from the anxious stone that pressed down inside his chest.

Whatever this was, whatever tragedy Nan faced, it surely couldn't be as bad as his gut was making it out to be.

Could it?

The red light blinked to green, and Steadman let off the brake, moving forward enough to get a slight breeze across his sweaty brow. Another ten minutes and the robotic GPS voice let him know he was arriving at his destination.

He pulled into the first parking spot he came across, not caring how far he had to walk. He needed that time to decompress and prepare.

Nan had texted him a room number. After checking in at the front desk, he caught the elevator up to the third floor and passed a nurse's station where a solitary head bent over a stack of medical files.

The hallway was deserted. Only the smell of rubbing alcohol lingered there, following him as he made his way down the corridor to stop outside room 324.

He took a deep breath and let it trickle out, readying himself to push open that door and be strong for his sister.

But before he could reach out a hand, the door swept inward, and Steadman was staring at two cops in uniform. They hesitated, looking him over, and Steadman knew what they were thinking. It was all the things he would be thinking.

The way you get after years on the job.

Nan pushed between them and folded Steadman in a tight embrace.

"I knew you'd get here quick," she said.

He pulled away enough to look her in the face. A reddened lump swelled beside her right temple, and the eye was shadowed by bruises, black turning purple.

"What happened?" he asked. "Were you in a car accident? Is Hank okay?"

Steadman looked beyond her to the hospital bed, swathed in sheets and shadows. The sleeping form was her husband, Hank, and Steadman got a quick impression of tubes.

Lots of tubes.

Nan closed her teeth over her upper lip in that bulldog way she had and Steadman saw a pleading look in her eyes before her gaze dropped away. He noticed she was shivering.

"This is my brother, Chief Deputy Randall Steadman," she told the policemen. "He drove down from the Seattle area."

Steadman shook their hands, and they exchanged professional courtesies before he turned back to Nan and lifted his fingers to her damaged cheek.

"What happened?" he repeated.

There was a pause before she answered. "It wasn't a car accident," she said. "We were attacked."

"Attacked? What—"

"I'm sorry, Rand." She staggered under his grip and raised a shaky hand to her throat. "I really need some coffee and something to eat."

She turned to the officers. "If there's nothing else you need from me, I think I'll go to the cafeteria."

"Of course, Mrs. Meninger. We'll be in touch."

They nodded their goodbyes and left. Nan clutched Steadman's arm as she watched the policemen stride down the corridor.

He felt her tremble like a sapling in a windstorm, but she didn't speak until the men stopped at the elevator and punched the call button.

"I'll go get my purse," she whispered. "We need to talk."

Chapter 2

Nan's cup of coffee sat untouched on the table in front of her, the rising tendrils of vapor waning as it grew cold. Steadman watched her face, the leaden lump in his stomach growing with each moment that passed.

She was tough, his sister, and the bones of her skull stood out under pallid skin like a Mt. Rushmore monument, solid and unmoving. But there was fear in her eyes, tinged with despair.

That alarmed him, and the swelling at her temple and blackened eye sent anger swirling through his growing sense of dread.

"Tell me what happened, Nan," he prompted. "When, where, and—if possible—who."

A wash of color came into her face, and he was relieved to see there was still some spirit left in her.

"Oh, I know who well enough," she said, her voice shot through with acid. "They made no effort to disguise themselves."

"Did you tell the police?"

She pressed her lips together, blanching them white. Her nostrils flared as she drew a breath through her nose. "I did not."

The heavy lump in his gut sank. "What's going on, Nan? I guess you've got a lot to tell me, but first I want to know about Hank. How bad is it?"

She closed her eyes, face twisting as she wrestled her emotions. Steadman covered her shaking hand with his own and waited.

Almost a minute passed before she swallowed hard and opened her mouth to speak.

"They kicked him. Two vicious bastards taking turns with their heavy boots."

Her voice went squeaky, and she paused, taking a deep breath. "He's got four cracked ribs, a broken arm, a broken nose, and a ruptured spleen. He lost three teeth, and his face is unrecognizable. He'll never again be the pretty boy I married."

Steadman squeezed her hand. Bad as it was, he had feared worse. "Well, Nan," he said, hoping to lighten the mood, "that ship sailed a long time ago."

She gave him a weak smile. "Don't I know it. But—" A little sob escaped her lips, and she bit down hard, staunching the flow. "I love him so much, Rand."

"I know, Sis. I know."

A loud clatter reverberated through the room as an attendant deposited a load of clean trays into a rack at the head of the cafeteria line. Steadman watched an elderly couple pry one from the top of the stack and begin working their shaky way along the path of options, consulting each other with every choice.

Hank and Nan would grow old together like that—sweet to each other, caring, united.

He turned his gaze back to Nan. "Hank will be okay, then. His prognosis is good, right?"

Her lips thinned to a grim line and again he saw that spark of color come into her face.

"He'll survive. Until they come for him again."

"Why would they do that, Nan? Who are these guys?"

"They're sharks."

Steadman wasn't sure how to take that remark. Was it a reference to the cold and brutal nature of Hank's attackers, or was she telling him their profession?

"You mean, like loan sharks?" he ventured.

5

She nodded. "Yes, and worse. I'm not sure what all they're into, but they're bad news."

"How on earth did Hank get mixed up with them?"

She sighed. "You know Ronnie's in his second year at MIT."

Steadman stared at her. "Hank borrowed college funds from a loan shark?"

She leveled that big sister glare at him across the table. "He's not stupid, Rand. It didn't happen like you think. Hank got sucked in, little by little, by pros who knew just where to put the pressure."

Despite the anxiety that gnawed at his gut, Steadman admired Nan for standing by her man. They might be going down, but they were going down together.

He hoped he could find a way to throw them a lifeline.

"Start at the beginning, Nan," he said, trying to keep his voice free from any trace of judgment, "and put me in the picture."

She canted her lower lip and blew out a frustrated sigh that reached her bangs, fluttering them as it passed.

"As you know, Hank's a night manager at the Hilton. In the course of his business, he became aware that these guys were running an illegal high-stakes poker game from their hotel suite. Their leader is a man called Abe Lizardo. He offered Hank a thousand dollars to look the other way."

She broke off, swirls of red staining her cheeks.

"It sounds terrible, the way I put it." A pleading note crept into her voice. "But you've got to understand there was a lot going on for us. We were squeezed pretty tight with no room to breathe or see our way clear. Car broke down, late on the mortgage, bills coming due, and time to pay another round of tuition. College costs more than a house, these days. Hank thought it would be a onetime deal. He let it slide."

Steadman saw all too clearly where this was going. It was like letting the camel put one foot inside the tent. Pretty soon you've got the whole animal on your lap and you're drowning in sand.

"I can see the wheels churning inside your head, Rand, and whatever you're thinking, it's probably not far off the mark. The games continued, the payouts got bigger, and by the time Hank realized how deep he was in, he couldn't get out. He was complicit. So when they stopped paying him there was nothing he could do about it. They had him by the balls."

Steadman grimaced. "Ouch. So why'd they beat him up? Did he end up ratting them out?"

Nan clenched her fists on the table in front of her, nearly spilling the cup of congealing coffee.

"I only wish he had. No, we'd come to count on that extra money, and when they stopped paying for Hank's silence, it hurt. But Abe wasn't finished with Hank. He brought him into his fancy suite, buttered him up, told him the hush money had stopped because he was one of them now, part of the team, and he was welcome at the table. They'd even stake him the first game."

Steadman groaned. "You've got to be kidding. What the hell was he thinking, Nan?"

She scowled at him, her teeth going up over her lip in that classic Nan expression of stubborn annoyance.

"You don't know these guys. They're urbane and charismatic. Car salesman types that can convince you they're your best pal while they're sizing you up for a coffin. Hank figured it wouldn't hurt to play that first game, with their money. He cleaned up, too. Brought home a pile, that night."

Steadman snorted. "Naturally, Nan. That's how it's done. He was hooked, right?"

She sighed. "By the nose. They sucked him dry, and then some." She rubbed at a spot on her forehead with two shaking fingers. "We're putting the house on the market and hoping it sells before they come back to break Hank's legs."

"Oh heavens, Nan," Steadman felt a vein of cold misery spreading through him. "Why didn't you tell the police?"

She gave him a pointed look. "That's the first thing they warned us about. Told us they had police protection, key officers on the payroll, and it would only go harder on us if we squealed."

Steadman swallowed and tossed through his mental inventory for some way to bring her comfort.

"They're not going to hurt you so bad you can't cough up the money. They want you operational, Nan. It sounds like they're giving you some sort of deadline?"

"Six weeks. They said if we didn't pay up in six weeks, Hank's a dead man."

He patted her hand. "They're not going to kill him, Sis. That's just to scare you."

Her face crumpled, and she bit her lip, silent tears spilling from her reddened eyes. She brushed them off and stared across the table at Steadman, her jaw hardening.

"Jeb Openshaw, the man Hank replaced at the hotel—he died in a hit-and-run accident. A newspaper clipping about the incident was left in an envelope on Hank's desk. If they don't get their money, they cut their losses and make an example."

Steadman saw the shudder that ran through her. He moved his chair next to hers and wrapped his arms around her, rocking her, wondering what the hell his next move should be. After a few moments, she pulled away and smoothed the hair back from her face, sitting taller in her chair, chin lifted.

"I spent a lot of time thinking," she said. "While Hank was in surgery, while I waited beside his broken body for you to arrive." She speared Steadman with her big sister gaze.

"And I came up with a plan."

CHAPTER 3

NEWLY CHRISTENED DETECTIVE CORY Frost tried balancing his breakfast in one hand while pulling open the door to the training room with the other.

The two slabs of peanut butter toast were no problem, held firmly together, face to face, and wrapped in a paper towel. And the pint of chocolate milk rested firmly against his wrist.

It was the orange that defeated him.

He lost his grip on the soft-ball-sized fruit, and it bounced, then rolled into the path of a sergeant in a hurry who kicked it back in Frost's direction.

"Sorry about that," Frost mumbled, bending down to retrieve the orange.

The notebook tucked beneath his elbow slid down the side of his uniform trousers and splayed open on the floor. He sighed. Picking it up, he used it as a tray and arranged the breakfast items on top, except for the orange, which he tried to cram into the pocket of his jacket.

Again, it escaped him, but he managed to scoop it from the air before it hit the floor, bringing him into a crouching position like a catcher at home plate.

Before he could rise, a shapely pair of ankles appeared in front of his face.

"That's some impressive juggling, Detective. Do you do birthday parties?"

He stood, feeling his face go hot. The uniformed woman regarding him with an expression half scorn, half amusement, was a heart-stopper. Glowing cocoa complexion, glossy dark hair cascading in a smooth sweep over a perfect brow, lips a cover girl would kill for.

Frost stared.

The woman raised an eyebrow. "I'll hold the door for you," she said, reaching for the handle, "but I get half the orange."

Frost froze like a deer in the headlights. Not a single clever response came to him, but he was saved from saying something stupid when the door burst open, nearly knocking them down, and Sheriff Polander glared at the both of them.

"Hurry it up, people. We're about to start."

Frost waggled his eyebrows, getting a grin in return. He held tight to his breakfast and stepped into the room after the woman, getting another glimpse of her stunning figure.

His heart sank when he saw the crowded tables with no two seats together. He'd started to imagine sharing his day—as well as his orange—with his captivating colleague, but they were forced apart, to opposite sides of the room.

He took a seat at the front table to the left of the podium and laid out his items, noticing that the woman was across the aisle and well behind him.

He hadn't seen her before, but he was brand new in the detective division and still had a lot of people to meet. In the brief moment he'd been with her, he noticed she wore no ring on her left hand and the name on her tag was longish and started with a J.

And she was gorgeous and witty and...

He crushed a mental boot down on these thoughts. He needed to reclaim his focus, get his head in the right place or he'd end up back in Patrol for another rotation. He'd worked hard for this promotion, and it jazzed him to be part of Investigations.

Opening his notebook, he wrote the date at the top of the page, ready to record the salient points of the training.

"Jamieson!"

The sheriff bellowed the name to the back rows. "Did Chief Deputy Steadman come over with you?"

"No, sir." Frost recognized her voice and turned in his seat.

Jamieson.

"He's on emergency leave," she continued. "Had a family issue down in Portland."

"Why am I just hearing about this now? He's supposed to give the potential hazard report."

"Yes sir, I know. He asked me to apologize, and he prepped me to do it."

"Is that right?"

The sheriff took a sip of coffee. "I want you here up front, then. Dooley," he gestured to Frost's table mate. "Trade places with Jamieson, if you would."

"Sure thing, Sheriff."

And just like that, Frost was sitting next to the most beautiful girl in the room, trying to listen and stay focused on the subject at hand. His peanut butter toast went untouched, cold and forgotten.

But he peeled the orange, keeping the skin intact, and laid a perfect half on top, sliding it in her direction like a supplicant's offering to his goddess.

CHAPTER 4

STEADMAN CHOKED ON A mouthful of lukewarm coffee, getting half of it down, spewing half of it back into the cup. He coughed, working to clear his throat so he could spit some words out, though he had no idea what he might say.

The suggestion his sister had just made was the most ridiculous thing he'd ever heard.

"There's no need to be so dramatic about it, Rand," she chided, handing him a napkin. "It's a pragmatic plan that has a good chance of working."

"In what universe?" Steadman asked, his head reeling. "I don't play poker, Nan."

"Yes, but how hard can it be?" she countered. "For you, I mean. You're trained to observe and interpret body language. You know when people are lying, all the little things they do to give themselves away. Nobody can bluff you."

He stared at her. "Nan, this isn't television. Poker is a whole different world—and listen carefully because here's the important part—I don't play it. I barely know a full house from a straight flush."

"But you can learn. You live right around the corner from that big casino. You can do some research on the internet and practice the skills at your friendly neighborhood poker tables."

"For Pete's sake, woman—have you gone insane?"

Steadman felt a pressure building inside his chest. He took a deep breath and let it roll out of him, rubbing the muscles at the back of his neck in an effort to relax.

"Nan, I understand you're upset and worried, and you have every right to be. You're looking for solutions to what feels like an insurmountable problem. I get that. But this plan sounds like a recipe for even more trouble. I can't believe—"

"Rand, just shut up for a minute. I told myself all these same things while I sat in a cold, hard hospital chair waiting for my husband to come out of surgery after being beaten within an inch of his life. These are very bad men, playing a whole lot of angles, and the only way to escape this is to beat them at their own game—and that's poker."

Steadman sighed and dropped his head to rest in the palm of his hand. How did she still have this ability to reduce him to younger brother status, reminding him she was in charge?

"It takes money, Nan, to win at poker," he pointed out. "And we don't have any."

She was nodding. "I know. I had mom's jewelry appraised when this whole mess started. I hoped I wouldn't have to sell, but I can get close to six thousand dollars for it. You can take that to the local casino and parlay it into a bigger stake. Hank said the buy-in at Abe's table is ten thousand."

She really had been thinking about this, scrambling to cover all the bases.

"This'll be second nature to you, Rand," she continued. "I know it will. I heard you telling Hank about that non-verbal communication seminar you attended in San Diego. Four days, Rand. Four days of intensive training so you can read the unintentional signals people give off. If anyone can do this, it's you, little brother."

She dropped her hand over his and squeezed. "And you're the only one who cares about me enough to even try."

And there it was.

Nan going for the heart string, twanging away on familial duty, love, and the ever-powerful chord of guilt. They both knew she still held an ace up her sleeve, a card she could play with perfect assurance he'd comply. A card with Thad's name on it.

He wouldn't make her do that.

Reaching that deep into a painful memory would leave a gash in both of them that might never heal. He dug the palms of his hands into his eyes and rubbed, hardly believing the sentence that was forming on his lips.

"You sell mom's jewels, Nan, and I'll see what I can do about learning some poker."

As he spoke the words, he made a promise to himself as well. He'd do some digging behind the scenes.

There had to be another way around this problem.

CHAPTER 5

FROST KEPT HIS EYES forward, working to stay focused on Lieutenant Sharpton's report on search and rescue operations in the county. It was a lost cause.

The delicate scent of shampoo or shower gel, floral with a hint of spice, teased at him, reminding him how close she was. So close he could almost feel the radiance of her body heat.

He made notes and tried to formulate an intelligent question he might ask if the opportunity presented. The lieutenant pointed to lines on a chart and spouted figures Frost tried to pay attention to, but he couldn't help worrying about the golden half of the orange he'd peeled. It sat untasted on the curl of rind, slowly dessicating.

Like his ego.

She hadn't touched it, had only given him a glance and the faintest, fleeting smile as he'd passed it over. He stamped down on his disappointment and opened his chocolate milk, determined to appear as nonchalant as she did.

The lieutenant finished, and the sheriff motioned with his pen like a symphony conductor. "Jamieson. You're up!"

Rising gracefully from her chair, she rounded the table and turned to face the roomful of officers. She smiled and Frost's pulse ramped up, despite his best intentions.

"Thank you," she said. "Chief Deputy Steadman sends his regrets, and I'll do my best to cover the material like he would."

Her brow furrowed, and she took a few steps as if gathering her thoughts before addressing the room. When she spoke, her voice was clear and authoritative. Frost's admiration climbed another notch.

"We all know that the destruction and loss of life will be catastrophic if Rainier erupts. But Chief tells me it's not a matter of if—only when. And it could be any day now. He believes that, and he's got me convinced. Here's what we can expect."

Frost took another swig of his milk while she brought up a map of western Washington on the screen at the front of the room.

"Scientists predict an eruption will go sideways—blowing out the western flank of the mountain. Ash and gas will spurt as high as six miles into the sky, and we'll talk about that in a moment, but our first and biggest concern will be the mud."

"Really?" questioned a sergeant in the second row. "When I think volcano, I think lava, magma, balls of fire. You're saying mud is our primary concern?"

"There will be plenty of hazards vying for attention, Sergeant Givens," she said, leveling her gaze at the questioner, "but this mud is no joke. Thirty-five square miles of ice and snow sit atop Mt. Rainier. If a pyroclastic eruption hits that snowpack with a thousand degrees Fahrenheit, melting that snow and mixing it with clay, rock, ash, and debris, the potential devastation is unimaginable. That tidal wave of mud will grow in size, speed, and power, plowing down everything in its path and traveling up to forty miles an hour, with the consistency of wet concrete."

"Holy crap," said Givens. "I have a newfound respect for mud."

A titter of nervous laughter skittered among the lawmen.

"As you should," the beautiful lieutenant said, nodding. "And if you care to use the proper name for those rivers of mud—out of respect—they're called lahars."

She tapped on the map. "Situated as we are, on the opposite side of the inlets, the lahars are unlikely to reach us. However, we'll feel their effects in profound ways."

Jamieson advanced the image on the screen, flashing through photos of utter destruction to illustrate her next points.

"That wall of mud—carrying the wreckage of trees, bridges, buildings, cars, and all manner of debris—will slam into the Point of Tacoma and will likely travel down the Nisqually valley as well, spilling into the Reach. When it hits our waterways, it will force our water to go elsewhere and we'll have flooding of disastrous proportions, cutting off transportation routes and disrupting power and communications."

"Sounds like it will set us back a hundred years in the space of a couple seconds," shouted someone from the back.

"It may do exactly that," Jamieson said. "We're used to ease and convenience, but if this catastrophe happens, it will rock our little corner of the world."

Frost felt a niggle of misgiving. Could something this momentous really happen here and now? It seemed unreal, but harsh things had happened in his life before and he was under no illusions about them happening again.

"What about the ash?" asked the sheriff. "I was a kid when Mount St. Helens blew and I remember ash raining down for weeks afterward, suffocating people, caving in roofs, clogging jet engines, making it cold and dark and causing all sorts of trouble."

"Absolutely," Jamieson agreed. "Ash is a big problem, but the degree to which it affects us will depend on the direction of the wind. If it's blowing our way, we can expect greatly reduced visibility and air quality. Everyone should be stocking filter masks as well as all the usual emergency prep items."

"Both Home Depot and Lowes are sold out," said a sergeant from the table behind Frost.

"That's your typical good news/bad news situation," the sheriff said. "The good news is people are paying attention and stocking up. The bad news is—you're going to choke, sergeant."

Another scattering of laughter echoed in the room and the sheriff stood. "Anything else for us, Jamieson?"

"No sir, except to say I hope everyone will take this matter seriously."

"Thank you, Lieutenant. All right," he said, glancing at his wristwatch, "let's take a ten-minute break. Back in your seats by half past."

People rose and started moving around the room, chatting and stretching. Frost stayed where he was, thinking about his mother, deciding he'd check on her after work and make sure she had emergency provisions, including filter masks.

The lovely Lieutenant Jamieson sank into the chair next to him, releasing a long sigh and letting her head fall back, a tendril of raven hair escaping a pin to bounce against her cheek.

"Whew!" she said, pulling the peeled orange toward her and taking a big bite. "This hits the spot."

Frost perked up, pleased and surprised.

"I was starting to fear you'd turned your nose up at my gift," he said.

"Gift? What gift? This is payment—remember, juggler boy?" She laughed. "No, I was just so nervous I couldn't eat anything this morning and now I'm starving."

"Nervous? Why—about that?" Frost asked, gesturing toward the podium.

"Yes. Chief left me big shoes to fill and I'm terrible in front of a crowd."

Frost shook his head. This woman continued to amaze him.

"I'm a trained detective, ma'am, and I saw no evidence of that whatsoever. You were fantastic."

She smiled, and Frost noticed a dimple appear in her left cheek, sparking a little flame somewhere inside him. He considered this an auspicious moment.

From the time he was small, he'd had a consistent answer for those who asked what he wanted to be when he grew up. A sheriff's detective, like his Granddad.

His years in traffic and patrol, the hard work and study he'd put into his exams, all the stress and angst over getting this promotion was worth it, and he couldn't wait to get started on his first real investigation.

And now, like a cherry on top of it all, Lieutenant Jamieson comes along as part of the team he'll be working with. Maybe he should buy a lottery ticket on his way home.

He smiled big and opened up his packet of peanut butter toast.

He was going to love this new job.

CHAPTER 6

THE CLACK OF POKER chips combined with the flutter of shuffling cards to create a gentle backdrop of noise. Steadman hoped it was enough to cover the rumbling inside his gut.

The growls stemmed not from hunger, but from nerves, and the soft green baize of the game table in front of him stretched out like a minefield, ready to blow him sky high with every faulty step.

He sat—tethered by a mixture of fear and obligation—in a chair with squeaky wheels in Garth Rafferty's basement, three blocks from his own clapboard house. Light filtered in through the half-drawn blinds, gilded by the setting sun, dust motes floating in the beams like lazy ballerinas.

He felt like a fool.

He still couldn't believe he'd let Nan talk him into this, but after some discreet investigation and a hard examination of what he'd discovered, he realized Nan's portrayal of the situation was spot on. Hank was in the tight grip of some dangerous people, and they hadn't left him any wiggle room.

At least Nan's plan offered access, a way to crack open the impenetrable shell that surrounded their operation. After a long and emotional discussion with Vivi, his wife, he'd stepped off the edge of his own universe and into a strange new world.

Vivi's feelings about his involvement were strong and varied, changing from one moment to the next. She was indignant over Hank and Nan's situation, wanting justice done and vengeance dispensed, but she wanted someone other than her husband to be the hand that dealt it.

They were expecting their first grandchild, and she was feeling protective. In the end, she conceded that Steadman wouldn't feel right if he didn't do what he could to help his sister, and she couldn't sleep next to a man who tossed and turned all night.

It took Steadman less than an hour surfing the internet for poker wisdom to realize he needed a hands-on mentor, someone who could coach him through the nuances of the game.

That's when he thought of Rafferty.

Garth Rafferty was a legend around the station. Retired ten years since, his name was still spoken in reverent tones within the taupe-colored walls of the department. He'd closed more cases than anyone else in the city's history and put away some pretty heinous criminals.

After wrapping up a nasty human trafficking case involving young Guatemalan girls, he hung up his uniform and donned a series of Hawaiian shirts while he quietly made a fortune in the local casinos.

Most of it in poker cash.

Rafferty had been Chief Deputy when Steadman came in at the bottom rung of the detective division, and though they'd never directly worked a case together, Steadman had a lot of respect for the man and a lot of confidence in his abilities.

They'd gotten to know each other in a mostly after-hours way, grabbing a beer after a shift or at one of Rafferty's famous backyard barbecues. While they'd never grown beyond a casual friendship, Steadman felt he could go to the man, hat in hand.

It took some doing, but he talked Rafferty into taking him on as an apprentice. The older man balked at first, stoking the fires of Steadman's desperation so that he leaked a little more information about Nan's predicament than he probably should have.

But something he said must have resonated because once he agreed, Rafferty took to his task like a bulldog with a bone, right from day one.

"Poker is not a game of cards," he told Steadman as they settled in at the table. He pulled the perpetual toothpick from between his molars, stabbing it into the air to drive his point home. "It's a game of people."

He shoved the toothpick back in and spoke around it. "Let the lesson begin."

He shuffled and dealt out a hand of Texas Hold'em, two cards each, including a dummy position on either side of him, making it effectively a four-player game.

"Meet Deadpan One and Deadpan Two," Rafferty said, motioning to the dummy hands. "You won't be able to read a thing on their faces. Good poker players wear a mask you can't get behind."

"You mean all the training the department invested in teaching me to read faces won't help at the poker table?" Steadman asked, fuming at Nan and her hare-brained idea.

"I didn't say that," Rafferty replied. "You'll pick up on some body language, and your instincts are well-honed, but top-notch players are guarded and may even deliberately send a false message if they think you'll bite. My point is that playing style and behavior will be better indicators, giving you a more accurate pinpoint into reading your opponents."

Rafferty chewed on the toothpick and gave a rueful chuckle.

"Beyond that," he said, "I was really just making a joke, Steadman. You got to lighten up. I mean, how much do you really think you'll get out of those faces?" he asked, gesturing to the empty spaces above the dummy cards.

Steadman laughed, but the tight-sprung wire within him didn't loosen. He had a lot to learn, and so much was hanging on this education.

"All right," said Rafferty, "let's play through a hand. I'm the dealer this time, so that means I'm on the button." He indicated a round, white token a bit larger than a poker chip in front of him.

"Now, that doesn't necessarily mean I'll be the one handing round the cards. In fact, the nominal dealer rarely does. It's just a way of keeping track of the rotation as play moves around the table."

"Okay," Steadman said. "I'll take what you're saying and hope it makes sense before too long."

"No time at all, my friend. You'll be playing like an old pro by week's end. Okay, so I'm on the button, and the player to my left is the small blind. That makes you the big blind."

"Sounds like a term that fits," Steadman said. "What does it mean?"

"A blind is a forced bet. In a 5/10 game, it means the small blind is forced to lay out a five-dollar bet and you, as the big blind, must double that."

"So I have to bet ten dollars, whether I want to, or not?"

"Them's the rules."

"Why?"

Rafferty tossed the chewed-up toothpick into a cut-glass ash tray and placed both hands, palm down, on the table in front of him. "Think about it, Steadman. Let me know what you come up with."

Steadman squirmed. He didn't want to think about it, but remembering why he was there brought the reason to his mind with crystal clarity.

"Okay, I get it," he said. "There's no point in playing if there's nothing at stake. Still, I hate someone forcing my hand."

Rafferty gave him a piercing look. "Then don't get in the game," he said.

A moment ticked by as the older man continued to scrutinize him and Steadman knew he was talking about more than poker. At last Rafferty cleared his throat and asked, "Are you in?"

Steadman thought over the arguments he'd had with himself, Vivi's tortured conclusion, Nan's riven face. He remembered Hank in that hospital bed, full of tubes, with more and worse to come. He wished he could formulate a better solution, but big blind was all too apt a description for the way he felt.

He picked up his cards. "I'm in."

"All right," Rafferty said, helping himself to a new toothpick and advancing a red five-dollar chip from the dummy player to his left. "Ten, to you."

Steadman pushed forward a blue chip.

"And now the action starts with the player to the left of the big blind. This guy," Rafferty said, jerking a thumb toward the other empty seat. "He has three options. He can fold. If he's got a couple of lower, non-consecutive unsuited cards, that's what he should do. There are plenty of other times when it might be smart to fold, and you'll learn those as we go along."

Steadman rubbed the bridge of his nose.

"He can call," continued Rafferty, "meaning he matches what the highest betting player has put up. In this case, that's you, and he would match your ten." Rafferty placed a blue chip for the dummy.

"Just for fun," he said, "I'll exercise the third option, and raise. That means I have to at least double the amount of the previous bet. So if I raise, I have to bet at least twenty. I'll do that." He placed two blue chips in front of his pile.

"And so the action moves around, coming back to the small blind. How deep is he in?"

Steadman calculated. "He's in for five, so that means he's got to toss in another fifteen to stay in the hand, right?"

"You got it. And now it's back to you. Will you kick in another ten to call?"

"My other options are folding or raising at least forty."

"Correct."

"I'll call."

"All right, and Deadpan Two will follow suit. Each player is now in for the same amount, and that ends this round of betting. It's time for the flop."

Rafferty tossed aside the top card on the deck, "burning it," and flipped the next three face up, placing them in a row.

"Okay," he said, "you're starting to learn some basics, but you're going to have to reach way deeper to meet the challenges of your situation."

He dropped the deck on the table and leaned back in his chair. "What are you thinking about right now? What are you basing your decisions on?"

Steadman glanced down at his cards and compared them to what lay on the table.

"I'm trying to figure out my chances of putting together a winning combination between what's in my hand and what's in the flop."

"Okay, and let's say your two cards plus three on the table make for a strong hand. Then what?"

Steadman shrugged. "Then I bet big."

"And what about your opponents? What do they have?"

Steadman stared at him. "I have no idea."

Rafferty nodded, grinding the toothpick between his teeth. "Uh-huh, and that's a problem. You should know what your opponents are holding."

"How can I possibly know that?" Steadman asked, trying to rein in his exasperation.

"What's the first thing I said to you when we sat down at this table?"

Steadman tried to remember. "You said poker wasn't about cards. It's about people."

"That's right—people, Steadman. If you base all your decisions on the cards you hold, you make yourself predictable. Easy prey."

Rafferty tapped two fingers against his skull. "You've got to get inside your opponent's head while keeping him out of your own."

He worked the toothpick around to the opposite side of his jaw.

"It doesn't matter what cards you hold in your hand. Nine times out of ten, you can play a winning strategy, regardless. But only," he said, jabbing the toothpick once more for emphasis, "only if you've got a fair idea of what your opponents have and how they'll play it. You've got to put them on a hand, and you do that by reading their behavior, gauging their style of play, and making sound judgments based on your observations."

"Oh hell, Rafferty—I've only got a couple of weeks to get this down. Sounds like I'd need a lifetime."

"Maybe," Rafferty agreed, "but I think you'll catch on quicker than you give yourself credit for. It's not all that different from reading a suspect under interrogation. I've got some cronies coming over tomorrow to take you out for a test drive. But you need to be aware there are even deeper levels of play. Remember—while you're reading them, they're reading you too. You have to ask yourself—what do they think I have?"

"Oh marvelous. And then I suppose it's what do they think I think they have, and it just goes on and on, like looking into a set of mirrors facing each other."

"Yes," Rafferty admitted, "but don't lose heart. You only have to go one level deeper than your opponent. Anything more than that is wasted effort."

"Cripes," Steadman said, shoving back from the table and coming to his feet. "This was a bad idea, Garth. I'm sorry I wasted your time."

He sighed and tossed his cards onto the table, rubbing a hand through his hair before turning toward the back patio slider.

"Sit down, Rand."

Steadman shook his head and took a step for the door.

"I said sit down!"

Rafferty's voice thundered through the low-ceilinged room. Steadman froze, startled enough to break through his frustration. He turned back, staring at the portly man in the flowered shirt.

"If I read you right," said Rafferty, and there was no toothpick bobbing now between his teeth, "and I'm pretty damn good at reading people, Rand—you're backed up hard against a wall and you need a way forward."

He motioned toward the chair and Steadman fell into it without argument.

"Now, I know you for a smart man, Chief. I'm not apprised of the details of your situation," he held up a hand, "and I don't want to be, but you wouldn't have come to me if you didn't think I could help. We have two weeks to get you ready for that casino, Rand, so scoot that chair up to the table and let's get started."

Steadman swallowed. He felt that wall at his back, lined with razor blades and dripping with acid. He sorely needed that way forward, and he didn't know if this was it or not, but he saw nothing else on offer.

The wheels of his chair squeaked as he rolled it back into place and picked up his cards.

"I sure hope you can work a miracle, Rafferty," he said. "Because you're going to have to teach a blind man how to see."

CHAPTER 7

MADDIE SWENSON STEPPED WITH care, moving between the trunks of towering conifers, keeping to the soft carpet of moldering leaves and pine needles.

The late September sunshine fell in slices across the forest floor, diffused and tempered by the lofty firs, oaks, and alders, its touch feather-soft against her cheek. She divided her attention between tracking her target and watching the ground for the dried, curling leaves and brittle sticks that would give her away if she stepped on them.

The brown squirrel froze, its ears perked, bushy tail poised like a plume of pampas grass above its head. Its nervous chitter, half question, half scold, rose on the crisp, pine-scented breeze.

Maddie nocked an arrow, steadying her hands and drawing back the bow. She released, imagining a mighty *thwang* as the arrow launched and she watched it curve through the air, homing in on the target.

The squirrel scurried away, spiraling up the trunk of a Douglas Fir and disappearing into the bunched needles at the top. The arrow bounced and skidded along the ground, coming to rest against a moss-encrusted tree stump.

Maddie sighed and went to collect it, regarding the blunt-nosed tip with disgust. She'd never be able to nail a target with this babyish bow, but her parents wouldn't let her shoot a real bow until she was twelve—ten whole months away.

28

She yearned to survive in the wild, to hunt and forage for food, to build a simple shelter, and defend herself against predators and other hazards.

Building a fire from what she could scavenge, finding enough wild berries to bake a pie—these are things she'd done multiple times. She was tough and strong, quick and smart, moving through the forest with confidence and verve. Another Katniss Everdeen, warrior queen of the wood.

She'd read all the *Hunger Games* books, and *The Knife of Never Letting Go*. On a rainy day last summer, she'd found some old books in a box at the back of her mother's closet, and buried herself in *My Side of The Mountain* and *The Sign of The Beaver*.

She read plenty of non-fiction, too. Every book she could find about people surviving in harsh environments against terrible odds. The subject fascinated her.

Maddie gauged the slant of the sun through the leafy boughs and turned north, working her way along the ridge to the brook that flowed down into the Case Inlet. The faux-leather quiver full of light-weight arrows flapped against her shoulder blade in a way no genuine quiver full of arrows would do.

Shrugging with contempt, she picked her way down the rocky embankment to scoop a handful of cold water from the stream. She was at least two miles beyond the house now, maybe three.

Up ridge, to the south and west, lay unfamiliar territory. Maddie wasn't supposed to go out that far, but the Saturday afternoon beckoned. Homework could wait. She'd been putting off the sixth-grade math assignment all weekend, reasoning that she could do it after dark.

The afternoons were getting shorter now that another school year had begun, and daylight was precious. She'd stay out just a little longer, though she knew she'd be in big trouble if she wasn't home by sundown.

Turning, she started downhill, slipping on the thick pile of dead pine needles. Her feet flew out from beneath her and she hit the ground on her back, cushioned by fallen leaves and the soft soil.

Giggling a little, imagining what she must have looked like and wishing she could have seen herself make that ungraceful descent, she stared up into the interlacing branches overhead.

Oh, how she loved the forest!

The other girls in her class spent their free time on X-Box and nail polish, but to Maddie, those things seemed so trivial. This was real. This mattered.

The dirt beneath her and the sway of the trees, the buzzing and humming and twittering of wildlife. She could still hear the music of the brook as it spilled over the rocks on its way to the inlet.

As she strained her ears, she heard another sound, a stealthy rustle. Raising up on her elbows, she looked behind her where the shadows under the pines seemed to shift in the dimming light. Her skin prickled.

Something had moved there, she was certain. Pushing herself to a standing position, she surveyed her surroundings and saw nothing to alarm her, but the woods now seemed brushed by a shade of menace.

Sweeping the clinging needles from the seat of her pants, she started homeward, keeping her eyes and ears on the alert. Bears and cougars were often sighted in the area and though they rarely attacked humans, she was small enough that a hungry predator might think her a juicy target.

She picked up her pace, now suddenly anxious to get home, remembering how abruptly darkness falls in the forest where the trees form a barrier against the sun.

She heard it again, that furtive whisper of sound, and she froze, listening hard. Something stalked her, moving in the shadows behind and to her left.

She felt the uselessness of her childish bow once again, wishing for a solid weapon to defend herself. Casting her gaze over the forest floor, she looked for stones she might throw, wishing she had a slingshot.

She ought to practice using a slingshot, and make it part of her customary gear. Arrows are hard to come by for an eleven-year-old with a measly allowance, but rocks are free for the taking.

The creature, whatever it was, moved again.

Maddie hadn't seen enough to identify it, but it was something big. Bigger than she was. Its movement dislodged a stone the size of a softball and it tumbled down the hill toward her.

She scooped it up like a seasoned infielder and held it in a ready fist as she hurried toward home.

The sounds of pursuit grew more pronounced. She'd been half-convinced it was her imagination, but now there was no denying that something followed her.

She turned, stone raised, eyes squinting into the dimness.

Should she shout and throw the rock to scare the creature away? If that didn't work, she'd have lost her best weapon. As she stood, indecisive, a flurry of guitar chords burst out from behind the trees.

Maddie was so startled she nearly dropped the rock clutched in her shaking fist.

A cell phone!

Whatever stalked her in the forest, it was human.

CHAPTER 8

STEADMAN WATCHED AS THE dealer swept his little pile of poker chips into the pot, each one representing a little piece of lost hope as he endured round after round of bad calls and worse timing.

He thought he'd learned something during those two weeks under Rafferty's tutelage, but classroom instruction didn't always hold up against the battering ram of real-world experience.

Nausea rose within him. The strident dings and trills of a hundred slot machines, with their flashing lights and occasional rush of coins, did nothing to help settle his stomach.

He tried to block out the permeating stink from filth-encrusted ashtrays and the mingling smoke of a dozen brands of cigarettes, tinged by cheap cigars and the unmistakable scent of marijuana. Staring again at the dwindling pool of chips that held the last of his sister's worldly wealth, he felt the weight of failure crushing down on him.

Six stacks of chips he'd thrown into that drain, and Hank's life depended on getting them back tenfold.

That wasn't happening.

Tossing his cards onto the muck pile, Steadman let his eyes go out of focus and drew deep breaths into his lungs, trying not to think too much about second-hand smoke. He needed to clear his head and keep his nerve.

One off the button now, in the small blind, he placed the obligatory five-dollar bet and without much hope, peeled up the corners of his hole cards, fighting to keep his face neutral when he saw that he had a pair of queens.

One by one, the other players folded as the action moved around the table until only Steadman and the big blind player to his left remained.

That's the way his luck had been falling—he finally got a decent pre-flop hand, and no one stuck around to play.

Somewhere, devils were laughing.

Steadman raised, like Rafferty had taught him. Three times the big blind plus one, in the hopes the last remaining competitor would see him through. He tossed down forty dollars in chips.

And the big blind called.

Steadman struggled to keep the surprise and relief from showing in his face or demeanor. The man he faced was whippet thin, with sunken cheeks and a forehead that stood out like a shelf above Marty Feldman eyes. A very hard read.

Steadman studied his opponent as the flop went down and thought he detected a flicker of excitement. The cards on the table were an ace, a five, and a queen. Steadman now had three queens.

Rafferty had schooled him in how to observe the players whenever he wasn't engaged in figuring out his own hand or deciding how to bet.

In fact, Rafferty had reiterated that he needn't worry about his own hand—that it didn't matter so much what he held, only what the other players thought he had. But that was a level of strategy above what he could manage at this point. He concentrated on trying to read his opponent and guarding his own reactions.

His experience of the man next to him suggested he had a loose aggressive style, a difficult type to play against. He bluffed often and lacked consistency in his betting patterns, making it hard to predict what he'd do or what his hole cards might be.

And that face!

How do you read a man who always looks like he just swallowed a firecracker? Steadman figured the guy for an ace and probably a face card. The ace in the flop would have him chasing the pot.

Sure enough, the man threw in a hundred. Steadman swallowed and tried not to look down at his dwindling stack of chips.

He raised to two hundred. The man with the Eyes reraised to four hundred, and Steadman called. The reraise suggested to Steadman that the man now held two pair, probably aces over fives.

That still wasn't good enough to beat Steadman's set of queens.

The dealer burned the top card and placed the turn. A nine.

Steadman's opponent bet two hundred, Steadman raised to four, and the Eyes called. Now, everything hung on the last card to be flipped.

The river.

It came up a five.

Steadman's heart squeezed inside his chest. The best he could figure, his opponent now had a full house, three fives and two aces. But Steadman had a full house, too. Three queens over fives

Making his the winning hand.

He controlled his breathing and tried not to let his hand tremble as he raised the bet and watched the Eye man reraise. Steadman called, pushing all but a handful of chips into the pot.

Straining valiantly to keep in check the huge grin that wanted to bust out across his face, Steadman flipped over his pocket queens.

And his opponent showed a pair of fives.

A stab of shock, like a rain of pins and needles, crossed Steadman's chest. Feldman Eyes had beaten him with four of a kind, a freak occurrence that couldn't be happening.

But it was.

Somewhere, those devils were having a knee-slapping good time.

Steadman hadn't seen it coming. This whole thing was a lousy idea, and he should have worked harder to find a better solution, or talk Nan out of this one.

But everything in him shrank from forcing her to play the guilt card, though he knew she would have done it to save her husband in the only way she knew how.

Thad's name had hung unspoken in the air between them, and that was enough.

The tips of Steadman's ears burned as shame and disappointment flooded through him. He thought of the hours of instruction Rafferty had lavished on him, the confidence expressed, the expectation rendered.

He remembered that first game with Rafferty's cronies. The old guys had fleeced Steadman, cleaning him out of plastic money and taking great delight in it.

But at the end of the evening, when Rafferty shooed the grinning grandpas out the door he told them, "Come back in two weeks, fellas, and the fish'll take every chip you got."

And it had happened almost that way.

Steadman got a top-notch education out of Rafferty, but it hadn't stopped him from losing all but six hundred bucks of Nan's stake. She was depending on him to do this and the thought of going back to her, empty-handed and bereft of hope, was more than he could bear.

He wasn't in the right state of mind for playing poker, leaning far too heavily on emotion rather than reason, but an irresistible force made of equal parts despair and resignation pushed him toward the bitter end.

Still reeling from the shock of his defeat, he pushed forward the big blind bet, his hand seeming to move without his conscious volition.

The dealer distributed the hole cards and Steadman peeked at his, registering a five and six of spades. A flicker of hope flared deep in his chest as the dealer laid out the flop—a four and a pair of sevens—but he allowed the wave of negativity within him to douse it.

Two women sat across from him. The first met the pot requirements, and the second raised the bet. Her neighbor—a man wearing an ascot printed with spear-wielding pygmies—called, and the gum chewing man to Steadman's right, who'd dispatched an entire pack of Wrigley's Spearmint in three rounds of play, also stayed in.

May as well end this now.

Steadman set his jaw and ground his teeth, knowing he'd lost his grip on rational thought and gone fatalistic. Rafferty had warned him against this.

He felt his cheeks flame as he pushed the last of his chips to the center of the table, going all in. The dealer set up a side pot for the other players and flipped over a jack for the turn. The players made their bets and Steadman watched the dealer place down the last card.

An eight.

Steadman stared, not daring to believe. He had a straight—a fine, strong hand. His opponents settled up the side pot and Steadman showed his two cards, good enough to win the main pot, a little over three thousand dollars.

Some of the heaviness floated out of his chest. He'd just made a huge step toward recovering Nan's stake and her hope for Hank's future.

Before anyone at the table could move, the lights flickered and went out, plunging the windowless room into inky blackness. A siren wailed in the distance, and then another.

Flaring red lights strobed into the darkness, striping a sea of frightened faces with crimson splashes, reminiscent of blood. Steadman's heart lurched, sending little electric shocks through his veins.

Something bad was happening.

A murmur, and then a roar of panicked voices rose, and people ran in the dark, slamming against tables, scattering chips and knocking over cocktail glasses.

A woman screamed. Someone heavy plowed into Steadman's table, sprawling over the top of it, and the pot of chips—his chips—flew out into space.

"What's happening?" shouted a man's voice, harsh with fear.

"It's Mt. Rainier," someone screamed back. "It's gone and blown. A tidal wave of mud is headed our way!"

Chapter 9

Maddie tensed every muscle to run.

The shock that had pulsed through her when the jangling ring tone shattered the silence of the forest spurred a rush of adrenalin that zinged through every part of her body. She sprang away, like an arrow released.

"Wait! Maddie, don't go!"

The sound of her name and the pleading tone of the half-familiar voice tamped down some of her panic. She slowed enough to turn her head, locating the dim figure among the shadowed trees.

"Wait up just a minute."

He was still nothing but a darkened shape, but his tone was friendly and reassuring.

"You scared me as much as I scared you," he said. "And besides, I got something I want to ask you."

He stepped forward, and a ray from the setting sun spilled enough light across his face for Maddie to recognize him. She came to a full stop, stunned into stillness.

Dart Rosedale.

What was he doing here, and what could he want with her?

He held up one hand in apology, the other still wrapped around his cell phone as he gaped down at the screen. "Sorry, I got to take this."

Maddie stared, watching as he turned his back and spoke into the phone. First, he makes her practically jump out of her skin, and now he's putting her on hold? No way.

She wasn't waiting around for this. Everything she'd ever heard about the guy led her to believe he was a dirtbag and he wasn't doing anything to change that opinion.

Making sure she still had the quiver and all her arrows, she started down the hill. Dusk was falling fast now, and she didn't want to pick her way through the dark woods with just the penlight she had in her pocket.

Maddie realized Dart must have seen her when she fell. That had been a minute or two before his phone went off, but he hadn't stepped forward to ask if she was okay, or laughed, or made a sound of any kind.

He'd been unnaturally quiet. Her cheeks flooded with heat and she felt angry, embarrassed, and—

Creeped out.

"Hold on, Maddie! I'm sorry—that was my mom."

She cast a glance back, taking in his shamefaced grimace. Maddie guessed he was uncomfortable about still living at home after his twenty-first birthday. She kept walking fast.

"Yeah?" she said, "and if I'm not home before dark my mom will be calling me, too."

"Do you have your phone with you?" he asked, jogging to catch up with her.

"No," she admitted. "It rings at the most inconvenient moments."

He laughed. "I see your point."

Keeping pace by her side, he let a moment pass before saying, "I've got a bow you can use. It's nothing fancy, but it shoots good."

She stopped walking. "What kind of bow?"

Shrugging, he said, "I think it's called a recurve. But here's the thing, Maddie. I'll let you shoot it, and I can teach you how to skin and clean your kills."

"Why would you bother?"

It was tempting to believe his offer, but she squinted at him hard, letting her doubt show through.

He pursed his lips, seeming to consider her question. "I can see you're interested. It's something I learned to do when I was a squirt like you. I'm just trying to...give back."

She snorted. "Yeah, right."

He was standing in her path now, and the trees hemmed them in. The forest had grown quiet in the twilight hour, scented by a hint of wood smoke from a faraway fireplace. She scowled and tried squeezing past him on the right, but he moved to block her.

"Come on, Maddie. I won't tell anyone. You won't get in trouble."

A tiny tremor passed through her. She didn't like being alone with him here in the gathering dark. How long had he been following her? Had he been stalking her?

"Let me pass, Dart. I want to go home."

A few seconds ticked by as he studied her, his forehead scrunched beneath the fringe of straight-cut bangs. She remembered going to see Planet of The Apes at the theater with her big brother. This guy could have been an extra in the movie and he wouldn't even need make-up.

His head was wreathed in an unbroken round of fuzz—beard, sideburns, thick, oddly textured hair the color of an orangutan. This formed a circular frame for his features, which seemed to crowd together in the center of his facial region, except for the large ears that poked out from the tufts of hair on either side.

He stepped out of her way. "Okay, no problem. I just thought I'd make the offer."

He paused and Maddie hunched forward, pushing past the bulk of his body, determined to get home without further delay.

His next words caught her broadside. "Seeing as how the bow belonged to Matt."

Maddie's heart clutched into a rigid ball inside her chest. She turned and stared at Dart Rosedale.

"What did you say?"

CHAPTER 10

Pandemonium.

Darkness prevailed, punctuated by scarlet flashes that made the whole scene feel like a B movie cut together by a drug-crazed film editor.

Steadman drew in a deep breath and pulled himself together. The shock of holding a winning hand and watching it get kicked to oblivion by the sudden blackout fell away, and his lawman's training came to the fore.

Mt. Rainier was erupting; he had things to do.

In the dark, the rustling and grunts of blind and frantic movement came across as if amplified through high-fidelity speakers. Squeals, scrapes, and strings of profanity rose in ever-increasing volume.

To his left, Steadman heard the thunk of a chair hitting the floor and a woman's cry of pain. People were getting hurt. Bracing his palms on the padded edge of the table, he hoisted himself up, planting a knee in a half-filled ashtray, grinding the remains of a soggy cigar into his new pair of khaki chinos.

The pungent odor of crushed tobacco reached his nostrils as a darkened figure, illuminated for a split second by the blood-red light, smashed into the table, pitching Steadman sideways.

He steadied himself and raised his hands, cupping them around his mouth.

"Attention! Hold up, everybody!"

42

His words were sucked into the void. The frenzied activity swirled around him, unabated. In little snatches of silence between the screams and crashing of bodies, Steadman heard someone reciting The Lord's Prayer.

Light flickered, then came in a steady stream that hurt his eyes after the thick blackness. The generator was up and running.

The sudden light acted like a splash of cold water, freezing people in their tracks, and Steadman took advantage of the opportunity. Standing atop the table and holding up his badge, he summoned his most authoritative tone.

"Attention, please! You are in no immediate danger. Panic will only get people hurt."

The roomful of faces turned to him, seeking assurance, and he gave it to them.

"We are sixty-nine miles distant from Mt. Rainier—outside the primary danger zone."

He believed this was true but knew about the very real threats bearing down on them. He'd been to training after training about what to expect and how to handle it.

About half the people waited to hear what else he had to say, while the rest hustled toward the exit. Most folks had cell phones in hand, fingers flashing with lightning speed across the tiny screens.

He needed to give them a few simple instructions to get them moving in the right direction. The window for effective action was small and closing fast.

"What you need to prepare for is flooding. And heavy ash. But there's a time delay before that will hit us. Go home, gather your families, prepare your property for flood damage, and stay off the streets."

He was losing them; he could see it in their faces.

"At this distance, we'll escape the worst of it," he assured them, "but you'll need to batten down the hatches."

"What if my house is on the beach, officer?" shouted a red-faced man with a beefy chest and a Harley-Davidson tattoo. "How do I batten down those hatches?"

Steadman nodded. "Good point, sir. If your house is on or near the water, get your family out and head to high ground. But don't panic and don't clog the roadways. We've got a couple hours before we'll feel the effects of the eruption."

Again, there was a flicker and a few seconds of darkness as the generator faltered before the power came back up.

"Oh, yeah?" snickered a woman, and Steadman felt the blush creeping over his face. He dipped his head in sheepish acknowledgment.

"There is that," he admitted. "We're likely to lose power—and probably cell reception—in advance of the flooding. If you've got camping gear—lanterns, cookstoves, and such—you're going to need it. Batteries and bottled water, folks. The word on this has been going out over every media channel for months. I hope you paid attention and stocked up."

"And toilet paper!" squealed a woman, her fine red hair streaking away from her scalp in a frizz of static electricity. "You'll wish you'd stocked up on that."

She broke into a manic cackle that raked across Steadman's nerves.

He continued reassuring the crowd, and his words seemed to dissolve the worst of the panic, a sullen silence taking its place as the crowd filed out the doors and into the parking lot. Steadman climbed down from the table and brushed the shreds of tobacco from his pants, noting the dark brown stain with regret. His wife would give him hell for that.

Or maybe she wouldn't.

By the time this was done and over, they'd be looking at things through a whole different frame of reference. He had a bad feeling that in the aftermath, Vivi wouldn't even raise an eyebrow over a ruined pair of chinos.

He stood in the empty room and surveyed the wreckage.

Broken glass, tables and chairs awry, and endless tumbles of mutilated cards. Not a chip to be seen.

Even amid the chaos, folks had the presence of mind to scoop up the cash, or its plastic equivalent.

Casino security would guard against looters intent on robbing the one-armed bandits and cash cages. Of that, he had no doubt. But all those loose, unguarded chips in the dark...

Gone.

And the last of Nan's nest egg, too, though this was not the time to fret about that. As pressing as her situation was, circumstances had changed, and he needed to shift his attention to the matter at hand.

He shoved his worry for Nan and Hank aside and hurried for the parking lot. But as he neared the exit, a white-faced woman still seated at a Blackjack table caught his eye. The casino's logo stitched onto the breast of her polo shirt and the scattered cards, two of them mangled in her tight-clutched fist, marked her as a dealer.

She was biting her lip so hard that a trace of red had started down her chin, and a wild, clouded look shadowed her eyes. Steadman felt a chill go through him. Those eyes were focused somewhere far away, haunted as hell.

"Ma'am, are you okay?"

She seemed not to hear him, and he waved a hand to get her attention.

"You should get moving ma'am. Best get home and prepare for a rough ride ahead."

She yelped as if he'd slapped her and dropped the contorted cards to the tabletop, burying her face in her hands. Muffled words slipped out between her fingers, but her sobbing was so agitated that Steadman could barely make them out.

My son. My little boy.

"Where is he ma'am? Your son. Is he at home? You should head there now."

She dropped her hands and stared at him with a look that would prickle at the back of his mind and heart for the rest of his life.

"He's in Orting. His dad has him this weekend." Her voice cracked and her face went back into her hands.

Steadman's heart wrenched inside his ribcage. He recalled the scenarios from his training courses. Orting lay directly in the predicted pathway for the volcano's main destructive thrust as it raged toward the Nisqually delta.

The first town to be obliterated.

He did the math and reached the inescapable conclusion that this woman's son was likely moments away from certain death. The thought of it forced him to consider the thousands of people about to be buried alive in a modern-day Pompeii. The magnitude of pain that would be suffered by those who loved them and survived to mourn them, took his breath away.

Almost paralyzed by the painful reality, Steadman fought to clear the creeping dread from his mind, but even as he grieved for the suffering of so many, a finger of relief twisted into him—relief that his own family was out of harm's way. That brought him a pang of shame, and his anxiety for Nan flooded back, taunting him.

He should go.

There was so much to do and so many others who needed help if they were to pull through this thing, as a community. But this woman in front of him was alone. Never in her life can she have felt so alone as she must right now, knowing her son was dying or dead and there was nothing she could do about it.

He gripped her hands tight, willing her his strength, and clenched his jaw against the howl he felt rising in his own throat. He didn't know how long they would have stayed, frozen in that moment, if two of her co-workers hadn't come looking for her.

"Shawna, sweetheart," said one of them, wrapping the grieving mother in her arms. "Come on, let's get you home."

The other one hung back, chewing on her thumb in an effort to stem the tears in her eyes as she spoke to Steadman in a low, quavery voice.

"Poor thing. Her divorce just went through last week and this was Toby's first official weekend with his father. She—"

Her words choked off, and she hugged herself furiously, working to get control. At last she simply said, "This will kill her."

Steadman watched her move forward to take her friend's other arm as they led the sobbing woman into a dark and painful future.

A great heaviness settled over him and the effort of putting one foot in front of the other seemed more than he could muster. His entire world, turbulent as it had been, was now tipping over the edge, everything changing in the space of a few moments, and it could only get worse.

He took a deep breath and straightened his spine, throwing off the malaise. His puny efforts may not amount to much against the massive force of Rainier's catastrophic disaster, but he determined to do all he could.

Pushing through the door, he hurried across the near-deserted parking lot. He couldn't spare time to run home and change, but he carried an extra uniform shirt in the trunk of his car and took a moment to put it on, tucking it into his khaki pants.

He beeped open the locks and wrenched wide the door of his car, pausing before he leaped in. A familiar shape on the pavement caught his attention. Near a crack in the sidewalk, a single blue poker chip rested, dropped and forgotten.

The big blind.

He stooped to retrieve it, holding it up to the light so he could read the casino's logo printed on its face. He tossed it up and caught it before slipping it into his breast pocket. Fastening the button, he fingered the chip through the fabric of his uniform shirt, convinced it was somehow significant.

That chip was an amulet, or an omen.

He just didn't know which.

CHAPTER 11

DETECTIVE CORY FROST TEASED the crumpled slice of bread from the toaster, burning his thumb. What was it about the appliance that always warped whatever he put in the left-hand slot? The right side worked just fine.

He took a stubborn pride in using the toaster, the microwave, and the blender because they were his, tokens of his independence. With his promotion to the detective division, and the little bump in pay, he'd moved out of his mother's house and into the tiny garden apartment.

He had his own place, and a job he loved. Now all he needed was a girlfriend who could cook like mom, and he'd be kicking his shoes off on cloud nine.

He wondered if Lieutenant Jamieson knew her way around the kitchen and felt himself blush.

Running his toasted thumb under cold water, he thought about his gorgeous associate in the detective division and decided she could botch his dinner every night and he'd be okay with that.

He buttered the burnt piece of toast, slathering it with enough raspberry jam to override the charred taste. Late Saturday afternoon and here he was cooking up a scrambled egg supper—one of the few things he knew how to fix—and learning the hard way that girlfriends don't magically materialize when the lease is signed.

He took a big bite just as his cell phone chimed out with the uh-oh ring tone that meant business on his day off.

He chewed and swallowed before hitting the talk button.

"Frost here."

"Hey, Frost, it's Peg, from Dispatch. We've got an all hands on deck situation. Mt. Rainier just blew her top, and we're in a state of emergency. Suit up and get down here ASAP."

Holy smokes—it had finally happened.

"Copy that. On my way."

Frost punched a button to end the call and flew down the hallway to the bedroom, skidding to a stop on the threshold. He pounded a fist against the door frame.

"Bat scat!"

He'd forgotten it was laundry day. He'd thrown all his uniforms into the dryer fifteen minutes ago and he didn't have anything dry to put on. Pacing in little circles, he scuffed up the carpet between the bed and closet, torn over what to do.

He might as well eat. He'd need the nourishment and maybe by the time he finished, the clothes would be dry.

Running back to the kitchen, he forked scrambled eggs into his mouth and chewed with mechanical concentration as he thought about what the night might bring. His mother had warned him a thousand times that the life of a law enforcement officer is a whole world different from how it's portrayed on TV.

And she ought to know.

She'd spent eighteen years married to Cory Senior, Frost's Dad, an MP in the US Navy. And she'd been raised by a father who'd been in the Sheriff's department for twenty-five years.

Nineteen months after retiring, he was killed while attempting to rescue a family from a submerged car during a flash flood. The mother and two-year-old boy drowned in the car, but before the raging torrent washed him away, Frost's grandfather saved the baby girl and her father.

The Frost family still got a Christmas card and a gratitude-filled letter from them every year.

When Frost was fifteen, his Dad shipped off to Afghanistan on a mission to help local Afghan governments set up police forces and organize their court systems.

On his sixteenth birthday, Frost received a gift from his Dad, a journal he'd been keeping, with photos and descriptions of the local landscapes and native animals. On the last page, his father had written a letter telling Frost how proud he was of the young man he was becoming, and entrusting him to look after the family.

As Frost read his father's words, he'd felt like a man for the first time, and was filled with an assurance of the love and confidence his father had in him.

Eight days later, enemy forces ambushed a desert convoy, blowing it apart, and killing Cory Frost Senior. Frost knew, as well as anyone, that bombs and bullets are real, and TV is TV.

He had a great deal of respect for his mother, and no wish to be the third great tragedy of her life, but he'd be damned if he let the risk keep him doing from his job.

He threw his plate and fork in the sink. He'd be damned if he let anything keep him from doing his job.

And that included wet laundry.

He maneuvered open the creaky louvered doors that concealed the old washer and dryer in a hallway closet and yanked open the dryer door. As he thrust his hand into the mass of still-moist fabric, the lights sputtered and blinked out, casting the narrow hallway in variants of gray.

The laundry was as dry as it was going to get.

Detective Frost pulled on a damp uniform and headed for the county complex at top speed, wondering if he'd see Lieutenant Jamieson there.

CHAPTER 12

MADDIE STARED AT DART, her heart thumping like a machine on overload. He took a step closer, one hand held out as if calming a skittish animal.

"The bow was Matt's," he said. "We used to go target shooting together."

The blood sizzled in Maddie's chest. "Bull crap, Dart! Matt never hung out with you."

The fist of anger loosened a little and Maddie swallowed hard, ramming down the rising lump that always came whenever she thought about her big brother.

Even the good memories.

It pushed its way hardest into her throat whenever she allowed herself to remember that awful day when Matt was late for dinner and the Sheriff rang the doorbell while mom was cutting the meatloaf.

"He did, Maddie," Dart insisted. "Not at first, and not for a long time. But just at the end there, before he...before he died."

"Shut up!"

Maddie turned, jogging fast toward home, eyes blurred by tears. She didn't see the root that tripped her, bringing her to her knees. Dart laid a hand on her shoulder and gripped her elbow to help her up, but she shook him off.

"Don't touch me!"

He had to be lying. Matt had called Dart a creep and a bully and never spoke his name without a curl in his lip. He often referred to him as "Old Blue." Maddie had once asked him why.

Matt and his friends, Kurt and Joey, had been hanging out in the rec room, playing video games. She'd come down to watch. Matt was seven years her senior, but he didn't mind having her around. He knew she had a crush on Joey, and he teased her about it mercilessly, but only when it was just the two of them.

He'd never betray her to Joey.

She sat on the sofa beside Matt and studied Joey's profile while he worked the controller, intent on the game. A figure burst onto the screen whirling a long spear. Joey's fingers flew over the buttons as he launched a defense.

"Hey, who invited Old Blue to the party?" Kurt said. "Dude looks just like him."

Matt laughed and Joey managed to grin and fend off the attack at the same time.

"Who's Old Blue?" Maddie asked.

"Dart Rosedale."

"Dart? He's a ginger with muddy brown eyes. Why do you call him Old Blue?"

Kurt snickered, and Matt got that look on his face that told her he was assuming his big brother role in an official capacity.

"Here's a little poem for you, kid. I say Blue, you say Dart. All you need to know is it rhymes with fart."

Kurt and Joey busted up and Matt reached out and gave her hair a little tug.

Maddie giggled, but she was honest enough to show her ignorance. "I don't get it," she said.

"Good. That's one part of your education that can go neglected, as far as I'm concerned."

And no amount of begging would get him to budge on that.

Maddie adored her brother. It tore her apart when an inattentive truck driver veered into oncoming traffic, killing Matt on his way home from football practice his junior year. He was the coolest, and Dart was a jerk. He had to be lying about the two of them hanging out.

But what if he wasn't?

"He'd want you to have it, Maddie. He knew how much you like all that stuff."

"If it was Matt's bow, what are you doing with it?"

"Come on, Maddie. You know how your parents are about that kind of thing. He didn't want them to know about it, so we kept it at our hideout."

"Hideout?"

"Yeah. We found an old, abandoned hunter's blind where nobody ever goes anymore, and we used it for our own."

"Matt died two years ago, Dart. Why are you just telling me about this now?"

His face was cast in shadows, and she couldn't see his expression, but his voice came out sounding full of regret.

"I walked away from things for a while. I didn't want to see the hideout or any of the things we kept there. A couple months ago, I started going back, and seeing the place brought memories of the good times. One day, I saw you in the woods with your own bow, and I knew what Matt would want me to do. I just didn't know how to approach you."

He paused, rubbing a hand across his face. "I've been thinking it over for a couple of weeks now, and today I thought I might talk to you about it. I was standing behind a tree, wondering what to say, when my phone gave me away."

She wanted to believe him so much. If Matt truly had a bow and was learning how to shoot it, she knew he'd done it for her, that he'd intended to teach her from his own experience.

She didn't fully trust Dart, but the lure was too much for her.

"Okay, I'll come back tomorrow and get the bow from you. It's too dark now, anyway."

"Nah, I got to work tomorrow. The hideout's not far from here. Let me show you where it is and you can either take the bow tonight, or let it stay in the blind, like Matt did. Up to you."

A whirlwind of considerations flashed through her mind. She was already late getting home, and if she stayed any longer, she risked getting grounded.

But Matt's bow, so close, drew her like a beacon. If she didn't go with Dart now, she'd have to wait days before she had another chance at it.

Still, her original suspicions against him lingered, a prickling awareness. She agonized over the decision, but knew she had to give in to the call of the bow.

"Okay, but we've got to do this quick. My parents—"

"Yep, I know." He took a small flashlight from his pocket and started walking. Maddie followed. "Matt told me they're a mite overprotective."

"They're not that bad. They just worry about me. Don't all parents do that?"

"Not mine."

"Then why did your mom call?"

He stiffened. "What? Oh, you mean back there. She wanted me home for supper."

"We'd better hurry. Are we almost there?"

"Another five minutes is all."

Even in the gathering gloom, Maddie could tell they were beyond the boundaries of her own exploration. A twinge of unease passed through her, and she knew it would be wise to turn back, but they had to be nearly there, and her curiosity was now too strong to deny.

She walked along beside Dart, following the bobbing of his flashlight and listening to his almost tuneless whistle. After a moment, she realized the melody was familiar, though she didn't know all the words of the song.

Oh my darling, Clementine.

The off-key whistling irritated her but just as she opened her mouth to ask him to stop, his pace slowed, and the flashlight's beam focused ahead. Something solid loomed against the last of the sun's ember rays, an old wooden structure, leaning a bit to the left.

"Here we go," Dart said.

"I'll never be able to find this again on my own."

"You can take the bow with you. Then you won't have to come back."

He paused. "Unless you want to."

Dart stuffed the flashlight in his breast pocket and dialed a combination into a padlock on a sturdy-looking hasp, yanking it open.

"Come on in. This won't take a moment."

He swept his arm in a grand gesture, inviting her in, and she stepped through the doorway, brushing off a strand of spider's web that wrapped across her face.

The feeble gleam of his light gave her a glimpse of a card table and two folding chairs, a filthy braided rug on the floor next to a rolled-up sleeping bag, and two pillows. As she swiveled her gaze, looking for the bow, she heard a metallic scraping noise and the snap of a padlock.

She whirled, her heart jumping into her throat, and Dart's little light went out.

Into the utter blackness, she heard him speak, and his voice sounded different, like someone else entirely.

"Oh Maddie," he said. "I've waited so long for this."

CHAPTER 13

STEADMAN HEFTED OPEN THE heavy front door of the county building, noting the smell of maple donuts that always seemed to emanate from the lobby.

It had taken him an hour to drive less than ten miles from the casino. Confusion reigned on the roads, and it was like rush hour times three, with everyone leaving their places of business to gather their families and get home, stopping for supplies along the way.

When he reached the grid-locked blocks downtown, he'd pulled into a parking lot and walked the rest of the way, saving himself twenty minutes.

He nodded to Fred Winter, the sergeant manning the front desk. Fred lifted his left hand in his customary two-fingered salute. He was missing all but the pinky and thumb, so the hand formed a natural "hang loose" sign, but Fred's face was far from tranquil. His right hand was busy punching numbers into the keypad of the desk phone, and his hair stood on end as if he'd been raking at it.

"Hell is descending upon us," he said as he buzzed Steadman through the security door.

"Wouldn't that be ascending?"

"Huh?"

"We raise hell, don't we? I always thought of hell as some dark place below."

Winter rolled his eyes, addressing the ceiling. "The sky is falling, and he's worried about semantics. Beat it, Steadman—the sheriff's waiting."

Most of the team was already assembled around the large conference table, consuming coffee and energy bars as they listened to Sheriff Polander coordinating their assignments.

Steadman pulled a chair from against the wall and inserted it into the space between Jamieson and the new guy, Frost. The sheriff's cheeks were mottled with red, his blue eyes slightly bulging under the pressures of the situation.

Steadman looked around the table, noticing rumpled uniforms, whiskered chins, and shaking hands. Everyone looked a little wired. He knew he was.

"We're spread way too thin out there," Sheriff Polander said. "Parking lots at Walmart and Fred Meyer are jammed and folks are making a run on bottled water, paper products, and canned goods. This makes Black Friday look like a baby's birthday party. Morris, Beck, Danforth, and Collins—get out there and restore some order, try to keep the casualties to a minimum."

"Yes, sir."

The four officers hurried out and Polander turned his attention to policing the downtown area. "Jamieson, I want you and—"

The door burst open and Peg from dispatch, one floor down, stood on the threshold, her face a dangerous shade of scarlet, eyeglasses sliding down her sweaty nose.

"Sheriff, I—"

She broke off and bent forward, coughing and panting.

"What is it, Peg?"

"The radio, sir. It's..." a pause for breath, "out of order."

The sheriff nodded, unperturbed. "Well, I can't say we didn't see it coming. That mountain will wreak all kinds of havoc—"

"But that's not all," she said, holding up a hand. "A call came in from a Bellevue detective just before the radio went down."

"Bellevue? That's eighty-five miles across the Sound. Besides dealing with the volcano, they've got their hands full trying to find a serial killer. What do they want with us?"

"Well, sir, that's the thing. There was a lot of static and I'm not sure I heard him right. It sounded like he said he was calling from the Ferguson estate."

"Rico Ferguson's place? Here, on the Case Inlet?"

"I suppose it must be, but it gets crazier, sir."

"All right, Peg. What's the rest of it?"

"He said there's been a murder."

CHAPTER 14

Frost felt like his guts were on a seesaw between terror and euphoria. He barreled down the stairs behind Chief Steadman, trying not to chafe his thighs between his still-damp pant legs.

Holy smokes—he never dreamed he'd see this much action so soon after putting on his detective badge.

Despite the state of emergency, murder still took precedence for the detective division. Chief Steadman headed up investigations into major crimes and since Polander had already dispatched most of the force to deal with the disaster, he'd pegged Frost to accompany Steadman on the case.

Frost had mixed feelings about that. He thought the sheriff had been about to send him downtown with the lovely Jamieson, an idea that held some attraction for him.

But a murder case promised to be interesting in other ways.

He halted on the landing for a second and grabbed a deep breath, steeling himself. The scrambled egg supper he'd ingested an hour ago threatened to come back up and he needed a moment to screw his courage and his brain together in the same socket.

"You all right, partner?"

Frost marveled at how unruffled the chief appeared to be. He guessed it came with the name—Steadman. Quite a lot to live up to.

But then again, his name was Frost. If that should imply he was a man who knew how to keep his cool, he had a long stretch to go and he knew it.

The road started now.

"Got your service weapon squared away?" Steadman asked.

"Yes, sir."

"Good. Who knows what we'll be facing out there. We'll bring an evidence collection kit and all the fixings. If we find a crime scene, I doubt we'll get a unit out there. Have to do the job ourselves, most likely."

"Sir?"

Frost cringed a little under Steadman's cool gaze. He hated to expose how green he was, but figured trying to hide it wouldn't help either one of them.

"The serial killer the sheriff mentioned," Frost said. "Is that the Puget Sound Slasher? And who's Rico Ferguson?"

Steadman's dark eyes studied him, and the chief gave a slight nod that might have signified approval.

"Fair questions, Frost, and I don't know how well I can answer them. Why don't you start by telling me what you know about the Slasher case."

They'd reached Steadman's office, and Frost watched as the chief pulled a large canvas "go bag" from a closet and started packing a few extra items into it.

"Only what I've seen on the news. Two murders in Seattle the police think are related—first, a guy who worked for Boeing, and then Senator Brown. Their throats were slashed, and there's speculation it might be connected somehow with the occult."

"Right. I don't know much more about it myself, except that the death of Coby Waters—"

"Wait, what? Coby Waters, the rock star? He's dead?"

Steadman's glance held regret. "Guess you missed the bulletin, Frost. He and his entourage camped in their RVs outside Bellevue Thursday night. Sometime early yesterday morning, Coby stepped out to smoke a joint and got his throat slashed. Same M.O. So now it's officially a serial case and detectives in Bellevue have joined the task force."

Frost felt like he'd just fallen down a rabbit hole. The world was tilting at a dangerous angle, stretching his grasp on reality.

He remembered dancing at sock hops during his middle school years to the music of Downed Illusion, with Coby Waters on guitar and vocals. Heck, their Six-eyed Bandit album had practically formed the soundtrack for his after-school homework sessions.

Now the man was dead, presumably at the hands of a serial killer, and it looked like Frost was about to become involved in the investigation.

In a thousand years, he wouldn't have seen that coming.

"Okay, chief. While I try to wrap my head around all that, can you explain why they'd send a detective clear over here?"

"Well, remember we don't really know if it is connected. Peg wasn't able to get any details before the radio fritzed out. It's just that, with all the media coverage, the Slasher case was the first thing that came to mind when she mentioned a Bellevue detective."

"Okay. And Ferguson?"

"Are you telling me you've really never heard of Rico Ferguson?"

"The name seems familiar, but—"

"Scherzo designer jeans? Pavillion suits and ties?"

"That guy lives out here?"

"Sure. He's got an apartment in the city, but his main residence is on an island in the bay. He takes a helicopter to work."

"So how does he tie in?"

"Heaven knows. The killer took out a big-time Boeing executive, a United States senator, and a classic rock star. All high-profile victims. Seems he likes the limelight, so going after a major designer fits the bill."

"Wait a minute, chief. How are we—"

Frost broke off as the office door flew open, admitting Lou, the building's janitor.

"Sorry, Chief Steadman. The sheriff sent me to tell you Highway 3 washed out in six places, crumbled away into the drink. Even if you try the back roads, you'll eventually have to return to the highway if you want to get down to Ferguson's place. And the water's still rising."

"Hell, Lou, it's barely begun," Steadman said. "Travel by car will be useless. We'd better take a boat through the Hammersley Inlet."

"And no one's got cell reception anymore either," Lou continued. "Sheriff said to tell you once you're gone, you may be on your own for the duration."

Sheriff Polander appeared in the doorway.

"You good with that, Steadman?"

Frost watched the chief square his shoulders, one hand on his holstered weapon. The man's eyes turned in his direction, searching his face. Frost said nothing, but Steadman seemed to read something there and spoke up for the both of them.

"We're good, Sheriff. We got this." He sounded sure of it.

Frost only wished he felt the same.

CHAPTER 15

DART ROSEDALE STOOD IN the dark with his back against the padlocked door. His heart raced in his chest and feelings of rapture flooded through every part of him.

He'd done it. His trap had worked.

Maddie was his now.

For months, he'd been planning and preparing for this, but he'd believed the fulfillment of his fantasy was still weeks down the road. And then Rainier exploded, paving the way.

He'd be a fool not to recognize the nod from the volcano god.

He'd told Maddie the phone call was from his mother, but that wasn't true. His boss from the feed store, Mr. Horgan, had called with the news of the eruption.

"Traffic's tied up in knots and most folks are more worried about securing their homes and family than stocking up on chow for the animals. I'm shutting down the shop and heading home, and you'd do best to stay inside. It'll be a rough couple of days, and a person could get lost out there in all that mess."

Dart liked the sound of that. He'd been so taken with the notion he hadn't replied to Mr. Horgan's suggestion about filling the bathtub and charging the batteries.

And then it didn't matter. The signal cut out, leaving Dart and Maddie isolated.

In a world of their own.

He kept the news about Rainier to himself, just one more advantage he had over Maddie. He didn't quite have everything in readiness to take her, but he figured he was close enough, and no time like the present.

He just needed a ruse to get her into the blind, and a fictional bow belonging to her dead and adored big brother was an inspired idea. He'd spied on her creeping through the forest with her silly baby bow and arrows long enough to know how to hook her.

Under cover of the chaos, he'd keep her in the blind, show her how it would be. He thought that'd be all right for a few days.

Her people would search the water for her, or maybe the homes of her friends. They'd have no reason to suspect she'd been taken from them and locked away. They'd consider her the victim of a natural disaster, never suspecting what had really happened.

By the time they had the resources to put together a search party, he'd have moved her down into the hidden rooms in the basement where he'd been building her a cell.

Next to Ma's.

He heard her breathing in the blackness. Quick, shallow breaths, like an animal at bay. He liked that she was afraid and imagined her eyes, wide and frantic.

Keeping her in the dark was delicious, but soon he would switch on a light and see those marvelous eyes. That was what he most wanted to look at.

He remembered the first time he'd seen those eyes close up. Their translucent blueness had mesmerized him, warming him, making him think of the chest ointment his mother used to rub on him when he had a cough.

Her eyes were like crystal balls you could stare into and see through to another world.

He'd wanted to possess her ever since.

A piercing screech ripped through the stillness, sending a thrill down his spine.

"Let me out, Dart!" she shrieked. "Let me go!"

Her initial fear was giving way to indignation, and he needed to put an end to that without delay.

Three steps across the rough wooden boards closed the distance between them and he grabbed her by the upper arm, squeezing hard until he felt bone beneath his fingers.

With his other hand, he reached into his pocket and brought out the butterfly blade, flipping it open with a satisfying snick.

"You hear that, Maddie?" he asked into the velvet black.

"Yesss." Her breath was shaky again, and that was good.

"Do you know what it is?"

She said nothing. He slammed her against the wall, pinning her arm.

"What is it, Maddie?"

"I don't know," she cried.

"You do know. Say it! Tell me what I have here."

She made a little warbling sound. "It's a knife."

"Very good, Maddie. It's a knife. I'm going to turn the light on now so I can show you the knife, and I don't want you to move. Do you understand?"

He felt her nod, and he grinned in the dark.

The small flashlight still poked up from his breast pocket, and he switched it on. He let go of Maddie, leaving her to cower against the wall while he fired up the propane lantern. Once the light was glowing, he stepped closer to her and held the knife so its blade reflected the tiny flame.

"This is my Madame Butterfly, Maddie. Would you like to see how she flies?"

Maddie's eyes stretched wide in the dim radiance. So beautiful, achingly angelic, and full of fear.

A wave of exultation washed over him. Yes! This is what he'd waited so long to see, so long to feel. Those eyes, under his power.

Maddie hadn't answered his question, but he showed her anyway. Expertly, he manipulated the blade and handles of the knife in rapid, intricate patterns, savoring the metallic scissoring sound that accompanied the movements, knowing it would increase the fear factor.

When he finished, he pulled another knife—a switchblade—from his pocket and flicked it open.

"And this one is Harold."

He held it up so she could see the thin, sharp edge. "We'll save him for later."

He snapped the knife shut and slid it back into his jeans.

"What I want to impress upon you, Maddie, is that you should do as I ask. The first time I ask. Does that make sense?"

Her eyes simmered with a mixture of fear and hostility, but she nodded her head.

"Let's test your understanding."

Dart unbuttoned his shirt and let it drop to the floor. Still holding the butterfly knife, he stood a foot away from Maddie and pointed to the center of his chest.

"Do you see my purple scorpion?" he asked, indicating the tattoo over his breastbone.

Maddie nodded again.

"Give it a kiss," he said.

She recoiled, cringing against the wall.

"The first time, Maddie. Don't make me tell you again."

She squeezed her eyes shut, and he saw they were wet. Her lips trembled.

He opened his mouth to tell her again and then remembered he wasn't going to do that. He'd let his butterfly do the talking, teach her some manners.

Before he could tighten his grip on the knife, Maddie drew back her foot and swung it out, kicking him in the shin, the toe of her shoe connecting square on the bone.

Pain exploded, and he doubled over, rubbing the spot, a string of curses flowing from his lips.

They were getting off on the wrong foot and that made his blood boil. Maddie ran past him and was scrabbling at the door, trying to work the combination lock. He drew a deep breath and brought the anger to heel.

"You're going to be very sorry you did that, Maddie."

There was nowhere for her to run. He approached, knees bent, ready to spring at her or protect his groin, whichever seemed called for. But the fight had gone out of her.

He had her trapped, and she knew it.

"My butterfly's going to take a stroke on you for that, Maddie. Don't say I didn't warn you."

He gripped her arm and brought the blade to her face, pressing it against her cheek.

"What'll it be, Maddie? Your face? Or should I cut off the toe that bit me?"

Her eyes widened, filling with panic. He savored it, letting it wash over him. With a sudden move, he arced the knife down, slicing across the lower leg of her jeans. She flinched and screamed.

"No, we'll give as good as we got. Tit for tat, Maddie. How about that?"

He stepped back and let her see his handiwork, the dark stain spreading under the denim. She sank to the ground and sat, rocking and moaning, her hand pressed against the moistened fabric.

"Roll up your pant leg," he commanded. "Let's have a look."

Her hands were shaking so hard she could barely manipulate the material, but he was happy to see her doing as she was told. The first time.

Blood oozed from the sliced skin, but the cut was shallow, the heavy denim having shielded the flesh beneath.

"That's nothing but a scratch."

He fumbled around in a box of odds and ends and came up with an old rag. He tossed it to her.

"Put some pressure on it. I'll bring you something to clean it with and a bandage. Later on. Right now, it's time for a retest. Did you learn something, Maddie?"

Her head bobbed up and down in a fervent nod. He watched her wind the rag around her shin, tying it in place. The cut really wasn't much.

But it was a beginning.

"Get up."

She rose, whimpering a little when she transferred weight onto her damaged leg. He stood in front of her and presented his bare chest.

"Mr. Scorpion, meet Maddie. Maddie, say hello."

He watched her swallow, long and hard. Finally, she croaked out a wavering hello.

He laughed, his voice harsh in his throat. "You'll have to do a hell of a sight better than that, Maddie, but we'll let it slide for now. Put out your hands."

"What?"

"Your hands, Maddie. I've got to get home for dinner, remember? Ma's waiting."

She stuck out her hands, and he took a roll of duct tape from a cardboard box next to the sleeping bag and wrapped it three times around her wrists.

"Sit down," he said, pointing her toward a folding chair made of wood. He secured her ankles with more strips of tape and covered her mouth for good measure, making sure to leave her nostrils clear.

"I'll bring you something to eat when I come back. I shouldn't be gone more than a couple hours, so you'll barely have time to miss me."

He put his shirt back on and fastened the buttons. Unzipping the sleeping bag, he draped it around her shoulders. There wasn't much of a chill in the air, but she wouldn't be able to move around to keep warm and he didn't want her stiffening up.

He caressed her cheek with his thumb, drawing it across her lips, and let his hand circle her neck.

"Cheer up, Maddie. If Matt truly had a bow, he'd have wanted you to have it."

He extinguished the lantern and walked out, closing the door behind him and fastening the padlock on the exterior hasp. Darkness closed thick around him like a fluttering of raven wings. Shining the little flashlight ahead of him, he traversed the pine-needled path, delighting in the melting anticipation he felt inside him.

His dream of having Maddie had been with him so long, starting as just a half-formed illusion, but solidifying over many months into a full-blown fantasy that inspired his efforts to fulfill it.

And now it had tipped over the line from imagination to reality, and there was no going back. His destiny stretched before him, power hummed through him, and he embraced the course he'd chosen.

With a smile, he picked up his pace. He had to get home and feed Ma.

CHAPTER 16

MADDIE FOUGHT HER IMPULSE to struggle against the duct tape wrapped around her wrists.

The smothering blackness pressed in on her, like a stifling sheet full of static electricity, and the strip across her mouth made it hard to breathe. The chair Dart had forced her to sit in didn't have arms, and he hadn't secured her hands to it, either by design or oversight.

So, she simply raised her taped hands to her mouth and pulled off the gummy strip, gasping at the pain. Much worse than ripping off a band-aid. If Dart had taped her mouth as another test of her obedience, she had failed again and knew he'd punish her for it.

If she were still here when he returned.

Darkness.

And silence so loud it hurt her ears. She forced herself to pull in three deep lungfuls of air and focused on letting her eyes adjust, trying not to panic.

Trying instead to remember what she'd learned on that day so long ago with Matt and his friends.

It had been summertime, one of those broiling hot days that rarely hit the Pacific Northwest, and they'd all taken refuge in the basement with a plate of tuna sandwiches and cans of ice-cold root beer.

Maddie curled up on a beanbag chair with a book and divided her concentration between its pages and Joey's face as he bent forward over the laptop screen, punching keys. Matt and Kurt sat on either side of him and all three were absorbed in watching YouTube videos.

She half-listened to their laughter and conversation while she read until she noticed Matt taping Joey's wrists together with her pink elephant-printed duct tape. That got her full attention.

"Use your own duck tape, Matt," she complained. "I've got plans for that."

"What plans? Are you making a duck tape hat to go with your duck tape purse?"

Joey grinned at her, and she felt her face go hot. Matt always chided her for calling it duck tape, and a hat to match her purse was exactly what she'd been planning. Put in Matt's words, it now sounded like a stupid idea.

"None of your business," she said. "Hand over my tape."

"Come on, Maddie. It's the only roll I could find, and this is so cool. Watch!"

Joey stood, holding his fastened wrists in front of him. With the air of a salesman doing a product demonstration, he lifted his hands above his head, holding the pose for dramatic effect, then brought his arms down in a sharp motion against his chest. An *oof* escaped his lips and his hands bounced off his shirtfront, still securely taped.

"Epic fail, dude." Kurt slapped Joey on the back. "Guess I can help myself to the rest of your root beer, because you can't stop me." He grabbed Joey's soda can and stepped out of kicking range, lifting it to his lips.

"I can still club you, man." Joey came after him, arms held aloft like a baseball bat.

"Cut it out, guys! If you spill that on the carpet my mom will pitch a fit." Kurt held his hands up in surrender. "I was just playing with ya."

"Why didn't it work?" Joey asked.

They huddled around the laptop and watched the video again.

"Keep it tight," Matt said. "You want the tape real tight. I made it too loose."

"Me, this time," Kurt said, holding out his wrists.

Maddie watched the boys as they taped each other tightly and perfected their technique, swinging their arms down and breaking through their bonds every time. She didn't care anymore that they were using up all her tape.

"I want to try," she said.

"Sure!" Matt gave her a big smile. "You don't know how many times I've wanted to tape you up, little sister."

She stuck her tongue out at him and held up her wrists, watching while he wound the tape tight, securing them together. She copied the steps she'd seen the boys go through, holding her hands high and then bringing them down in a quick, chopping motion against her chest with her elbows pulling in opposite directions.

"Ow!"

All she'd succeeded in doing was roughing up her wrists and loosening the tape a tiny bit. And it hurt. After two more failed tries, she'd asked Matt to cut her loose.

"Nah," he said, leaning back and kicking his legs up on the ottoman. "I kind of like you this way."

She sank down beside him and put her head on his shoulder.

"Why couldn't I make it work, Matt?"

"You're just too little. You can't muster up enough force to break the tape."

Maddie looked up at him, putting on her best puppy dog eyes.

"All right," he said. Pushing her off him, he rose and retrieved a pair of scissors from the desk in the corner of the room. "You want to know the good news?"

"What's the good news?" She watched him cut through the pink elephants.

"You'll grow."

That had been over three years ago, and she had grown. But was she strong enough? Could she do it in the pitch dark with her legs strapped to a chair?

The tape felt tight around her wrists, but if it didn't work the first time, her efforts would only loosen the tape. Every time she tried and failed, her chance of succeeding would shrink. The fear generated by that thought almost paralyzed her.

But Dart said he would only be gone a couple of hours and the fear generated by that thought was worse.

She stood, grateful Dart hadn't tied her torso to the back of the chair like you always see in the movies. Her taped ankles made it awkward, and her balance felt off. She hoped she wouldn't fall forward, bringing the chair down on top of her.

Raising her hands high above her head, she drew a deep breath. She paused a moment to concentrate all her power, to send up a prayer of supplication, to banish her weakness, then swung her arms down. They hit her chest, and nothing had changed from that long ago summer day.

It still hurt, and it still hadn't worked.

Tears prickled at her eyelids, and she blinked them away, suddenly furious. She thrust her arms into the air and brought them down with an abrupt snap. Her elbows parted, and the tape broke with a satisfying *riiippp*.

Dropping back into the chair, she rubbed at her wrists. They were tender and raw, but her spirits soared, surging with hope and adrenaline.

Dart hadn't bothered searching her pockets to see if she had a knife. He would have laughed if he had.

Hers was a tiny penknife, a birthday present from Matt, engraved with her initials. It was small, but useful. She fished it out and cut through the tape on her ankles, freeing herself from the chair.

Heart beating like mad and disoriented in the dark, she moved carefully until she found the table with the lantern. She ran her fingers around the base of the lamp, finding and pressing the ignition switch. It flared, and she adjusted the flame until it lit the small, rugged space.

Running to the door, she saw that it was just a slab of plywood hinged to the door frame. It didn't even have a knob or handle, just the loose piece of metal that coupled with the loop to form a place for the padlock to go.

She pulled at the flappy metal plate, but the door wouldn't budge. Dart had secured it from the outside.

She kicked it, remembering how she'd kicked Dart in the shin. He hadn't liked that, and she suspected he wasn't finished making her pay. She had to get out of here before he came back.

She had to.

Frantic, she looked around the room and saw that there was another piece of hinged plywood, this one covering a window high on the wall. The metal plate was not loose, however, but threaded with a combination lock.

Maddie dragged the chair to the window and spun the dial, yanking at it with all her might, feeling a wave of panic crashing over her. She focused on her breathing, slowing it down, bringing it under control.

For a while, her father's nickname for her had been Cracker, as in safe cracker. He'd gone to Goodwill in search of a decent second-hand toolbox and come home instead with a good piece of luggage, a hard-shell Samsonite with a combination lock. He'd paid five bucks for it because no one knew how to open it.

"I'll give you ten dollars if you can figure out the combination for this thing," he'd told her.

For three weeks, Maddie spent her television time fiddling with the suitcase, methodically working through the possibilities. The case finally cracked open during an episode of *Sponge Bob,* and Maddie had noted down the combination, collected her reward, and earned her new nickname.

She didn't have three weeks now. Not even three hours, but she had to try.

She dialed in numbers, twisting left and right, trying not to duplicate combinations she'd already tried, but she was far too distraught to go the methodical route and was trusting to luck.

Luck was not with her. After a hundred futile attempts, Maddie let out a scream, pounding her fists against the plywood. The air felt thick and heavy, hard to breathe, and the walls were closing in.

She was in a box. Locked in a box, like an expensive toy or a piece of jewelry, and the madman with the key was on his way.

She pushed away from the wall and explored the rest of the room, looking for weak spots in the floor or walls and finding none. As she worked her way around the perimeter, the light began to flicker. The lantern was low on fuel.

Soon, darkness would return.

She went to the cardboard carton from which Dart had taken the duct tape and dumped it out onto the floor. Seizing the big square-shaped flashlight, she thumbed the on button, relieved to see a stream of light flow from the lens.

Switching it off, she rummaged through the rest of the box's contents, most of it rubbish, and found two packs of cheese crackers and a small coil of twine which she shoved into her pockets.

At the bottom of the pile, she found a wrench. She hefted it, noting how heavy it was. If she couldn't find a way out, she'd put the chair behind the door and stand ready to club Dart over the head when he came back in. He wouldn't expect her to be loose, so she'd have the element of surprise.

And a wrench is a lethal weapon. Just ask Colonel Mustard.

But she hadn't given up on getting out before he came. She climbed up on the chair and hammered down at the padlock. The heavy tool landed only glancing blows, sliding off one side or the other without much impact.

Maddie hooked the business end of the wrench into the U-shaped space above the dial and twisted. She thought the metal bar popped up a little, and she renewed her efforts, gritting her teeth with the strain, but made no more progress.

If she had two tools to squeeze into the space, she could leverage them against each other. She searched the room for something sturdy enough to do the job but came up empty.

She brought out her penknife. It might work, but the process would ruin the beautiful, polished handle, obliterating the engraved initials.

Her gift from Matt. But if it saved her life, he wouldn't want it any other way.

She shoved the unopened knife into the hole, next to the mouth of the wrench, and used them to counter each other, putting upward pressure on the metal bar of the lock. The wrench gouged and scraped against the carved handle of the knife and Maddie felt it doing the same to her heart.

She pushed harder, not willing to let the sacrifice be in vain. With a grunt of effort, she pried at the tools with every bit of strength she could muster.

The lock popped open with a snap.

CHAPTER 17

STEADMAN THANKED HIS LUCKY stars he didn't tend toward seasickness.

The boat bounced up and slapped down repeatedly on the choppy water as he manned the steering wheel, setting up a rhythmic stuttering that would wring the lunch out of a man with a weaker stomach. He'd sent Frost up front, armed with a telescoping pole for fending off hazards, and he felt guilty as he watched spumes of cold and frothy water break over the bow, soaking the poor detective.

He also felt a little bad about having to wrest the boat away from the officers in marine services. The department had only three other boats and every one of them was desperately needed.

Still, his mission took precedence, and the sheriff had cleared it. Steadman suspected the man would offer his personal craft to compensate for the shortage.

The water turned murkier and more restless as they traveled east toward Arcadia, drawing closer to the Nisqually Reach where the tidal wave of mud was even now slamming into the Puget Sound.

The buzz of the motor filled his ears, blocking out most other noises but every so often Steadman heard the thump of debris hitting the flank or underside of the boat. He slowed down. He wanted to get to Ferguson's island fast, but not at the expense of tearing open the hull.

A flash of light to the left caught his eye, and he turned his head, watching as the shore caved in, tumbling a utility pole toward the water, its live wire snapping and sparking like a writhing snake.

A final spurt of sparks flew heavenward and then it lay still, a foot or two from the lapping edge of the inlet.

"Did you see that, Chief?" Frost's voice, high and excited, floated above the motor's roar, his head still craned toward the downed pole.

"I did, but you need to keep your eyes forward, Frost. There's a lot of fast-moving rubble out there."

"Yes, sir!"

They traveled another five minutes down the stretch of water before Frost piped up again.

"Which way are you taking us around Squaxin, Chief?"

Steadman had been debating the point with himself. Their destination lay to the north, but Squaxin Island, home of the Squaxin Tribe reservation, stretched across the intersection of several waterways.

They had options, and Steadman knew there were sound arguments for taking the southern route around the island. He hesitated.

"We'll go north," he decided, shouting out the words, but the wind snagged and whipped them away.

Frost caught them though. "You sure, Chief?" he shouted back. "The passage that way is pretty narrow. Wreckage in the water could block it up."

"What do you suggest?"

Frost's gaze turned toward the opening of the inlet, but the tree-covered shore jutted into the waterway, obscuring the view.

"Maybe turn south? The Case Inlet is broader and deeper, less chance of clogging up."

"How do you figure? We'd be flying right into the mouth of the monster. Broader passage, but a lot more junk dumping into it, and more dangerous."

Frost didn't answer. Steadman considered the parade of dire variables marching through his head. He liked that the detective was thinking for himself, but the final choice was his.

"We'll go north," he announced. "I'm hoping the islands will act as a barrier against the worst of the mess. I hate to go the long way around on my way to a crime scene."

Frost gave a firm nod. "Roger that!"

Steadman steered to the left, and the waterway widened, opening out into the juncture where several inlets met.

The water here was more turbulent, and he felt the boat buck beneath him, smacking down on something solid. He winced, hoping the hull would maintain its integrity through what loomed ahead.

Daylight leached away into the leaden sky, but there was enough of it remaining for Steadman to see the masses of ruined lumber tossing in the shifting waves, dotted with all manner of detritus.

A car door floated by, snagged by the branches of a dead tree. Off the port bow, a sodden parka bobbed on a raft of splintered logs, a long gash exposing the down feather innards as they leaked into the thrashing water.

Steadman hoped its owner had not suffered a similar fate.

Squaxin Island lay dead ahead. This was the last chance for him to change his mind, but one glance at the litter-strewn waters to the south, with more muck cascading in at every moment, convinced him his initial assessment was their best bet.

He pointed the boat north and sent up a prayer.

Maneuvering along the Squaxin bank, he thought about the double homicide that had occurred there last month. A wrathful wife shot her husband and his lover in the backseat of the family car.

With all the devastation Rainier could pour out, the volcano could hardly rival the power of a human heart set on destruction, the families ripped apart by foolish choices and rash acts.

Steadman's associate, Detective Len Perry, had wrapped up the case with the help of a department liaison by the name of George Henry.

Henry was a bit of an icon in the region, and everyone around here knew him as Chief Redfish. His notoriety came partly by way of the big salmon-roasting festival he hosted each year on the Hood Canal. But more than that, folks remembered him for breaking a local curse and bringing a pair of scheming murderers to justice.

"Ho, chief! Steer left," Frost shouted, bringing Steadman's attention back to the perilous water.

As he nosed the boat past the northern tip of Squaxin Island, an influx of debris from the eastern passage converged on them. A knot of gnarled branches attacked their starboard flank like an angry sea monster and Frost jabbed at it frantically with the reaching pole.

Steadman turned the boat to the west, hoping he wouldn't run aground or impale them on a submerged tree trunk. Frost pushed away the dead trees and a bobbing rusted-out washing machine.

Skirting the floating hazards, Steadman nosed the boat up the channel. He drew a deep breath but before he could release it, a heavy thunk sounded beneath them and the boat lurched, throwing Frost down on his backside. Steadman throttled back.

"That didn't sound good," the detective cried, picking himself off the deck.

No, it didn't. Steadman pressed his lips together. What a useless waste this trip would be if they couldn't even make it past Harstine Island and had only a wrecked boat to show for it.

"You all right?" he asked Frost.

"Totally."

With a hair-raising screech, the boat tore loose from whatever had grabbed it from beneath and they skimmed ahead in the muddy water.

Steadman checked the instruments. None of them registered a problem and the amount of water accumulating in the bottom of the boat seemed no more than before, a testament to a bilge pump in good working order.

He let out that breath he'd been holding and slowly notched up their speed.

The last glimmers of daylight faded into the western tree line and a vee of wild geese flew across the sky ahead, forming an arrow pointing away from the danger.

Steadman wished he could follow, but his course lay in a different direction, and he must go where it led.

The sulfurous smell of marshland crept into his nostrils, and he squinted into the gathering darkness. The masthead light cut a swath through it as they edged forward, green and red sidelights twinkling like Christmas tree beacons.

A wave of weariness washed over him as he realized they'd only just rounded the bend with miles to go before they slept.

As if sleep would be an option.

CHAPTER 18

MADDIE SHOUTED IN TRIUMPH.

Her fingers were raw and sore and there'd be blisters, but she'd destroyed the lock. Her jaw ached from grinding her teeth while straining to pop the mechanism, and the tinny taste of blood spread through her mouth, making her gag.

Her little penknife had fallen to the dirty floorboards, disappearing into shadow. She scrabbled around and found it, scarred but more precious than ever, and returned it to her pocket.

With shaking hands, she slid the lock off the metal tab. Pulling up the hinged piece of plywood, she peered out into the night.

Fresh air and freedom!

With a surge of energy, she pushed her head and shoulders out the opening, but the heavy plywood flap fell against her back, digging into her skin, getting caught against the waistband of her jeans, making it impossible to wriggle out.

She had to find a way to hold the window open.

Switching on the big, square flashlight, she aimed it around the ceiling above the window, searching for something she could use as an anchor point. To her relief, a hook protruded at the perfect distance, a boon provided by some long-ago hunter.

A hunter much taller than she, it turned out.

Even standing on the chair and pushing up on her toes, Maddie couldn't reach the hook. It poked out from the ceiling, a maddening two inches from her grasp.

Her eyes roved over the room in a frantic search for something to use as a booster. She folded the sleeping bag into a square and placed it on top of the chair seat, but the slippery fabric made the layers slide off each other as she mounted the makeshift stool and the filling compressed under her feet, leaving her just short of reaching the hook.

Huffing out a breath made of equal parts anger and determination, Maddie spread the sleeping bag on the floor and rolled it into a bundle, securing it with the ties sewn into its seams.

Now it would not slide apart so easily, but it made an unwieldy perch. She felt like a tightrope walker as she crouched on top of it and carefully rose to a standing position, arms held out like a balancing pole.

A flood of exhilaration poured over her as she fastened the flap onto the hook and moonlight sprinkled into the room, filtered by pine branches swaying in the night breeze.

Jumping down from the chair, she kicked away the sleeping bag and turned off the lantern. Grabbing the flashlight, she climbed back atop the chair and lowered the torch as close to the ground as she could before letting go. She heard a muted thud as it hit the ground, but no tinkle of broken glass.

Now it was up to her to follow.

A flurry of panic swirled through her, and she felt certain Dart would arrive in time to grab her by the ankles and pull her back in. She bit her lip until the pain refocused her attention on the escape route before her.

Time to go.

Hoisting herself through the window was not fun. There was no sill and the rough edge bit into her palms and her stomach. She didn't want to drop headfirst, but there wasn't a lot of room for maneuvering her feet around.

In the end, she came out sideways, trying to tuck and roll, but landing flat on her back, knocking the wind out of her.

Sprawled on a bed of pine needles, Maddie stared up into the sky, finding a single star that wasn't obscured by clouds or branches. She watched it twinkle while waiting for the breath to come back into her lungs.

The night was quiet, except for a faint wavering whistle. Half-dazed, she lay listening as the sound grew louder and more distinct until it consolidated into a melody she recognized.

Oh, my darling.

Before she could even snatch a breath, she heard the rattle of the padlock on the door and a sea of chill water flowed into her veins. There was nothing shielding her from Dart but a sheet of plywood.

And an open window.

CHAPTER 19

DART FUMBLED WITH THE padlock.

The scant moonlight slanting down through the trees came from the wrong direction. Blocked by the bulk of the hunting blind, it cast nothing but shadow where he stood, lending him no help at all.

As he worked at the number wheel, the strap of the shotgun he'd slung over his shoulder slid down the silky sleeve of his down jacket, pulling at his arm, and the slight nip in the air stiffened his fingers, making them clumsy on the combination dial.

He stopped his whistling and paused to listen. On the other side of the door, he heard a rustling sound, and a faint thump. A thrill of anticipation coursed through him. She was scared and squirming, and with good reason.

He smiled.

He'd told Ma how he caught his Maddie, trapping her with the trick about the bow. Ma's black eyes had followed him as she chewed the hamburger patty he'd cooked for her.

He worked while she ate, slathering together another section of brick and mortar, preparing a place for Maddie. He'd been taking his time with the construction, thinking he had another month at least, but now he had to finish it fast.

Ma made a gagging noise. He'd cut the hamburger into tiny pieces, but she still choked twice before getting it all down.

She did that a lot.

He wiped her mouth and poured her another glass of water. He'd been almost as young as Maddie was now when his father had shut Ma into the basement cell.

After three days of listening to her screaming, Dad had gone in with a big kitchen knife and come out with a scrap of meat which he threw to the dogs.

Ma hadn't spoken a word since.

Dad taught him how to care for her. How to measure the medicine into her food and empty the slop pail, checking daily that the shackle around her ankle hadn't gone slack.

Dad was the one who changed her clothes and often took a long time over the chore. Dart's offer of help earned him a smack across the face.

"She's your Ma, boy. Show some respect."

Five times during those years, Dad had brought other women into the house. Strangers.

The first one, he carried in over his shoulder. Her long blond hair fell free, obscuring most of her face, but Dart saw the strip of tape across her mouth and caught a glimpse of her eyes, open so wide they showed white all around their blue-colored centers, mesmerizing him by their intensity.

Dad disappeared down into the basement with her, and Dart wasn't allowed in. For two-and-a-half weeks, Dad took over Ma's care. And then one day when he returned home from school, Dad was waiting for him.

"Your Ma needs feeding. See to it."

Dart fixed a plate and ventured down the stairs, his nose wrinkling from the battery of smells that grew stronger with each step. Bleach was the strongest, but mold and something coppery came through as well.

He wondered if he'd see the woman. She looked so young, not much older than he was. Maybe he could talk to her, touch her even.

But she wasn't there.

His mother didn't open her eyes when he came in. She lay curled on her cot like she did when she was sleeping, but her lips were moving, and her face was wet. A ray of light through the grimy window glinted off one tear-shined cheek.

"Ma? I brought you something to eat."

Her eyes squeezed tighter, and the moving lips pressed into a straight line. Staring down at her frozen face, he waited for her to relent, to soften her mouth or open her eyes, but she was like stone.

He left the plate and plastic fork beside her bed. Exiting her cell, he locked it behind him and turned to go. At the foot of the stairs a mop rested in an empty bucket. He looked in and saw the twisted sprawl of mop strands, stained the color of red wine.

The sixth time his dad brought home a woman, he'd invited Dart to join him in the basement.

A gust of wind stirred the pine needles at his feet and Dart felt an eager surge well up in his gut. He dialed the last number into the combination padlock, and it clicked open.

He tensed for a moment. If Maddie had somehow gotten loose, she might be fool enough to attack him when he came through the door. He prepared himself for the possibility as the door swung open.

A lacy rectangle of pale light fell across the rough wooden floorboards, and it took a second for him to realize its source as moonglow through the open window.

Anger speared through him, and he snatched the flashlight from his pocket and shone it into every corner.

Maddie was gone.

Howling and cursing, he ran to the window and looked out at the thick, darkened woods. Beneath the window, a few crushed blades of grass were struggling to attention, silvered by moonlight.

She couldn't have gotten far.

He tripped on the tangled sleeping bag and went down on one knee. She'd left behind a hell of a mess, and a quick search confirmed his fear that she'd taken the big flashlight. His little pocket-sized torch was running low on batteries and he'd forgotten to grab replacements.

Hitching the shotgun back onto his shoulder, he burst from the hut, fueled by fury, blood sizzling through his veins. Throwing another curse to the moon, he tore into the woods, dodging trees and pumping his legs until his lungs burned. He bent forward, heaving in great gulps of air, and tried to think.

Maddie would run downhill, toward the water. Almost no one lived this high up in the forest, but houses dotted the waterfront, and she might find somebody home.

He couldn't allow that.

He scanned the downhill sector, straining to detect a trace of light, and thought he saw a tiny pinpoint bobbing in the distance.

He set his face in that direction and ran.

Chapter 20

Frost strained his eyes, peering down into the darkened water, pole at the ready like a knight at a jousting tournament. Defending the boat.

He shivered and gave a rueful, inward smile. He'd worried about coming to work in wet clothes. Now his uniform stuck to him like a second skin, sodden with sea water, cold and scratchy.

He sniffed at it, wrinkling his nose. It smelled of bog and dead fish. He was almost glad Lieutenant Jamieson wasn't around to see him in all his glory, and hoped she was safe, wherever she was.

What he wouldn't give for a thick, dry towel.

He had the best towels in the world at home, courtesy of his mother. She'd presented them—generous-sized sheets of fluffy brown Egyptian cotton tied with a satin ribbon—as a housewarming gift when he got his own apartment, and she'd paired them with a foil-wrapped pan of shepherd's pie. His favorite.

He remembered the twinge of guilt, tempered by gratitude. It had been hard moving out.

Part of him felt like a deserter. His mother had lost both parents, and then his father. He was all she had left, but he needed his own space, the room to be a man. She understood that, but he could see it pained her to let him go.

He thought about those towels, lovingly selected and passed to him with a hug and a tearful smile. They seemed to him like an extension of her arms, wrapping him in love and comfort.

He should tell her that the next time he saw her.

Something loomed out of the darkness, drifting fast toward the starboard bow. A tire, rimmed and fully inflated. Frost wondered if the rushing mud had ripped it from a fleeing carload of people. Banishing the thought from his mind, he pushed the tire away from the prow and focused his eyes on the dashing waves.

Behind him, the motor sputtered and cut out. Frost turned to see Steadman frowning down at the wheel, fiddling with the ignition.

The engine coughed, caught, and let out a roar that lasted all of five seconds before choking off into silence.

"Need a hand, chief? I can check the motor for you."

"Good with an outboard, are you?"

Frost hesitated. His experience with motorboats was occasional and mostly limited to watching someone else perform the hands-on stuff. Why had he piped up like that?

"Not really," he admitted, "but my uncle lives on the canal, takes me out sometimes in his boat."

Steadman shrugged. "Sounds about as good as what I got. See what you can do."

Frost felt his ears burn as he passed the pole to Steadman on his way back to the outboard. It was big, far larger than Uncle Stan's, its fine points shrouded in darkness.

"Here, take my Maglite," Steadman said, passing him the small flashlight. "Just don't drop it overboard."

Afraid now that letting it splash down and disappear into the murk was exactly what would happen, Frost gripped the cold metal cylinder in one hand and fumbled around with the other, trying to find the lever that would allow him to raise the motor.

He pushed against a flat bar and felt a slight give in the housing. With a flood of relief, he shoved the flashlight into his pocket and used both hands to tilt the motor, raising it up into the back of the boat.

Wads of muck clogged the blades—thick strips of bark, shreds of fabric, an old shoe, caught by the laces. He cleaned them away the best he could, grateful he hadn't turned out looking like a bumbling fool.

He lowered the motor, locking it into place, and gave Steadman the thumbs up.

They resumed their positions, Frost in front with Steadman at the wheel, and the motor rumbled back to life. The floating debris seemed thicker here, and Frost remembered his warning about the passage becoming blocked. He wanted to prove himself competent in the presence of a superior officer, but he sure hoped he was wrong about that prediction.

He kept the pole constantly busy now, staving off every manner of drifting obstacle. They traveled northward for another mile before the engine bogged down again and Frost repeated the procedure, clearing the blades.

The third time the boat stalled and Frost lifted the motor out of the water, the propeller was so congested with a mangled mass of garbage he knew he'd never be able to free it without tools and a better light source.

Like the sun.

Dejected, he stared at the mess. A slight shift in the balance of the boat signaled Steadman's approach, and Frost felt the faint prickle of heat emanating from another body as the chief stood looking down over his shoulder.

"It appears we got us a rowboat, Frost," Steadman said.

Tearing his gaze from the fouled propeller, Frost watched the chief rummage through a storage locker. He fished out a pair of telescoping oars and passed one over, a grim smile tugging at the corners of his mouth.

"Let's get paddling, Frost. And put your back into it. That crime scene isn't getting any fresher."

Chapter 21

Maddie slammed into the tree with a force that knocked her off her feet.

With a gasp of pain, she rose to a kneeling position and massaged the growing knot on her forehead, feeling the tender bump and the beginnings of the headache that would follow.

Something chattered in the tree above her. A squirrel perhaps, woken by the vibration of her impact.

Enough of this. It was too risky running through the unyielding blackness. Her arms were scraped raw from bouncing off the rough-barked pines, and twice her long hair had become tangled in branches, precious seconds ticking by while she freed herself from their grasp.

With the frantic hope that she'd created enough distance between herself and Dart to hide the beam, she switched on the flashlight. Head wounds were no treat, but a broken ankle might prove fatal. She could move faster and safer with the light.

Even illuminated, the terrain was tricky to navigate. Thickets of thorny bushes sprang up at irregular intervals, making it necessary to backtrack and find a way around.

And the ground was uneven, dropping steeply in spots, spread with a thick layer of pine needles. The resinous smell rose all around her, closing in, mixing with the scent of her panic.

Maddie slid and slithered downhill, trying to keep her feet, sometimes scrambling sideways along the ground like a demented crab. She dislodged a clutch of stones and listened as they tumbled into the gully below, warning her not to follow.

She set a course along the ridge, looking for a reasonable way down. If she could get to the waterfront—

Maddie froze. She hadn't seen or heard him coming, but she felt him there, on the slope above her.

She snapped off the light and crouched, ears straining to catch any sound of his approach. Only the soft sigh of pine boughs floated on the night air.

She held still and counted to twenty, flashing back on her days of playing hide and seek. The stakes now were higher than she'd ever envisioned during those easy days of play.

Now, she was hiding for her life.

The silence remained undisturbed for another count of twenty. Maybe she'd been wrong about his presence, misled by her terrified imagination. She drew a deep breath and tensed to move forward but before she could take a step, a rock the size of a softball bounced down from above.

He was there.

Maddie sprang from her crouch and ran. The layers of needles shifted under her feet, making it hard to gain traction, slowing her flight, and she needed her hands free to fend off the grabbing trees and bushes and to catch herself when she slipped or teetered.

She couldn't use the big flashlight now anyway, but she was smart enough not to leave it for Dart. Heaving it toward the gully, she heard it crash to the bottom accompanied by the frozen shimmer of breaking glass.

A surge of terror rushed through her, swelling her pounding heart and sending it up into her throat.

For a moment, her mind blanked, washed clean by panic. Her arms and legs operated on autopilot, pistoning out and back, throwing her forward.

But as she started coming back into herself, she realized she had a great advantage over Dart. A couple of them.

Many of the trees had low-hanging branches—easy for her to duck under. Harder for him.

And she could squeeze through gaps in the close-growing masses of underbrush where he would find it difficult to follow.

Her size was a point in her favor, and she was more nimble, too. She heard him stumble, curse, and scramble to regain his footing.

Also, she was in better shape. Before long, Dart was panting so hard that she could easily track his location. He was running behind her and to the left.

She veered right and put on a burst of speed, plowing head-on into a thick bank of bushes, too tightly clustered to push through.

She groped along the dense foliage, her frenzied fingers searching out a bolt hole for her escape. She found a spot that seemed promising and pushed forward, trying to keep as quiet as possible, but she heard Dart's breaths close behind.

"Stop running, Maddie. You'll get nowhere. I've got a shotgun and if I have to, I'll use it."

She swallowed, but her throat was so dry it hurt going down. Did he really have a gun or was he bluffing? It didn't matter—she wasn't stopping.

Clawing through the tough leaves and branches, Maddie forged ahead and almost sobbed with relief when her hands plunged through into open air. But as the rest of her tried to follow, her shirt snagged on a branch, bringing her to a halt.

Dart couldn't follow her through the cramped tunnel she'd made, but his noisy panting told her he was working his way around. She had to get free.

She strained to get at the branch which held her but couldn't reach her arms behind her back with any kind of strength behind them. She twisted and pulled, her own breath coming in frantic gasps.

"What's wrong, Maddie? Are you stuck?"

She stopped struggling and considered backing up. Maybe the branch would let her go that direction. If she was quiet enough, maybe Dart wouldn't realize she'd doubled back along the route they came.

"I think I'm going to pluck me a big, juicy berry. That's what it sounds like to me, Maddie."

His voice had moved farther off to the left, but at any moment he would find a break in the foliage and pick her out of the bushes just as he threatened. He started singing, his voice soft and taunting.

Oh my darling, oh my darling, oh my daaarling Madeleine.

With a desperate burst, Maddie gave up the idea of backtracking and wrenched against her leafy prison. The stubborn branch released her, scraping a long stripe in the skin on her back and keeping a piece of her shirt for itself.

She was off and running hard, the blood pumping madly through her veins. A glorious hope flooded over her as the distance between them grew. And then, all too soon, she heard that panting breath again, diminishing the hard-earned gap.

As her heart sank, her foot found a protruding tree root, and she sprawled headlong, her lungs knocked breathless for the second time that night.

With no time to rise and find a hiding place, Maddie flattened herself to the ground, pinning her hopes on shadows and silence. She struggled to keep from gasping as the breath came back into her body and she drew shallow, soundless sips of air.

She heard Dart crashing through underbrush, his stamping boots and labored breathing giving away his position.

And then it all stopped.

The woods fell silent save for the gentle creak of limbs overhead and the distant hoot of an owl. Where was Dart? What was he doing? Was he creeping ever closer, or waiting for her to move and give herself away?

Darkness embraced everything. Maddie realized it must be two or three o'clock in the morning and the air was laced with frost.

A shiver ran through her, but she held herself still, not daring to move an inch. Her skin tingled and burned where the greedy branch had ripped away her shirt and her nose started a slow drip, but she gritted her teeth and remained motionless.

An eternity passed.

A dry rustling, stealthy and subdued, broke the silence, coming from some-place very near. Maddie felt the hair on her arms rise like snakes summoned by a charmer's pipe. Her eyes drilled into the impenetrable dark, but it was a featureless canvas, showing nothing.

And then she heard his furtive advance, his whispered breathing as he moved toward her, not more than ten feet away.

She held her breath and prayed that he would pass on. His muffled footsteps, slow and steady, came closer. So close.

And then his heavy boot crushed down on her arm.

A bolt of pain raced along her nerves, and she bit down on the gasp that rose to her lips, summoning every bit of her strength to hold still. He stood there, pressing her arm into the cold earth for what seemed an hour.

Her agony was eclipsed only by her fear that she'd been caught, but a bubble of wonder rose inside her as she understood another advantage she had in being small; he counted her skinny arm under his boot as nothing more than a fallen tree branch.

Tears welled up and spilled down her cheeks but still she didn't move or make a sound.

She could smell him, a sour odor that made her think of Matt's gym bag after a long football practice. The smell merged with the agony in her arm to create a unique sort of torture and she bit her lip, wondering how much longer she'd be able to endure.

Just as despair threatened to overwhelm her, he lifted his foot and took another step. The sudden release of pressure sent a new spear of pain rocketing through her arm before blessed relief descended.

Pressing her lips together, she squeezed her eyes shut as the blood flow in her arm returned to normal.

When she opened her eyes again, a flash of illumination startled her, so sudden in the total gloom. Not ten feet in front of her, a tiny pane of light shone against Dart's face, painting it an eerie blue before he turned it away, sweeping it across the darkened forest.

His cell phone.

In its glow, she saw he hadn't been lying about the shotgun. It hung from a strap over his shoulder, and it seemed to her big enough to take down a grizzly.

Please, please, please don't turn around.

She sent the prayer heavenward, her heart swelling with the plea. He took a step forward, moving the light from side to side, short snatches of Clementine floating on the air.

You are lost and gone forever.

Maddie's scalp prickled. She lay still, almost faint with tension, and continued her urgent prayer.

Something moved, up-ridge and to the left. A night animal, or an angel.

Dart heard it, too. He gave a shout and crashed off through the woods. Maddie scrambled up and moved fast in a downward angle to the right, any sounds she made covered by Dart's noisy pursuit in the opposite direction.

She was free and running.

CHAPTER 22

STEADMAN STARED, HIS HEART sinking like a ball of lead in his chest.

He and Frost had finally made it to the island where Rico Ferguson lived but the sight that greeted them was not encouraging.

The piers of the bridge had vanished, completely submerged, and several pieces of decking floated in fragments, creaking as they strained against each other in the tossing water. Only traces of the railing remained to show where the bridge had once stretched between the two land masses.

Steadman wasn't surprised to see it, but he couldn't crush the wave of frustration that washed over him. If murder had been committed on the island, the logistics of processing the scene and transporting the victim would be greatly complicated without a connection to the mainland.

He glanced at Frost. Steadman couldn't see his partner's face, but the man's posture told the story.

In the main, Steadman approved of Frost's resilience and upbeat attitude. The man was an unknown in the detective division and Steadman had been testing the new guy, prompting him for ideas about how best to navigate and giving him a crack at fixing the motor when it protested and shut down.

Frost hadn't disappointed him.

And he couldn't blame him now for the dejected droop of his shoulders. Last night, after rowing through muck for over an hour without making any headway, they'd each wrapped in a blanket and hunkered down to catch a few winks before daylight made it possible to try again.

At the first glint of dawn, they'd slogged ahead through five more hours with dogged determination and now that their destination lay in sight, it was clear their trials were far from over.

Steadman knew the stately homes along the island's shore featured private docks and boathouses, but the rising waters had nearly obliterated most of them. In fact, the shore itself had disappeared, and the flood rose right up to, and in some cases beyond, the houses.

He'd never visited the island and had no idea which of these mini-palaces belonged to Rico Ferguson. He knew the designer's street address, but saw no numbers obligingly posted waterside.

Sighing, he motioned toward a house set farther back with a narrow strip of sand still separating it from the frothing waves.

"Let's drop anchor here and wade ashore."

While Frost guided the boat and heaved the anchor over the side, Steadman checked his Glock to make sure the weapon was ready to go. He tucked an extra magazine in his jacket pocket, zipping it shut, and decided to leave the Remington 870 shotgun locked up on the boat.

Once on land, he and Frost made their way toward the series of large glass sliders at the back of the house. There was no sign of anyone in residence.

He watched Frost stop to untangle shreds of garbage from his water-logged shoes. The junior detective slapped handfuls of sodden muck onto the beach, flinging mud from his fingertips, his face twisted in disgust.

"Which way to the Ferguson place?" he asked.

"I'm not sure," Steadman admitted. "I thought we'd knock some doors and ask around. Or we could look..." He paused, scanning the neighboring homes. "For that," he said, pointing to a property jutting out about a hundred yards west.

The rising tide covered the wide expanse of the backyard, lapping against a garage large enough to hold two RV's. Or a helicopter.

Steadman was willing to bet a cement landing pad stretched beneath the sheet of writhing water.

Frost's gaze followed the direction of his finger. His brow puckered, then cleared.

"Of course." He tapped his forehead in a quick salute. "That's why you're the boss man."

"It's not conclusive evidence," Steadman said, "but it's a good place to start."

They trudged through a muddy, debris-clogged mess, the water lapping halfway up Steadman's calves. When they arrived at the garage and peeked through the windows, he found his hypothesis proven.

A blue and white Bell helicopter took up half the space and behind it, in the shadows, rested a low-slung sports car of Italian design. Fashion posters featuring bored-looking models in Scherzo Jeans and stylish Pavillion suits plastered the walls of the hangar.

"Bingo!" said Frost. "Where's that Bellevue detective? I thought he'd be meeting us here."

"I don't know. Let's see who's home."

The water at the level of the house was at least ankle deep and Steadman's shoes squelched with every step, mud oozing between his toes, the stink of it rising to wrinkle his nose. He rapped loudly at the rear door and got no answer.

"Let's circle around and meet at the front. Look for signs of a break-in," he said, gesturing for Frost to go left while he went right. "And be ready for anything."

The doors and windows appeared to be secure, though by the traces of mud and silt griming them, Steadman suspected the floodwater had made its way into the house. He saw nothing else to cause alarm.

Arriving at the front of the house, he surveyed the front yard before peering into the narrow windows on either side of the entry door. This end of the house was on higher ground and the lavish foyer looked undisturbed by man or nature.

He pressed the doorbell but heard no echoing ring. Raising a fist, he pounded against the solid panel of a door. No response.

Frost rounded the corner of the house, his voice raised in excitement.

"Chief! Kitchen door's been forced."

"Did you go in?"

"No. I thought we should do that together."

"Good man," Steadman approved.

He trailed his partner back to the broken kitchen door and drew his weapon, watching Frost follow his lead. He nodded, signaling for Frost to push open the door. They filed in, and Steadman was happy to see Frost cover the area according to procedure.

A faint odor of rotting flesh tainted the air, the buzz of flies audible in the quiet of the abandoned house. Steadman dreaded rounding the corner from the mudroom into the kitchen proper, but gritted his teeth and made the turn.

A sizable puddle of blood stained the pale terrazzo floor, despite the thin layer of silt and water that had washed over it, and more blood smeared the lacquered cabinets, but no body was apparent.

The darting flies congregated around a plate of raw chicken breasts on the kitchen counter. Beside the spoiled poultry, a pile of half-chopped vegetables and an assortment of pinch bowls filled with colorful spices showed that someone had been preparing a meal.

Steadman controlled his impulse to stop and take a closer look and was pleased to see Frost moving on, as well. Their first priority was to ascertain whether anyone, victim or perpetrator, remained on the premises.

They moved from room to room and Steadman realized it would take some time to clear the house. It was bigger than it looked from the outside, and filled with closets and man-sized cabinets, each in need of checking.

The center of the house opened onto an elaborate atrium. It was deserted but splashes of dried blood on the hardwood decking told Steadman this was another area that would bear closer inspection.

They finished clearing the ground floor and Steadman motioned with his head for Frost to mount the large, curving staircase to the upper level. He followed close behind as the passage widened into a gallery at the top of the stairs.

They checked a few rooms that opened off the gallery, and he saw the tension in Frost's shoulders as they approached the corridor that led to the bedrooms. Hallways could be a funnel of trouble, providing little cover.

At the first closed door, Steadman saw a sheet of paper tacked to its surface. He ignored it for the time being and gave Frost the nod, gliding in as his partner threw the door open.

They encountered no living being, but three large sheet-wrapped bundles lay in the center of the floor and a heavy, oppressive odor floated on the air. Steadman had no doubt the linen-shrouded shapes were bodies.

"What's going on here, Chief?" Frost asked. In the dim light through the drawn blinds of the windows, his face looked as white as the sheets on the floor.

Steadman kept his voice gruff. "Let's finish our circuit."

They cleared the rest of the house, finding nothing else of note, and re-turned to the room with the mysterious sheet-covered forms.

This time, Steadman removed the paper tacked to the door, taking it to the window for better light as he read it out loud. The writing scrawled across the paper, becoming increasingly difficult to read as it drew down the page.

To the sheriff and deps in charge:

I am Det. Nate Quentin, BPD, Homicide. I apologize for disturbing your crime scene. Water's rising and time is short, forcing me to preserve what evidence I could and move it to a safer location.

I've tried to be thorough, but the bridge is moments away from a washout, so the details will have to wait. Here's a quick summary:

I'm working the PS Slasher case and I followed a lead to Mt. Vista where a conversation with Ms. Riley Forte alerted me that Mr. Ferguson might be in danger.

She was right. You'll find his body, along with two unidentified, wrapped in sheets. We moved them out of reach of flooding. Sorry.

I took pictures and collected what I could—

No more time. Get to MV. The suspect is a resident, but radio cut out before I got a name. That's where I'm headed.

N. Q.

Frost whistled, low in his throat. "Holy smokes, does this sort of thing happen a lot in homicide investigations?"

Steadman rubbed the bridge of his nose. A headache was trying to work its way under his skin. "Pretty much never, Frost. Guess we're just lucky."

A tri-fold of wrinkles rose on Frost's forehead and Steadman figured the young detective was trying to decide if that had been sarcasm or sincerity.

"What do we do now, boss?"

Steadman didn't answer right away. Anger, prompted by feelings of helplessness, flooded over him. He'd failed to help Nan and Hank. He'd failed to make a timely arrival at a murder scene under his jurisdiction. Extenuating circumstances aside, a deep rift tore at his store of confidence, tangling his emotions and eating at his gut.

Irritated that he and his team hadn't been the ones to handle the scene, he was grateful that someone had, before the layer of muddy water obliterated its finer points.

But it left him with a new set of problems. What was he supposed to do with three bodies he couldn't transport? What course of action was best to take?

He looked down at his soaked and mud-streaked boots.

"I don't know about you, partner, but my first order of business calls for borrowing a pair of Mr. Ferguson's very fashionable socks. I don't suppose he'll mind."

He ran a hand over his grit-crusted forehead and squared his jaw.

"After that, we head for Mountain Vista."

CHAPTER 23

FROST AND STEADMAN WADED through cold muck and floodwater to reach the boat, each miserable step accompanied by the scolding cries of seagulls. The greedy birds squabbled over the remains of dead fish carried up by the flood tide, chasing one another in querulous spates.

The odor was appalling and Frost was surprised to discover that despite the awful stench, he was hungry. The energy bar Steadman had passed him that morning seemed a long time ago.

His feet were like two blocks of ice at the end of his rubbery, gangling legs. It was just after noon on what should have been a sunny Sunday, but rays from the faint yellow orb in the sky had to poke their way through an ever-thickening gloom cast off by the volcano.

As a result, the air had a bite to it, and Frost longed for a fluffy blanket and a seat by a crackling fireplace.

He thought of the warrior his father had been, certain he'd endured harsher conditions for longer periods while still discharging his duties with honor. Frost drew a deep breath and straightened his spine, determined to ignore the goose flesh and growling stomach.

He climbed aboard the swaying boat.

"Take off your pants," Steadman said as he topped the ladder.

"What?"

"Come on," said the chief, gesturing impatiently. "No one's looking. We'll do what we can to get warm and dry before we press on. Let's hang our pants and change into Rico's socks. That polyester blend dries quickly."

"Not that quickly," Frost mumbled, remembering the state of his uniform when he'd put it on—had it only been yesterday?

Steadman gave him a look and Frost decided not to protest. He removed his holster and stripped off his pants, handing them to the chief who dropped his own trousers and arranged both pairs over the T-top covering the console, securing them with a clamp, like an industrial-sized clothespin.

The day was not windy, but a stray gust blowing their britches overboard would be the icing on this not-so-tasty cake and Frost appreciated the chief's forethought.

He sighed. If Lieutenant Jamieson had been along on this crazy jaunt, he bet it wouldn't be happening like this. He wondered once again what was going on in her world and hoped she was okay.

He and Steadman had taken not one, but two pairs each from the plentiful supply in the sock drawer of Rico Ferguson's bedroom closet. Frost peeled off his own sodden socks, wringing them out over the side of the boat before tossing them to the side. He slipped the dry socks over his frozen toes, moaning with pleasure and pulling both pairs as high up his calves as he could get them.

"Here," Steadman said, tossing him a packet. Frost was glad to see it contained an emergency blanket made of thin layers of Mylar. He wrapped himself in the woolly blanket he'd used last night and added the lightweight Mylar as another layer. He grinned at the chief, giving him a thumbs up.

"Feeling better?" Steadman asked.

"So much better. Now all I need is—"

"Something to eat?"

"You said it."

"Indeed, I did. Got anything?"

Frost felt his face sag, disappointment seeping into his newfound warmth. He'd been so excited at the prospect of his first murder investigation that he hadn't seen ahead to a situation such as this.

"I'm just yanking your chain, Frost. I brought the eats, but you might not like what you get."

Frost caught the little brown box the chief flipped at him. An MRE. He'd be dining like his dad today. He studied the label. Shredded Barbecue Beef with Seasoned Black Beans.

"Sounds decent," he told Steadman.

"At least it'll be hot," the chief replied.

"It will?"

"Sure. It's got a flameless heater in there, which can also do double duty as a hand warmer."

"Oh man, I sure hope you're not yanking my chain now, boss."

"Cross my heart."

Frost watched as Steadman showed him how to position the pouch containing his entrée with the packet of magnesium shavings and pour a little water down into the bottom of the bag, starting a chemical reaction. He folded the bag shut and slid it into a cardboard sleeve. Soon the bundle was putting out an impressive amount of heat.

"Bless you, Chief Steadman. You're a man in a million."

The chief looked pleased, but rolled his eyes in a way that let Frost know the compliment was over the top. Still, as they ate in silence, Frost thought he'd rarely appreciated a meal as much as this one.

By the time he'd finished every last bit, he felt more warm and dry and satisfied than he would have believed possible and found himself fighting to stay awake. His field of vision blurred, narrowing to twin slits as his eyelids drooped like they were filled with lead shot.

A sharp blast of noise next to his ear jerked him to attention as the chief snapped his fingers.

"No time for a nap, partner," Steadman said. "We've got an important chore to do, and then we move out. Got to make it to Mountain Vista before nightfall."

Frost shook the fuzz off his brain. "What's the chore, boss?"

Steadman pulled a kit box from the storage locker. "We're cleaning our weapons."

"Now?" Frost said, surprised.

He looked around the boat, at the mess that littered the deck from filthy waves crashing over the bow and all the crud he'd cut off the propeller blades. Their dirty trousers flapped gently in the whisper of a breeze.

"Here?"

"Yes, now and yes, here. Let's get to it."

Steadman wiped the bench seat with a blanket and laid out bottles of cleaning fluid and lubricant, along with rods, brushes, and pads, before ejecting the magazine from his Glock and clearing the chamber. Frost shrugged and fetched his own gun.

"You sure this isn't just because you like the sight of me in my boxers, Chief?"

"You're funny, Frost," Steadman replied, "but this business isn't. We've been out wading in mud and muck all afternoon. It's no joke what that can do to a firearm. You've met Fred Winter, the guy who usually works the front desk on day shift?"

"Yeah, I know him."

"Ever wonder how he lost those three fingers on his left hand?"

"Ah," said Frost, "I begin to see where this is going. Hunting accident or line of duty?"

"Hunting. Laid his shotgun down on the muddy floorboards of Dale Franklin's truck and didn't think to check the barrel before he made his shot. Shredded the crap out of his brand new Remington and he kissed those three fingers goodbye."

"Dang!" Frost had heard of such things, but thought they were pretty rare. "Okay," he said, "but that was a shotgun. This Colt belonged to my granddad, and it's a tried-and-true piece. Never misfired."

"Be that as it may," Steadman said, giving him a stern look, "I take proper gun care very seriously. I've personally witnessed two incidents where obstructions caused injury and my trainer went so far as making us use gun condoms when we were out in the field in inclement weather."

"No kidding?" Frost couldn't help the grin that crossed his face. "Did you keep one in your wallet?"

Steadman just grunted, but Frost saw the corners of his mouth quiver before he held out his hand, palm up like a surgeon giving orders to a nurse. "Bore brush."

Frost handed over the instrument and began stripping down his own weapon. They worked in companionable silence, with just the snick of metal on metal and the soft rhythm of cleaning pads and shop cloths.

Only the occasional drift of garbage bumping against the side of the boat and the swirl of air against his bare legs reminded Frost of the highly unusual situation which faced them.

He imagined telling this story to his kids some day and doubted they'd believe it. He and the chief, cleaning guns in their underwear while an exploding volcano and a serial killer hovered in the background. They'd think he was making it up and he wouldn't be able to blame them a bit.

Steadman finished first and fetched his pants off the makeshift clothesline. He dressed while Frost reassembled his granddad's service weapon and packed up the kit.

"Time to get back to it," Steadman announced, tossing Frost his trousers, still slightly damp. With a sense of deja vu, Frost zipped and buckled, replacing his holster and shiny, clean weapon.

"Let's see if you can get that motor running," Steadman said, nodding toward the outboard.

Frost tipped the motor up out of the water and used a long-shafted screwdriver and a set of heavy-duty scissors to free the blades from the twisted mass of gunk that held them captive.

From the corner of his eye, he watched Steadman bring up the anchor. Cutting away the last of the wreckage from the prop, he lowered the motor back into the water and listened as Steadman cranked up the engine. It roared to life.

"Yes!"

He made his way up to the front of the boat, high-fiving the chief as he passed. Grasping the reaching pole, he resumed his duty as defender of the prow.

The water still churned, rich cocoa waves with cream-colored tips. It made Frost think of the fudgy river on Willy Wonka and The Chocolate Factory, but this water was contaminated by far more than one fat German kid.

Frost pushed logs, uprooted bushes, and entire trees out of the way. Soggy cardboard drifted by and a toilet seat, somehow kept afloat by a puffy cover fashioned from pink plastic roses.

Though Steadman kept the speed down, they made good progress, following the shoreline toward the dock that lay just a half-mile shy of Mountain Vista.

Frost wasn't surprised when the motor started to sputter. They'd made it farther than he'd dared hope. The engine buzzed and died, and in the interval, Frost thought he heard something odd.

The chief fired up the ignition again, drowning out the unexpected sound, but as the motor coughed and faded, Frost became certain.

"Hold on, Chief!" he said, pressing his palm to the sky. He cocked his head and strained to hear it again. "Listen to that."

A voice, like that of a child, wafted through the air in what sounded like a cry for help.

"What in blazes? Where's it coming from?" asked Steadman.

Frost held his breath and tried to determine the source of the cries. He focused on a heap of junk floating twenty yards off the port bow.

A jolt of shock ran through him when he realized the sodden shank of fabric draped over a Styrofoam cooler was a sleeved human arm. And it was moving.

"There!" he pointed.

Steadman squinted, his face a mask of amazement. "Well, I'll be danged. Let's get over there."

Frost grabbed a paddle and he and Steadman maneuvered the boat until they reached the makeshift floating device. The hand clutching it was small, tinged a faint blue.

Fear rippled through Frost and his stomach roiled with dread. He tapped the curling fingers with his paddle.

"Grab hold and I'll pull you aboard," he shouted.

The hand shifted, grasping, and was joined by another. Two little hands clung to the paddle, and the Styrofoam cooler bobbed away to reveal the most beautiful child Frost had ever seen. Hair like dark, molten gold slicked down on either side of a water-beaded alabaster face, and eyes the color of sun-gilded cornflowers stared back at him, unblinking and terrified.

Relieved to see the life in those eyes, his heart ached nonetheless, thinking how cold and scared she must be. Gently, he pulled her to the side of the boat and leaned down to lift her aboard.

A loud *booooom* tore across the water and Frost saw three holes appear in the smooth plastic of his paddle, with more marring the fiberglass side of the boat.

Before he could even process the meaning of this, the air filled with the sound of more gunfire.

CHAPTER 24

DART SWORE, DUCKING BACK behind the thick-trunked pine tree as a piece of it splintered off with a ping, narrowly missing his eye.

A feeling of unreality dragged at him, stirring his gut like a sludgy cup of coffee. The nightmare that had started with Maddie's escape had just grown several shades darker.

"Drop your weapon!"

The strident voice came bounding across the water, and the swirl of nausea troubling his stomach became a tsunami. As soon as Maddie had a chance to speak, she'd spill everything to the men in the boat.

And by the look of it, they were law. He had no choice but to shoot, and they were shooting back.

"This is Chief Deputy Steadman, and I repeat—drop your weapon and move out where I can see you. Keep your hands up."

Adrenaline spiked through Dart's veins. His hands shook like spindly branches in the wind and his mouth felt as if it had been sucked dry by a bitter sponge.

He spared a dark thought for his old man. Nothing like this had ever happened to his dad. For years, he'd somehow snagged women without drawing the notice of the police and Dart knew he must still be at it.

Somewhere.

Six weeks after high school graduation, his dad had packed a bag and disappeared. If he'd been caught practicing his chosen lifestyle, it would have made national news and Dart knew he sure as hell hadn't quit.

He was either dead, or still at it. If the old man had seen fit to take Dart with him on his hunting expeditions, given him any proper training, this wouldn't have happened. Damn the man for giving him a taste for it and leaving him to flounder.

Another shot rang out, and leaves fluttered as the blast landed around him. He whipped his Mossberg around and pulled the trigger with desperate abandon, watching as one of the men in the boat worked the paddle, pulling the boat back.

His target was moving out of range. If he wanted a hope of hitting anyone in that boat, he'd have to run down onto the open shore.

He crouched behind the tree and surveyed the beach. A grouping of rocks rose about fifteen yards out, their base concealed by swirling water. If he could make it to that cover without getting hit, he might have a chance.

His only chance.

He gripped the shotgun and tore across the muddy, pebbled beach, his boots slithering atop the slime. One of the men on the water fired and shot rained down, rattling against stone, driving holes into the mud, but falling short of Dart.

The next thrust of his legs would bring him in range, and he cringed while the momentum carried him forward, expecting to feel the piercing sting of metal tearing into his soft parts.

And then, he was behind the rock.

He drew one quick breath, steadied his aim, and fired. A thin scream rose up, floating on the air.

Maddie.

A savage satisfaction welled up within him, heating his blood as he fired again. He couldn't tell how much damage he'd inflicted, but he was committed to doing all he could.

One shell left. He pulled the trigger before the boat could pull back any further and was rewarded by a shout of pain from one of the men.

Two clear thoughts sprang into his head. He had hit at least one of them. And it wasn't near enough.

Under the circumstances, he thought he could count on their means of communication being shut down, limiting the dangerous knowledge of his deeds and identity to the three of them in that boat.

His next course of action had to be keeping it contained and blotting out the stain before it spread.

Where would they come ashore?

They had Maddie, and she would be their primary concern at this point. They'd be heading to Maddie's house to reunite her with her worried parents and those who would keep her safest.

Dart chewed off a piece of thumbnail that had come loose and spat it into the murky water, making up his mind.

He would be there to greet them.

CHAPTER 25

MADDIE STARED AT THE blood dripping onto the floor of the boat.

Black spots crowded at the edge of her vision. With all she'd endured over the last twenty-four hours, she held onto a stubborn pride that she hadn't fainted or become hysterical. But this last assault, hearing all those bits of metal pinging at high speed all around her, seeing them open up holes in all they hit—it was too much.

She blinked her eyes and clenched her fists, determined not to collapse. The man who'd been hit dropped the shotgun and clapped a hand over the wound in his arm. She saw blood pool up and spill over between his fingers.

"Get us out of range, Frost!" he shouted to the other man.

Both wore uniforms, so she knew they were some kind of police and that made her feel so much better. A sob worked its way up into her throat and she swallowed it down. Stooping, she crab-walked over to the bleeding man.

"It's okay, honey. It's not as bad as it looks."

He smiled, pressing the corner of a blanket over the wound, and some of the fear eased out of her chest.

"You're not hurt, are you?" he asked.

She shook her head.

"I saw how you stayed low, coming over here. You're a smart girl. I don't think he can reach us anymore but keep your head down."

She nodded. The other man, the one who had pulled her out of the water, stopped paddling and hurried over.

"Shooter ran off into the woods," he said, guiding the bleeding man to a bench seat. "How bad are you hit?"

"Just burned a trench down my arm. Stings like the dickens, but shallow. Should be able to control the bleeding pretty quick. Why don't you see to her first?"

He tipped his head toward Maddie and the man who'd rescued her turned his gaze in her direction, his face pasty beneath short-trimmed reddish blond hair. His eyebrows, light as they were, stood out in contrast to the pallor of his skin, making the astonished look on his face even more pronounced.

He pointed to himself. "I'm Detective Frost, and that's Chief Deputy Steadman. I just call him Chief and I bet you could too, if you want."

Maddie nodded again, not yet ready to speak, though she wanted very much to tell them about Dart so they could hunt him down and put him in jail.

"What's your name?" he asked. When she didn't answer right away, he said, "Did that man hurt you?"

She opened her mouth, but the words stuck in her throat.

"Let's get you warmed up," he said.

He wrapped a scratchy blanket around her that smelled a little like campfire smoke, and over that he tucked a big sheet of foil, making her feel like a giant baked potato. To her surprise, a giggle rose up and escaped her lips.

"Dart Rosedale," she managed to say, quivering inside her protective covering.

"That's your name? Dart?"

The hold on her tongue let go. "No!" she shouted, glowering at him. *"His* name. I'm Maddie. Maddie Swenson."

"I'm pleased to meet you, Maddie. Are you okay?"

"Now I am," she said, and the tight crunchy feeling in her chest lifted a bit more as she realized it was true. She wasn't alone anymore. "Thank you for coming," she said.

"I'm so glad I did, Maddie. When you're ready, I'd like you to tell me all you can about that man." He paused. "Are you feeling warmer now?"

She wasn't cold anymore, but she couldn't stop shivering. She thought if she tried to speak again her teeth would chatter, and she didn't want him to think she was falling apart. She dipped her head toward the Chief.

He understood. "Will you be okay while I help the Chief for a few minutes?"

She gave a firm nod, and watched while the man called Frost got a first aid kit and cleaned and bandaged the Chief's arm, which had mostly stopped bleeding.

Objects in the water bumped and battered the boat as they drifted by. From her position on the boat's floor, she couldn't see them, but she remembered her bewilderment at all the floating garbage on the water when she'd plunged in.

She didn't understand how all the junk had gotten into the inlet and worried that maybe a plane had crashed into the Sound. Swimming through the shifting masses had terrified her, yet she was grateful for the cover they'd provided, allowing her to hide from Dart.

The deputy finished with the first aid, and the chief asked for her address and phone number but didn't try contacting her parents.

"Aren't you going to call my mom?" she asked.

She saw a look pass between the two men and it scared her. The chief knelt down and put one warm hand on her shoulder.

"Do you know about the volcano, Maddie?"

A wave of dizziness shimmied through her. Volcano? Was this a dream, the continuation of a long, confusing nightmare, each piece more unreal than the last?

She felt those black spots blooming at the edges of her vision again and the chief gave her a gentle shake.

"Stay with me, Maddie. I know you've been through a lot, and you just want to go home. We'll get you there, but I'm afraid we can't call your parents. Cell coverage is down. Mt. Rainier erupted yesterday, and it's knocked everything out."

She couldn't breathe. Her chest squeezed up again and she fought off a smothering wave, pushing it away, refusing to give in. At last, she pulled a gulp of air into her lungs and the dizziness disappeared.

She raised her chin. The chief said the eruption had knocked everything out, but she was here, and she was okay. She'd made it this far, and she was going home.

"I want to tell you what happened."

She let it all pour out of her. How Dart had followed her in the forest. How he'd tricked her and trapped her. How she'd escaped, and he'd stepped on her in the dark, and she got free of him but then he somehow found her again and chased her right down to the water.

She told how she'd decided he would not catch her again, even if she had to drown to get away from him.

She saw the Adam's apple go up and down in Detective Frost's throat, and the Chief's face got redder and redder the more she talked. She remembered the purple scorpion tattoo and told them about that, and Dart's Madame Butterfly and how he'd cut her with it.

She talked and talked until her jaw grew stiff and tired and her eyes felt scratched and heavy like they were full of sand.

And when she couldn't talk anymore, she curled up in the bottom of the boat and let sleep cover her like a soft, dark blanket.

CHAPTER 26

STEADMAN FORCED HIMSELF TO swallow past the bitter lump in his throat as he stared down at the sleeping child, her cheek cushioned against one curled fist.

Seeing her there like that, so vulnerable, her face shadowed by copper-colored lashes against pale, smooth skin, the tip of her nose tinged pink, brought a stab of memory too painful to face in that moment.

He slapped it away.

The late afternoon had finally warmed to something above sixty, and the fetid odor of fish-stained mud wafted across the churning water, doing unkind things to his stomach. Shimmers of rage and sorrow clashed within him as he thought about Maddie's situation—and about Nan's—making matters worse.

He squeezed his eyes shut and massaged the bridge of his nose. Time to button down the emotional conflict and make a good decision about how to move forward.

"Let me go after him, boss," Frost said, his voice wound tight. "I can paddle over and wade to shore. He can't have gotten far—"

Steadman opened his eyes, rubbing a layer of grit from beneath them with a tired hand. "Not going to happen, partner. You and I are sticking together, and neither one of us is leaving her," he said, gesturing toward Maddie. "Let's concentrate on getting her back to her family and go from there."

"But—" Frost stopped, spluttering, his eyes echoing the fury that pulsed through Steadman's own veins. "He's getting away. He shot you, he tied up a little girl and cut her with a knife. Lord knows what else he had planned—and we're just letting him go?"

"Not at all, Frost. Thanks to that brave little girl, we know something about this guy. We know his name, where he lives, and most importantly, we know where he's going."

"We do?"

"Here's something maybe you didn't know about me, Detective. I've spent every free moment of the past two weeks training with one of the wiliest minds in casino poker this side of Vegas. If there's one thing Garth Rafferty's pounded into my head, it's this—you've got to base your strategy on your read of the other guy."

Steadman focused his gaze on his partner's indignant face. "He's got one play, Frost. Tell me what it is."

Frost looked blank for a moment and Steadman watched as comprehension dawned. "He's got to head us off at the pass, stop us before we spread what we know."

"Which means—"

"He's headed to Maddie's house."

"Right on target, Detective."

Frost groaned. "That means we've got to turn around and go back the way we came."

"I'm afraid so, and we'd best not waste time. That boy's not what I'd call mentally stable. Who knows what he might do if he gets there first. Start paddling, Frost. I'll see what I can do about the engine."

Steadman knelt at the rear of the boat and lifted the outboard, tilting it up on its mount. A tangled mass composed of seaweed, rope, scraps of fabric, and any number of unidentifiable strands coated the blades. Using his pocketknife, he sawed and picked at the knotted mess until the last of it fell away.

The propeller was a sorry shadow of the fine piece of machinery it once had been, the blades bent and discolored. Steadman lowered it back into the murky water and settled himself in the captain's chair.

He pressed the ignition button and listened to the engine hack, cough, and die. He tried again and managed to keep the motor running long enough to get another three hundred yards back along the shoreline, the way they'd come.

Just as he was feeling like they had a hope of making it to Maddie's address before Dart could arrive, the boat bucked, slewing up and sideways, and a hideous scraping noise emerged from beneath. The engine choked out. Steadman ran aft and stared down into the water as chunks and shreds of chewed-up wood eddied and spun in a choppy froth.

"Damn! A submerged tree."

"Sorry, boss. I should have seen it."

"No way you could, in water as thick and brown as this. It's not your fault, Frost."

It took both of them struggling together to disengage the prop from the tangled limbs of the sunken tree and lift the motor out for inspection. The propeller was done for, two blades mangled beyond any reasonable use, and a third ripped clean away from the shaft.

"Well," said Steadman. "it's back to paddling."

They each took an oar—Frost at the starboard, Steadman on port—and dug into the mud-churned surface of the inlet. As he dipped and skimmed his paddle through the filthy water, the memory prompted by Maddie's sleeping face flooded back and with grim resignation he let it come. It had pushed free from the depths of his subconscious and though he hated to admit it, maybe it had something to say that he needed to hear.

But it was hard, thinking about those years—the squalor of the unkempt house, the smell of unwashed laundry and empty bourbon bottles. The roaches ate better than they did, though Nan did her best to cook and keep the place decent.

He was nine, Nan twelve, and their little brother just two years old when their mother packed a bag and walked out, without a kiss or a backward glance.

For a while, Steadman thought they were doing okay. He missed his mother, but only a little. She'd never been a warm or affectionate woman and he believed she'd found it easy to walk away, leaving a toddler and two pre-teens to be raised by the weak, ineffectual man who'd sired them.

Little by little, as the months passed, and the family accepted that she wasn't coming back, liquor took what was left of their father.

The man steeped himself in alcohol. Never a violent or abusive drunk, he nevertheless couldn't be depended upon to work a regular job or do much about the wretched condition of his family. Caring for the youngest one, Thad, fell almost entirely upon Steadman and his older sister.

Nan was the glue.

She provided the sticking power that held the family together. She was mother and sister, rolled into one, even though there were only three years between them. Nan managed to get passing grades in school while holding down a job and keeping house.

Despite the difficulty and drudgery, they had some happy times and both he and Nan felt a fierce attachment to their little brother.

Steadman gritted his teeth, regret searing through him like white-hot fire. He stabbed the oar with savagery into the tossing water as if that might kill the beast of memory. He longed to shove it away, but he continued to let it torment him—half believing he deserved it, half feeling like these thoughts were surfacing for a reason.

He'd been fourteen, on that darkest day. Nan had moved on from working the fast food circuit and had a job she was proud of, at a local boutique.

Dad was home that afternoon, but deep in alcohol-scented slumber, and Nan charged Steadman with watching over Thad while she went to work. But he'd made plans with a group of buddies, the sort of plans that didn't include seven-year-old brothers.

He was not about to miss out on fun with friends—not when all Thad had to do was stay at home and watch TV.

"I wanna go with you, Randy."

Steadman hated that nickname, insisting on Rand instead. Thad was the only one who got away with calling him Randy.

"Not this time, pal. I'll make you a peanut butter sandwich and you can watch cartoons until I get back."

"But I can keep up with you on my bike, Randy. Honest, I can."

Steadman remembered the tug inside his chest prompted by that earnest little face and funny lisp through missing front teeth. Now, he gripped the paddle and gnashed his own teeth together, forcing himself further down the dark road of that day.

"I'm sure you can, bro," he'd said, ruffling the little boy's hair. "But I need you to stay home this time. I'll let you play with my Legos. You can build a new bat cave."

"Don't wanna."

Thad pouted out his lower lip and gave Steadman the evil eye, but he hadn't caved. His friend Barry had a pack of cigarettes from his older brother, and John had stolen three Penthouse magazines from the stash his father kept in the back of the bathroom linen closet. Steadman had "man plans" and having Thad along would ruin everything.

He'd made the sandwich and poured half a glass of milk, settling Thad down with a TV tray and a bin of his best Legos before slipping out and peddling away on his thrift store mountain bike. The three friends spent an hour in the woods and Steadman had choked through his first cigarette, knowing at once it was a habit he'd never pursue.

John's mom had busted him with the magazines, banishing the whole stash from the house, so that was a washout. Still, they'd had a good time joking and playing and when dusk drew near, they mounted their bikes and headed home.

A thump shook the boat and Steadman stumbled against the side as it dipped under the tug of underwater detritus. He thrust his paddle into the roiling water, grinding his teeth together until he tasted blood.

But he let the rest of it come, let it sting into him like a wash of acid, stripping away the protective flesh until only the stark, white bone of memory remained.

Blood-red lights had striped across the tall pine trunks as he and his buddies neared the main road. There was no siren, only the silent, eerie spiral of flashing lights, but Steadman's stomach shrunk inside him, settling as if weighted by a giant stone.

He knew.

In that moment, he knew what he'd see when he emerged from the cover of the forest, and he wanted to burrow under the pine needles and never come out.

He stopped on the fringe and stood, straddling his bike, his heart thumping like a hammer in his chest. Leaning over, he vomited into the ferns. Barry and John went ahead, curious to see what the ambulance was for. He heard them calling his name.

When he forced himself to come out, the only thing left to see was the mangled remains of Thad's bike and the dark-stained pavement beneath it.

His little brother, a sweet seven-year-old who loved Legos and peanut butter sandwiches, was dead.

Steadman gagged on the taste of blood as the crush hit him beneath the breastbone, the pain as fresh now as it had been all those years ago.

Tortured by the memory of his poor judgment and selfish decisions, he twisted in the wind of his own derision, everlastingly unable to rewind or to stop wishing that he could.

He had a history of letting family down, and now he knew why the memory had surfaced. That would not happen again.

Not today.

Not with Maddie's family. He'd see her home and safely settled. And he'd track down her captor and bring him to justice.

He'd do right by her.

The vicious burn of anger and sorrow kept him warm as he worked the paddle through the water and the sun sank, inch by inch, below the tree line.

He thought about Nan, how hard she'd worked and how much she'd sacrificed for him. Even after he'd let her down on that disastrous day, breaking her heart, shaming himself, and effectively killing their little brother.

He thought about the husband he knew Nan loved with every fiber of her being and the trouble they were in. He thought about how she'd come to him for help, how much she was counting on him.

He'd give anything in this world to know how he was going to do right by her.

CHAPTER 27

DART HUNKERED DOWN BEHIND a clump of hydrangeas in Maddie's front yard, watching the windows of the house, the smell of damp earth crinkling his nostrils. Dusk was just settling over the landscape and the sky was an ashy gray, no stars peeping through to break up the sullen blanket.

Dart licked a finger and lifted it to the sky. Not much in the way of a breeze, but he detected a feeble eastward puff. If that changed, fallout from the volcano could shift in their direction, dumping loads of ash into the air. Best to be under cover in those circumstances.

The lawmen had been paddling, he noticed, rather than running the motor. With all the muck in the water, he wasn't surprised. He was about ninety percent sure he'd beaten them here and nothing he observed said any different.

He planned to get into the house, put Maddie's parents out of commission, and ambush the deputies when they came. By midnight, he'd solve his exposure problem and have Maddie safely locked in the basement cell next to Ma.

He ran his hands over his jeans, feeling the solid lumps formed by his precious knives, hefting the gun over his shoulder. He had all he needed. Rising, he took a deep breath and strode across the lawn to the front steps.

Maddie's mother answered his knock. Red spots mottled her pale face and Dart supposed she'd been crying. She tried to hide her disappointment when she saw him, but Dart knew she'd been hoping for news of her daughter.

"Oh, Dart." She peered into the distance behind him, biting her lip. "Everything all right at your house?"

"Yes, Mrs. Swenson. No problems. I just came over to see if you folks needed anything."

"Well yes," she said, her voice breaking, "we need Maddie safe at home. Have you seen her, Dart? She's been missing since yesterday afternoon."

"What? Oh, that's terrible. Is there anything I can do to help?"

He watched her features twist with the effort of keeping her emotions in check. A second or two passed before her jawline hardened and she pointed at him with her chin. "What's the shotgun for?"

He shrugged. "Just general security. You know, a lot could happen in a situation like this. Animal attacks, looting. I just feel better having it with me."

She considered, then nodded, taking a step back and holding the door open for him. "Yes, we feel the same. Please come in. I could use someone to talk to."

Dart hesitated. "Where's Mr. Swenson?"

"He took the dogs out looking for Maddie."

Dart stepped into the house and shut the door behind him. She was alone.

"I'm sure he'll find her. She's bound to be okay, Mrs. Swenson. Maybe she sprained an ankle or just got lost."

He followed her down a wide hallway into a kitchen at the back of the house. The aroma of coffee met them, and she offered him a cup.

He hung the Mossberg on a set of pegs just inside the back door, meant for coats and jackets. A lone pair of muddy green galoshes slumped on the floor beneath. She poured out a cup of hot brew for him and they perched on stools at the granite-topped island, sipping in silence while Dart's hand inched toward his pocket.

He played through it in his mind, picturing how it would all go down. Harold was the knife for this job. He'd flick open the switchblade and jab it up hard under her ribs before she could even speak. When Mr. Swenson came home, he'd be waiting.

But would the man be armed? And what about the dogs? Would they follow him into the house?

Dart looked around the room and noticed the dogs' food and water dishes next to the back door. They looked the size of hubcaps. So, not chihuahuas.

"You folks have a gun, then?" he asked, as if making conversation. "What kind?"

"We just have the one and Isaac took it out with the boys."

"The boys? Is that what you call the dogs?"

She looked startled, then gave a short laugh. "No, the dogs are female. Isaac took Marv Henderson and Dave Wilson with him to help find Maddie. Full-fledged men, not boys, but the way they sometimes act..."

Her expression was rueful, but the hard-edged worry in her eyes showed through.

Dart swallowed the rest of his coffee—too fast, too hot—and tensed, ready to rise. The search party could return at any moment.

He had to act now.

CHAPTER 28

THE SCRATCHY FABRIC AGAINST her cheek was the first thing Maddie became aware of as she drifted up from sleep.

She realized she was rocking slightly, like in a cradle or a swing, and wondered if that was part of something she'd been dreaming. She lolled, lazy, wrapped in warmth while remnants of her dream state swirled at the edge of consciousness, swimming out of reach before she could focus on any one of them.

She had a feeling it was better that way, and with that thought came full awareness.

Maddie shot upright, breathing hard. The blanket fell away, and the sudden rush of cool air brought gooseflesh out on her arms, prickling under her thin jacket.

She'd made some kind of strangled, frightened warbling sound with her mouth and the two men, each rowing with a long paddle, turned to her, their faces tight with concern. She remembered now—Chief and Frost.

And she remembered more than that.

A sudden, overwhelming need to be in her mother's arms flooded over her and she was horrified to find her throat clogging with tears. She would not cry.

Digging her fingernails into the palms of her hands, she concentrated until the physical pain drew her focus and allowed her to swallow and breathe. Just swallow and breathe.

If the men noticed her near breakdown, they gave no sign of it.

"Hey Maddie," the chief said, gesturing with his paddle. "Recognize this place?"

She swiped the moisture from her eyes and looked out over the boat railing, taking in the sight of the familiar shoreline. It was all she could do not to leap overboard and swim for land. They couldn't get her there fast enough.

Home.

As they pulled into the shallows, the hull of the boat biting sand, Maddie swung a leg over onto the ladder, ready to full-out sprint the ninety seconds it would take her to get to the house.

But the chief pulled her back and turned her to face him, his touch gentle yet firm.

"Let me tell you how this has to go, Maddie. I know you're anxious to get home, and we're anxious to get you there. But we have to be smart about this. Dart could be waiting, and remember, he's got a gun."

A gurgle of fear rose in Maddie's chest. "Could he hurt my parents?"

It seemed to her the chief hesitated a shade too long before answering.

"I don't think he's had time to do any mischief here, Maddie, but we need to be careful. We need to protect you. Detective Frost will cover us from the boat while you and I get behind the tree line. Then he'll join us, and we'll go from there. But no running ahead, Maddie. It's very important you understand that."

The weight of disappointment pulled at her heart. To be this close to home and have to move so slow was torture, but she knew the chief was right. She nodded.

"I understand."

"Good girl."

She watched him sling the long-barreled gun over his shoulder and pat a hip holster where she saw another smaller weapon nestled. Frost drew his own gun, holding it low and ready. Chief raised an eyebrow at Frost and the detective nodded back.

"Let's go then."

Chief went down the ladder ahead of her, landing knee-deep in water, and waited for her to descend a few rungs before lifting and carrying her to the shore. Setting her down, he took her by the hand and led her fast across the beach and into the waiting pines and alders, their faint and ragged shadows fleeing before them on the pebbled sand.

They startled an owl, and it hooted loud enough to make Maddie jump before it flapped away, deeper into the forest. The chief brought the long gun to the ready as they watched Frost run to meet them.

Slow and quiet, the three of them pushed forward with Maddie pointing the way. They didn't use a flashlight, relying instead on the sparse dull stripes of moonlight that fell between the branches.

Maddie felt excitement in her chest as they neared the border of her family's property, but she restrained the urge to shout out or move ahead.

The trees thinned, and she saw her house, lights burning in the wide array of windows spanning across the rear. A bubble of longing rose within her, bright and clear as the sun. She was about to step onto the back lawn when the chief stopped, putting out an arm to hold her back.

Shadows covered his face so she couldn't read his expression, but she saw him raise a finger to his lips.

"Listen," he said, in a voice so soft she almost missed it.

She stopped breathing, straining hard to hear what he meant. The crackle of dry leaves under a treading foot came to her and as she peered through the dark, the dim figure of a man appeared.

And he carried a gun.

Maddie's heart leapt in her chest. The chief held on to her, but she squirmed free with a terrific yelp and ran, a shout breaking from her lips.

"Daddy!"

CHAPTER 29

FROST MADE A SNATCH for Maddie as she rocketed out of Steadman's grasp, his heart beating in his throat as if it had wings and was trying to escape.

He'd seen the man materialize out of the shadows, the outline of the shotgun silhouetted in darker shades against the gloom. During the shooting, he hadn't been able to get a good glimpse of Dart Rosedale and he couldn't be sure that's who faced them now, but he felt the situation called for extreme caution.

Maddie's exuberance overcame both his and Steadman's efforts to restrain her, and Frost watched in dread as the girl sped into the night, closing the distance.

As she leapt into the man's arms, a baying of dogs burst into the night and two enormous mastiffs loped into view, pausing to sniff and lick at Maddie before moving on to investigate the two strangers in the yard.

Relief that Maddie had found her father—rather than the malicious Dart—vied with Frost's unease over the dogs' suspicious regard. They barked and growled, showing their teeth, daring him and Steadman to take one more step.

"Bella, Poppy, hush!"

The deep voice was almost smothered against Maddie's hair, but potent enough to calm the dogs. They sat on their haunches, eyes wary, still on the alert. The man released Maddie and came across to shake hands, wrapping Frost's cold palm in a warm, hearty grip.

"Thank you so much for finding Maddie and bringing her home. Her mother and I have been frantic, and I've been out searching for her since last night. I can't think what—"

He broke off and gave his daughter a look filled with equal parts exasperation and gratitude. "You've got some explaining to do," he said.

Steadman spoke up, his voice low and steady, but Frost sensed the undertone of urgency. "I think we should go inside and talk, Mr. Swenson."

"Sure, sure. Maddie's mom will be crazed with worry, wanting to see her. I can't think why all the racket from the dogs hasn't brought her out already."

A fist of dread squeezed inside Frost's gut, and he saw Steadman's lips thin to a grim line across the hard plane of his jaw.

Maddie took a few running steps toward the back door, but this time Frost was quick enough to catch her. She craned her head to peer up at him, her chagrined expression highlighted by stray beams from the porch light.

The girl's father saw the interaction and drew in a sharp breath. "What's going on? Maddie?" He turned to the chief. "What's happened that you're not telling me?"

"Mr. Swenson, we really should ge—"

Steadman broke off as the back door of the house burst open with a clatter and a red-haired woman streaked across the lawn. Maddie flew to meet her, and Frost's heart swelled as the three family members reunited, sharing a long embrace.

The last time his family did that was the last time his family would ever do that.

He shook off the little stab of envy by reminding himself that Maddie's family circle wasn't as big as it once had been either. She'd lost her brother, as he'd lost his father and grandfather. But family went on.

He was ecstatic to see this happening and to be a part of it, and the relief he felt at seeing Maddie's mother well and whole nearly overwhelmed him.

Steadman herded them into the house and secured the door. Frost sat with Maddie and her parents in the family room while Steadman checked to make sure Dart was not in the house and all entryways were locked.

Frost suffered the parents' frightened glances and mystified questions, putting off answers until the chief returned.

Steadman finished his circuit and gave Frost a subtle nod as he seated himself in a leather armchair.

"Do you feel up to telling your parents about it, Maddie," he asked the girl, "or would you rather have me do the talking?"

"No, I can do it," Maddie said, and the note of strength, the resilient determination Frost heard in her voice, told him she would be okay. It would take time and the love of good parents, but Maddie had both those things, and she was a survivor.

She sat between her mom and dad on the sofa, each family member sharing warmth and physical contact.

"Yesterday," she began, "I was exploring the woods on the hills above the house when I found out Dart Rosedale was spying on me. He told me—"

"Wait a minute," Mrs. Swenson interrupted, "Dart Rosedale? But he was just here, not ten minutes before you arrived. He didn't mention that he'd seen you, even after I told him you were missing. Why wouldn't he have—"

She stopped, a shadow creeping into her face, darkening her eyes. Frost felt awful, knowing the agony and guilt that were about to descend over her mother's soul.

"Dart was here?" Steadman asked.

"Yes, he came over to ask if there was anything we needed. I invited him in for coffee—"

She broke off and Frost watched all the color drain from her face.

"He sat right there," she said, gesturing over to the bar stools, "and drank my coffee. We chatted."

She stopped, putting her hands over her face and rubbing hard.

"What's the rest of it?" she asked, her voice turning brittle. "What happened, baby? What did he do to you?"

Maddie cupped her mother's cheeks between her little hands.

"I got away, Mom. I got away from him before he could really hurt me, and he's been chasing me ever since. But now I'm home."

"Oh, my—" Mrs. Swenson's face crumpled, and she burst into tears.

Maddie hugged her mother, and Mr. Swenson wrapped his arms around the both of them. Frost imagined how this could have ended—how he, or another one of the deputies, might have had to deliver news so much worse than this.

A wave of something close to actual joy flooded over him. How curious that he could feel such a thing amid this utter turmoil.

Maddie got the rest of the story out, punctuated by sobs from the mother and swearing from the father. Mr. Swenson got up and kicked the side of the sofa savagely when Maddie described how Dart had demonstrated his butterfly knife.

He paced in agitation until she got to the part about Frost scooping her into the boat, only then calming enough to rejoin his family on the couch. When Maddie finished speaking, silence stretched through the room, broken only by one of the dogs lapping from the water dish.

Mr. Swenson cleared his throat and said what they'd all been thinking.

"Now what?"

"Now, we need to make sure Maddie stays safe," Steadman answered, "and I don't think this is the best place for her. Let me give you my ideal situation, under the circumstances, and you tell me how close we can get to it."

"All right, Sheriff. Let's hear it."

"It's just Chief Deputy, sir. I doubt you'll find me running for the office of sheriff."

Pity. Frost thought Steadman could fill the sheriff's shoes with everything the job demanded. After working with the man over the past two days, Frost was learning to like and admire the chief as much as any man he'd ever met.

Barring his father.

"From what Maddie tells me," Steadman said, "Dart knows a few things about your family. He'll likely know about your closest friends in the area and might go looking for you there. Do you have any friends in the vicinity that Dart won't know about? Until roadways and communications are restored, I'd like to see you battened down at an anonymous friend's house. Is that possible?"

The couple thought for a moment, then Maddie piped up. "What about the Jenners?"

"Tell me about them," Steadman prompted.

"They just moved in a couple of weeks ago," Mr. Swenson said. "About eight miles away on the other end of the Loop. We see them at church on Sundays and have talked about getting together, but it hasn't happened yet. I doubt Dart knows anything about them."

"We can't just show up unannounced and expect them to take us in," Mrs. Swenson protested.

"That's exactly what you must do," Steadman said.

Mr. Swenson smiled. "It's what we teach at church. Let's give them the opportunity to show that Christian spirit."

"I think they'll be happy to take us," Maddie said, her voice firm.

"What about our friends nearby," said Mrs. Swenson, "the ones that Dart knows about? Are they in danger? Shouldn't we warn them or something?"

Steadman rubbed his chin. "I think ignorance is their best defense. Dart is interested in limiting the knowledge of his guilt, minimizing his footprint. If he goes there looking for you, it's best that your friends genuinely have no idea, so they won't telegraph their awareness. He'll sense that and move on."

Frost hoped Steadman was right about that. What a horrible mess this could turn into if Dart took it into his head to start pumping the neighbors for information. Common sense should tell him to flee the area, but Frost didn't put a lot of stock in Dart's powers of common sense.

"We have a plan, then," said Steadman. "Go pack a bag and let's get moving. The faster we're out of here, the better."

CHAPTER 30

Steadman straightened himself behind the steering wheel, experiencing a wave of exhaustion that was almost pleasurable, mixed as it was with relief and happiness for Maddie.

He had a good feeling about the Jenners and their location—distant enough from the Swenson home to add a nice buffer and yet situated in a small, tight-knit group of neighbors where a stranger would be noticed and regarded with caution.

He felt a little burst of warmth in his chest as he remembered Maddie's goodbye hug and her feather whisper in his ear.

"Thank you for saving me, Chief."

What a sweetheart of a girl and a real, honest-to-goodness trooper. He hated to think what she'd been through, but felt a tug of pride for her, knowing she was strong enough to come out on top.

The whole family had embraced both he and Frost before they left the Jenner home, and Mr. Swenson had pointed out the key to his house on the ring Steadman held.

"Use the house for a command post, if you need it," he said.

It looked as if they might need it.

A fine film of ash grimed the windshield, intensifying the gloom as Steadman stared forward, his weary eyes focusing on the roadway, scanning for hazards. He drove the Swenson's borrowed SUV at what felt like a crawl, passing many times through enormous standing puddles, maneuvering around water-logged trees and—in one instance—a smashed-up rowboat, stripped of paint and splintered beyond recognition.

They'd had to stop twice to clear obstacles where the water had risen high enough to deposit unpassable debris on the road. He switched on the windshield wipers, smearing sooty blue liquid across the glass expanse, and tried to ignore the marshy smell coming off both him and Frost, sour emanations from their filthy uniforms.

"Do you think Maddie will be safe with the Jenners?" Frost asked.

It was the first time the detective had spoken since they left the Jenner house and despite his good feelings, Steadman couldn't help the doubts creeping in. It was only natural.

"I'm positive," he said, with slightly more assurance than he actually felt. "With virtually no traffic on the roads, it was easy to see that no one followed us out there and Dart has no way of knowing where we took her. She is safely tucked away now, and Dart's got a big problem. He failed to keep the cap on his dirty little secret and if the boy's got two brain cells to rub together, he'll be hightailing it out of the state."

"We've got to stop him, boss. How can we rest until we've got him?"

"Take it easy, Frost. If he was stupid enough to run on home, we'll get him."

"And if he wasn't that stupid?"

"We'll cross that bridge when we get to it."

The detective slammed a fist against his knee and burst out with his peculiar version of a curse word. "Bat scat, Chief! Too darn many bridges are washing out in this disaster. What if we got nothing to cross?"

Steadman put a note of warning in his voice, hoping to steady his partner. "We'll deal with it as it comes, Frost."

Streetlights were scarce in this rural area, only two or three appearing on a mile stretch of road, and the glow of porch lamps was intermittent, scattered like a handful of tossed pebbles.

As Steadman drove forward into the night, even those few spots of illumination winked out and the headlights bored into thick blackness like twin drills to the center of the earth.

"Power outage," Frost said. "I'm surprised it didn't happen sooner, but I had fond dreams of getting a hot shower and running a load of laundry."

Steadman gave a regretful laugh. "I agree we both smell like the back end of a stink bug, but—"

"I know, Chief. That's why they were only dreams. Duty before creature comforts."

After what felt to Steadman like a decade, they neared the darkened house Mr. Swenson had pointed out as the Rosedale residence. He stopped well short of it, killing the headlights, and he and Frost exited the vehicle, pushing the doors gently shut rather than allowing them to slam.

Steadman locked the shotgun in the car, but checked to make sure his Glock was ready to go. Both he and Frost carried flashlights.

The box-shaped house hulked under a flat, heavy sky, moon shining like a tarnished silver plate, dull beams drooping downward through a dirty mist. A set of mournful creaks issued from the dilapidated gate as they pushed through, making their way to the front door, weapons drawn, ears pricked to pick up any sign of Dart's presence.

"Should I cover the back door?" Frost whispered.

"No. I'd rather we went in together, but if he busts out the back and runs for the woods, you can take point."

"Thanks, Chief." Frost cleared his throat. "It occurs to me we don't have a warrant."

"I don't think anyone will fault us for moving ahead without a warrant, Detective."

"I was hoping you'd say that."

Steadman tried the knob on the off chance it was unlocked, but knew it couldn't be that easy. He pounded a fist against the metal door, feeling it shake beneath his hand.

"Sheriff's deputies, Mr. Rosedale. Open up!"

Only silence for an answer, and Steadman detected no sounds from inside. Taking a deep breath, he landed a sharp kick just under the doorknob. The door shuddered but showed no sign of giving way.

In his experience, this rarely worked out the way it did in the movies, crashing open on the first kick, making the fellow on the screen look so slick. Instead, after five more attempts he was sweating like a Christmas ham, the perspiration stinging the long gash in his arm where Dart's shotgun pellet had scraped away the flesh.

He stopped to catch his breath.

"I got her started, Frost," he panted. "Why don't you finish her up?"

It felt like a rite of passage and Steadman remembered his first time, more than a few years back, when his own chief had ceded the satisfaction of the door's crunch and collapse, giving Steadman the chance to shine.

Frost wasted no time in smashing his boot against the resisting slab and Steadman heard the characteristic sound of the wooden frame weakening. The third time Frost raised his foot, wood caved and splintered, leaving the door to swing inward, hanging crookedly on its hinges.

Steadman went in first with gun and flashlight, fanning out, checking corners and behind furniture. The only thing that moved was a skitter of little brown roaches running for cover.

A rancid odor hung in the air, like lard gone bad. A lot of lard. Whatever had occupied Dart Rosedale's time in recent months, it hadn't been housekeeping.

A quick search of the premises yielded no sign of Dart or anyone else. Maybe the kid was smart enough to head for the border, but Steadman would feel better making that assumption if he could find something to convince him it was so.

"I'm going upstairs," he told Frost, "to look for indications he packed a bag. Check the kitchen and pantry. If he took food with him, maybe he left some sign of it behind. See what you can find."

Steadman climbed the scuffed wooden staircase to the second floor, shining his flashlight along the strips of peeling wallpaper and water-stained ceiling. Here, the odor of rancid fat yielded to the stench of unwashed sheets and clothing. He kicked aside a pile of dingy laundry, wondering if it hid anything interesting. It didn't.

A quick search of the bathroom turned up no toothbrush, toothpaste, or deodorant, which lent weight to his theory that the boy had flown. On the other hand, maybe his personal hygiene went as neglected as his household chores and their absence didn't mean a thing.

"Chief!" Frost's voice floated up, carrying a note of excitement. "I got something you should see."

Steadman hurried down the stairs and into the kitchen. Frost stood in the pantry doorway, holding the flashlight beneath his chin like a kid around a campfire.

"What'd you find?" Steadman asked, ignoring the theatrics.

"Well," Frost said, "there's this."

He indicated a spot on the pantry shelf where a thick layer of dust was interrupted, leaving three round shapes.

"Looks like he recently took some cans and other stuff."

He played the light over a similar rectangular vacancy, empty of dust as if a cracker or cereal box had been removed.

"Good work," Steadman said. "Smart money says he bugged out."

"Maybe," Frost replied, "but that's not what I called you down for. Look at this."

He shone the light over the back wall of the pantry, illuminating three pegs hung with aprons so faded and worn that Steadman could see right through to the wallpaper in the flashlight's beam.

Frost reached a hand forward, pushing aside one of the aprons and touching a spot on the wall. It slid open, a little swinging panel, to reveal a doorknob.

The skin on the back of Steadman's neck tingled, and he pulled the Glock once more from its place on his hip.

"The fox has a hidey hole after all," he said, keeping his voice low.

"And there's this," Frost whispered, holding out a key. "I found it under a fruitcake tin on the top shelf."

Steadman grinned. "Clever thinking, detective. That's the last thing anyone would think of disturbing. That cake has probably been up there since 1962."

He considered the situation.

"We need to be real careful here, Frost. If we open that door and shine our lights down, we present the perfect target. We're short-stacked."

"Huh?"

Steadman gripped his gun in one hand and the flashlight in the other. He nodded toward the key. "Open it quick and stand back, Frost. Do not follow me down until I give the all clear."

Frost hesitated, his mouth opening to voice a question or objection, but there was no time.

"Do it now!"

The detective turned the key in the lock and pulled the door inward, allowing Steadman access to the narrow stairway. He went in fast, using the flashlight's glare to blind and confuse, holding the Glock at the ready.

No shots rang out, no muzzle flashes in the dark. He drew a breath and shone the beam methodically over the area. Nothing moved or made a sound.

He descended the stairs, heart thumping in his chest like a galloping stallion. The basement consisted of a single, open room containing a worktable and an array of tools.

As Steadman neared the bottom step, he saw an alcove at the far end, partially obstructed with freshly laid bricks. Dart could be hiding behind the half-wall.

He approached with care, pausing every few steps to listen. He was three feet from the wall when an unearthly gurgling wail rose and surrounded him, shocking him so completely that he lost his grip on the flashlight and it fell, casting its beam in crazy, whorling loops as it rolled on the uneven floor.

"I'm fine," he shouted, for Frost's benefit. "Don't come down here."

He retrieved the light and aimed it into the space beyond the wall. He stared, not comprehending at first that the animal locked in the cage was human.

The wave of revulsion that washed through him was staunched by a stab of pity so sharp he felt like he might actually be bleeding.

"Frost!"

He meant to add some kind of warning, some words of wisdom stemming from his experience to prepare his partner for this, but his tongue was paralyzed, his throat swollen with bitterness.

He couldn't form a single word.

CHAPTER 31

FROST CLATTERED DOWN THE stairs into the dark cavern below, filled with equal parts dread and curiosity.

The chief's voice calling his name had sounded so strangled, like the gasp of a drowning man going down for the last time. Frost found his own breathing felt strained and painful, but he was bursting to know what was down there.

A putrid odor permeated the walls, and shadows writhed and danced under the bouncing beam of his flashlight, causing objects in the darkened basement to leer out at him like Hitchcockian special effects.

Frost caught a glimpse of rusty tools hung on pegs above a stained and battered worktable. He tripped over a bucket and knocked the mop from its mooring to smack against the concrete floor. As he reached the far end of the room, Steadman grabbed him by the shoulders, holding him back with a gentle squeeze.

"I would have picked a different way to break you in, detective, if the choice had been mine," the chief said.

After a pause, he sighed and released Frost's shoulders, stepping back so that Frost could see a set of bars encased in concrete. He pointed his flashlight into the cell and saw a figure, a woman encased in some kind of gown, cowering on a cot. She moaned and turned her face away from the light.

"Can you work your magic, Frost, and find the key for this?"

Incredulous, Frost stared past the bars, taking in the dank prison—the rough, filthy floor, the worn and shabby blanket, the blue plastic bucket that served as a chamber pot, contributing to the oppressive stench trapped in the room.

He wanted to cry. Saliva welled up in his mouth and he couldn't swallow it down, couldn't make the mechanics of his throat work, but knew better than to spit it out at a crime scene.

He and Steadman searched for a key, rifling through boxes of junk, combing over the encrusted tools. With a wrench of horror, Frost realized what he'd thought was rust was more likely dried blood.

What nightmares had taken place in this basement?

An enormous flood of relief threatened to break through his fragile composure as he thought of Maddie, safely delivered into the hands of friends.

Her—down here—was unimaginable.

Frost crawled beneath the metal worktable and shone his flashlight on its underside. In one corner, a black hide-a-key case clung like a cicada shell to the metal frame. He yanked it free and fumbled out the key, his hands shaking so he nearly dropped it.

"Here you go, boss."

Steadman spoke in soothing tones while he worked the key in the lock.

"It's okay," he murmured. "We'll get you out of here and get you someplace warm. Get you something to eat. You're going to be okay."

He kept repeating the words in a soft monotone, almost like a hum. A mantra. Something they could all believe in.

The metal bars swung open with a grating squeal and Frost wondered how long since Dart had visited his prisoner.

She was thin, though not emaciated, and he saw that she was older than he'd first thought, probably in her fifties, though her condition made it hard to tell. Circumstance might have added thirty years to her appearance.

She didn't move or look at them or react in any way when Steadman took her hand, rubbing it between his own. Her eyes were vacant, and Frost reflected that she probably lived in some internal, faraway world and he hoped she could be coaxed back into this one, once it became habitable for her.

Steadman scooped her into his arms and Frost lit the way as he carried her up the stairs.

The chief lowered her onto a tattered couch and arranged the blanket around her.

"Should I get some water?" Frost asked.

"I'll do that," Steadman answered, removing the Swenson's car keys from his pocket. "I need you to go to the nearest house and ask where we can find a doctor. Keep looking until you find one."

Frost ran to the SUV, the ash-crusted moon casting lacy shadows on the muddy road. It was after three o'clock in the morning. He'd have to pound hard to rouse people from sleep and he risked finding a shotgun leveled at his face. He'd take care to announce his affiliation with the Sheriff's department and hope folks took that in a positive light.

After half an hour, he returned to the Rosedale house with two people in tow. He led them up the front porch and found Steadman sitting on the couch beside the woman, tenderly clipping her fingernails by the glow of his flashlight, as if she was his own aging mother. Except, if it had been his mother, he probably wouldn't be depositing the clippings into a zip-lock baggie.

"Did you find a doctor?" was the chief's only greeting.

"No," Frost replied, "but I think I happened on a pretty good alternative. This is Hattie Higley," he said, indicating the woman. "She's a psychiatric nurse, and this is her husband, Bruce. He's a guard at the women's correctional facility in Purdy."

Steadman rose and shook their hands. "You folks are a godsend. Thank you so much for coming, and I hope you'll find it in your heart to help this poor woman. She's been through hell for who knows how long."

"Has she said anything?" Hattie asked.

"No," Steadman said. "And she won't. Her tongue has been removed."

The nurse made an indignant clucking and knelt down beside the couch. She ran efficient hands over the woman, taking her pulse, feeling for injuries. Steadman cleared his throat.

"It's not safe for her here. Is there any—"

"Of course she can't stay here," Bruce said. "Bring her to our house and we'll keep her until this volcano mess is straightened out and you make other arrangements."

The chief reclaimed the car keys and drove the five of them to the Higley house where Hattie made quick work of settling the woman down at the kitchen table for a meal. Frost felt his own stomach growl.

"I'm going to fix something hot," Hattie announced. "You gentlemen want to stick around for that?"

A battery-operated lantern lit the kitchen and Frost saw a camp stove set up on the counter. These folks were capable and prepared. He gave Steadman a look he hoped was filled with hunger and hopefulness. A gentle smile crept over the chief's lips and up into his eyes.

"We'd love to, ma'am. Thank you very much."

In minutes, they were sitting down to scrambled eggs, ham, and pancakes. Frost forgot about his filthy clothes, clammy against his skin, and the exhaustion that pulled within him like a leaden weight. He was in heaven.

The woman, who Hattie had dubbed Sweetie, ate a little but her eyes wandered, making contact with no one. His hunger sated, Frost found that looking at her made him feel tired beyond reason as he wondered about the human capacity for cruelty.

But watching Hattie feed her, patting her shoulder and keeping up a soft patter of soothing talk, he realized that as deep and dark as it went on the one end, it was balanced by the human potential for compassion on the other.

He and Steadman thanked the couple and took their leave. As they climbed back into the SUV, Frost remembered the burning question he'd had just before Steadman had barreled down those stairs into that cursed basement.

"Chief, what did you mean when you said we were short-stacked? I don't remember hearing that term in tactical training."

"You wouldn't," Steadman said. "It's an expression used in poker to mean you've got less to bargain with than your opponent. When that's the case, you have to get aggressive. There's really only one way to play it."

"How's that?"

"Don't speculate. Commit while you still have enough chips. And be first into the pot."

"Ah," Frost said. "That explains a lot. I think."

CHAPTER 32

MADDIE'S EYES FLEW OPEN.

A hand wrapped around her upper arm, and she fought against it, gripping and twisting, pressing her fingernails into the flesh while screaming at the top of her lungs. In the dark, she saw movement, a figure, a face lost in shadow, and she bucked and wrestled to free herself.

"Maddie!"

The sound of her name, exploding in the blackness of the room, shot her heart straight into her throat and she struggled to pull in breath for another scream.

"Maddie, honey, you're okay. We're here. You're safe. You're safe now, Maddie."

Her mother's voice.

The terror receded, melting bit by bit like a square of midnight chocolate on the tongue. She clung to the sound of her mother's voice and began to remember where they were.

She heard a click, and a little flame leaped into the gloom as her father lit a candle. Maddie leaned into her mother's chest, feeling the beat of her heart, fast but slowing. She breathed deeply and felt her own heart calm.

Her mother hummed soothingly and stroked her hair. "It's okay, baby." There was a pause and Maddie sensed a note of tension creeping back into the room as her mother spoke again.

"Who's Harold?"

Blood rocketed through Maddie's veins like traffic on the freeway, rushing and hot, even as her mind went blank, fighting against the memory.

Harold?

A soft whimper rose up around her, growing in intensity until she felt the vibrations in her chest and knew it came from her.

"Harold!" she screamed, pulling back from her mother. That's what she'd been dreaming about—Dart and his Madame Butterfly.

And Harold.

A ball of dread formed in her stomach and started a slow roll through her gut.

"I forgot to tell him about Harold," she said.

"What do you mean? Tell who?"

"I told Chief about Madame Butterfly, but I forgot about Harold. I should have told him!" she cried, her voice rising to a panicked squeak.

How much would it matter? Would Chief and Frost catch Dart? They knew he was crazy. They knew he was dangerous. They'd be ready for him.

But what if they weren't? What if they weren't ready for Harold?

It would be her fault.

The ball of dread settled into an ache that churned, making her feel like throwing up. She clenched her fists and pressed them against her eyes, willing away the tears as she made the confession to her parents.

"I forgot to tell Chief about Dart's other knife."

CHAPTER 33

WEAK RAYS OF MORNING sun fell against the windows of the Swenson's garage, almost like a normal day in western Washington. Except instead of rain clouds, an increasing screen of ash veiled the sky. Steadman surmised the volcano was still pumping it out.

It felt strange to be so cut off from all the usual channels of communication. Almost like going back in time to an era uncluttered, and unenhanced, by technology. When a man had to depend on himself, with the help of friends and neighbors.

He thought about the Jenners and the Higleys, and a ripple of gratitude passed through him. The help of good friends and neighbors was not merely a thing of the past.

The oil lamp hanging from a hook above him sputtered, emanating a gentle hiss, further fostering that feeling of being in times gone by. A dreamy sensation settled over Steadman, and he fought to keep his eyes from closing where he stood.

He stamped his feet and shook himself hard. He needed to stay alert and in the moment. Looking down at the disassembled shotgun on the workbench, he saw he'd spilled a small puddle from a bottle of lubricant. He grimaced and swallowed.

The heavy scent of gun oil permeated the air and coated his tongue. He mopped up the spill, but the oil-soaked rag he used sent the nauseating odor out in waves. He should open the garage door for ventilation but didn't want to give Dart easy access if he paid Maddie's house another visit.

He took the rag to the farthest corner of the garage and returned to the workbench. Frost was sleeping, getting some well-deserved rest while Steadman stood the first watch.

He smiled, remembering the detective's well-scrubbed face as he went off to bed. He'd gotten his shower, after all, and Steadman looked forward to one of his own when he got the chance. The power was still out, so the water was likely to be cold by that time.

Such was life.

Steadman pushed the rod and iron brush down the barrel of the shotgun, sweeping out a light buildup of dust. He really was determined to be diligent about keeping the guns in pristine working order, as far as it was possible. And besides, it helped keep him awake.

He had another four hours to go before he planned to wake Frost for his shift. They were both exhausted and needed to log some sleep time before they could press forward to any useful degree.

And after sleep, then what?

Steadman soaked a pad in solvent and thought about their next move. He and Frost had returned to the Rosedale house with the "go bag", thinking to collect evidence, but it seemed a futile task. There was no power to the house, they didn't have the tools to do a thorough job, and neither of their dampened phones was working properly to take pictures or video.

On top of that, his battery was about shot. In the end, he decided to secure the scene the best they could and leave it for the specialists.

In a shed behind the house, they'd found some old boards, along with a hammer and nails. Steadman made sure all the windows were locked, and he held the boards while Frost nailed them in place, sealing off both the front and back doors.

If he was dumb enough to come back, Dart could break into the house—but they hadn't made it easy for him.

Rest seemed the most prudent priority after that.

Steadman changed the cleaning pad and made another pass through the barrel. Both he and Frost had been running off of anger and a desire to nail Dart's skinny butt to the wall. Anger was a great motivator, but it could burn off as fast as it flared. And worse—it skewed your judgment.

A lot.

He remembered a training day in Rafferty's basement den when he'd been particularly exasperated by the game. After thrashing him for hours, his poker-wise mentor had leaned back in his chair and tossed his handful of cards to the table, a crafty look on his face.

"Ever play pinball when you were a kid, Rand?" Rafferty asked.

Steadman rolled his eyes, predisposed in the face of his frustration to consider it an asinine question.

"Sure. Whenever I had quarters rubbing a hole in my pocket and someone was hogging the Asteroids machine."

There hadn't been that many spare quarters when he was a kid, and Rafferty's reminder of that sent Steadman's irritation up another notch.

"Did it ever make you mad when the little ball didn't go where you wanted it to, heading into that dreaded gap between the flippers?"

Steadman snorted. "Never happened that way for me."

"Okay, hotshot. Let's pretend it did."

They both knew it had.

"Did you ever get so pissed that you took it out on the machine? Shook it, maybe, or slammed a fist into it?"

Steadman felt something boil over inside him. This was a useless enterprise. He'd never pick up the skills he needed to defeat a crack team of players in a couple of weeks. Or ever.

And he was about sick of the nuggets of wisdom Rafferty kept doling out through hand after hand of cards and numbers and statistics. The little devil inside him wanted to pound that smug expression off Rafferty's face and by some bizarre quirk of reasoning, he thought he could do it best by winning the pot.

Steadman threw his own cards on the table.

"Right now, I'm about ready to slam my fist into you," he said through gritted teeth. "Deal the cards."

Rafferty folded his hands in front of him and bowed his head, looking almost as if he were about to say grace.

"You're making my point, Rand," he said quietly. "Go home. Come back tomorrow, and we'll talk."

Steadman kicked the empty chair next to him, a wheeled affair that went spinning across the bamboo flooring to crash against the wet bar.

"I'm not quitting now, Rafferty. Deal the damn cards!"

Rafferty stood, the extra twenty pounds he had on Steadman poking out like a bulbous shelf under his Hawaiian print shirt. He looked thoughtful, rather than angry, and that made Steadman all the more furious.

He knew he was being petty, acting like a spoiled child, but he couldn't seem to put a lid on it. He pushed his chips to the center of the table with so much force that half of them went over the edge.

"Let's do this, Rafferty. I'm all in. How about you?"

Without a word, Rafferty simply lifted his arm and pointed toward the door that led out of the daylight basement and into the backyard where Steadman had enjoyed barbecues and games of horseshoes back in the days before Rafferty's retirement.

Steadman swallowed hard. He grabbed a handful of poker chips and hurled them at the older man's belly. They bounced off and rolled on the table, producing the only noise in the room.

Steadman left.

It took a lot for him to come back the next day. Not because he was still angry, but because he wasn't.

Mortified by his behavior, he didn't know what had come over him and felt deeply sheepish about the whole thing. He owed Rafferty an apology. His mentor may not want to continue their relationship, but Steadman meant to at least give him that much.

Rafferty answered the doorbell and took Steadman's proffered six-pack as if nothing had happened. There was no awkward funk in the air, no hint of resentment. Rafferty grabbed a bag of pretzels to go with the beer and they headed down to the basement.

Steadman saw the poker chips were back in their neat stacks, the deck of cards ready to go.

They took their seats, and he watched Rafferty pop the tab on a can of Blue Ribbon and knock down a long swallow, wiping his mouth with the back of his hand before letting out a sizable burp.

"So, Rand," he said, his voice mild. "Did you ever kick the pinball machine?"

Steadman had to laugh, amazed that what had so incensed him yesterday felt so innocuous today. Only his sense of shame remained, and that was fast dissipating in the face of Rafferty's easy forgiveness. He responded with honesty.

"I kicked a few," he admitted. "Slapped one so hard once, my palm was sore for a month."

"And what happened when you lost control like that?"

He thought about it, remembering those days. "The machine shut down. Game over."

"Ah," said Rafferty, lifting an eyebrow. "Tilt."

"That's right."

Steadman recalled the garish, hot pink sign that lit up just before the flippers stopped working and the ball zig-zagged down to an inexorable death. "Tilt."

"And that's what happens when you lose your temper at the poker table," said Rafferty. "You're toast. Once you start making decisions based on emotions rather than sound strategy, it's game over and your best course of action is to walk away. It's called tilt, just like in pinball."

Steadman whistled, low in his throat, and shook his head. "I was about as dumb as a rock yesterday, Garth. I apologize. I don't know why I acted like that."

"Players on tilt never do. It's near impossible to admit you're wrong when tilt's got you in its clutches. It's a kind of madness, if you'll pardon the pun."

"You've pardoned worse from me."

"I've been there, my friend, and I learned the hard way. You might be the brightest player—knowing every strategy and reading every opponent with dead-on accuracy—but it won't amount to a hill of beans if you go on tilt. You're done for. And it doesn't have to be anger that throws you off. Sometimes it's euphoria or fear. Any time emotion is calling the shots, you're on tilt."

"So, what do you do about it?"

"Well, like most things, prevention is worth a pound of cure. Ten pounds, maybe, in this case. Recognize your triggers—those things that set you off—and eliminate them or get away from the table before tilt takes hold."

"And if it's too late for that?"

Rafferty picked up the deck and started shuffling.

"Two steps," he said. "First, you got to know you're on tilt. And admit it to yourself. Sounds easy, but it's damn difficult. And if you can get past step one, step two's an even bigger challenge."

Steadman groaned. After his experience the day before, he had an idea how tough it might be.

"I hesitate to ask," he said, "but what's step two?"

"Leave," said Rafferty. "Cut your losses, walk away. Live to play another day."

"Oh, that's cute."

Rafferty shrugged. "I don't deserve the credit for that little ditty, but hell if I know who does. Lost in the annals of poker history, I suppose. Bottom line is this, Rand—do not chase your losses. Period. Keep your focus on the big picture, the long run, instead of getting trapped in the desperate compulsion to do something right now."

Sound advice, easy to say. Infinitely harder to back those words with wisdom in action.

A flutter of wings, followed by a soft thud, brought Steadman's attention back to the Swensons' cold, oil-scented garage. A bird, probably disoriented by the increasingly sullen sky, had flown up against the window.

Steadman looked out, craning his neck to see the driveway below. The bird—Steadman thought it was a chickadee—floundered on the gravel surface in an effort to right itself. As Steadman watched, another flash of movement caught his eye.

A cat.

The orange tabby crept across the Swensons' front lawn, and the poor bird's movements became even more frantic. Steadman slapped his palm against the window, but the cat paid no heed. In three blinks, the stalking feline would be in pouncing distance. Steadman cringed and gritted his teeth, willing the little bird to fly away.

And in that moment, it did.

Like a miracle—wings restored, balance regained—the chickadee flew up and out of reach, leaving the cat to yowl after it.

Steadman let the breath out of his lungs. He hadn't even realized he'd been holding it in.

He returned to the worktable and wiped down the shotgun's exterior, polishing it well before inserting the bolt assembly into the carrier. He finished putting all the pieces in place and checked to make sure everything was in working order.

Going back to the row of windows across the top of the garage door, he peered through, wondering if he'd even recognize Dart if he saw him again. He'd only gotten a glimpse of the man from a distance, and it was mostly the clothes he'd seen.

Dressed differently, Dart might not stand out to him at all. Still, when he scanned the tree line and the long driveway out to the main road, he saw nothing to raise his suspicions.

The cat was gone.

After that, he walked another circuit through the house, ensuring the doors were still secure, observing outside conditions through each window. He ate a can of cold pork & beans and found a box of Rice Krispies Treats in the pantry, figuring Maddie wouldn't begrudge him sharing her snack.

He munched down two bars and drank some water before doing forty jumping jacks and stretching his hamstrings at the kitchen bar to keep himself awake.

It was a long three hours until Frost's turn at sentry duty.

CHAPTER 34

THE TOE OF DART's boot caught on something in the darkness, and he stumbled forward, cracking his kneecap against a hard, exposed root.

He flung a slew of curses into the night and stretched out on the pine needles, trying to rub away the shock of pain by kneading at it through the thick denim of his jeans. A faint sigh of wind fluttered the boughs above his head, but that was the only sound he heard.

The crickets had stopped.

His knee still throbbed, and his ankle sent out tender shoots of pain, as well. From the last time he fell.

He'd grabbed a new flashlight from home, but the batteries were weak, and his quick search hadn't turned up any spares. The beam of light was pathetic, doing little to clear a path before him, but it was two hours to sunrise and Dart needed to log some distance.

After learning from Maddie's mother that her husband had two men and two good-sized dogs in search mode, he'd recalculated his odds and his strategy. Added to the two lawmen, it was more than he could handle, and he didn't know how many people they'd already told about him.

He decided his best bet was to get out of Dodge while the volcano ran interference for him. He left Mrs. Swenson to her coffee and tears and ran home to load a backpack with a change of clothes, a toothbrush, several bottles of water, and some food from the pantry.

He added a package of dust masks he found in the garage. The air was getting sooty and if the wind shifted, it would only get worse.

He wasted precious minutes standing inside the pantry, staring at the wall hung with a row of threadbare aprons. What should he do about Ma?

A thorough search of the premises would expose the hidden door and if Ma was still alive when they found her, she would have a lot to tell. Though he didn't know how they would get it out of her. She couldn't speak intelligibly.

He didn't know if she was still capable of writing or if any form of communication was open to her. And if anything was, would she testify against her own son?

He thought she might.

He should end her now. He should go down those stairs and guarantee her silence. But what about everything else they would find? There wasn't time to scrub it all out, even if he could. There was enough down there to tell a damning story and there really wasn't a thing he could do about it.

Except leave.

Dart sat on the cushion of pine needles long enough that the crickets started up again, sending out their hopeful mating song. He wondered how such a ruckus could attract an amorous partner. It was an irritating sound, grating on his nerves.

He stood up, brushing dirt and leaves from his pants, and readjusted the weight of the pack against his shoulder blades. He hated being on foot, but he'd had to leave his old Ford pickup back where the road had crumbled away into the Sound.

No one had placed orange cones or triangles to warn drivers about what lay out of sight just around the bend, and he'd nearly gone airborne, slamming on the brakes just in time. He'd parked the truck on the shoulder, at the far side of the eroding blacktop, but the way the muddy swirling water sucked at the tremulous shelf of land, he feared it might be floating away by lunchtime.

Not his problem, though. The truck wouldn't have gotten him far, in any case.

He flicked on the flashlight's feeble beam and pointed it forward. He believed he was traveling roughly parallel to the main road that led to Mountain Vista. It was time to veer off to the west and head up over the ridge that separated the inlet from the Hood Canal.

He aimed to avoid contact with anyone until he reached Highway 106. There, he figured to hitch a ride and get clear of the area before word got out and they tightened the net.

With luck, he'd be in Canada before the sun went down again.

CHAPTER 35

FROST SAT ON A bar stool at the Swenson's kitchen counter, swinging his legs and eating a bowl of Lucky Charms.

He couldn't keep still. Recharged by almost five hours of sleep and a sugar rush from raiding the pantry, he was eager to head out and track down Dart.

Giving Steadman a shot at a few hours of uninterrupted sleep was one of the hardest things he'd ever had to do. And now that the chief was awake, it was even more agonizing to wait.

He supposed it was only fair to let Steadman get a shower before they left. The hot water was gone, so it would be a short one, thank heavens. Frost couldn't wait to get on the road.

He swallowed the last bite of soggy marshmallow bits and tipped the bowl to drink the rest of the milk. It wasn't what you could call cold anymore, after sixteen hours in a powerless refrigerator, but it hadn't spoiled.

Frost licked the spoon, relishing the sweetness. He hadn't indulged in delicious but nutritionally barren kid's cereals in a long time, trying to be healthy and virtuous with shredded wheat and raisin bran.

As a child, the only time his mom bought "junk cereal" was when they went on a camping trip. Treating himself to that bowl made him feel like he had way back then, like he was setting out on an adventure and the world was his.

Dart Rosedale may be running for the hills, but he'd better be enjoying these hours of freedom, because they'd be his last.

Frost rinsed the bowl and left it in the sink. He stared out the kitchen window, chewing at his bottom lip in frustration. The sun, a dull golden disk, was sinking behind the trees, leaving only a few hours of daylight. Why couldn't the chief hurry it up?

He heard a gentle clink and turned to see Steadman emerge from the hallway, buckling his belt. At last.

"Where do you think he went, Chief?" Frost asked.

Steadman dropped to the couch and began putting on his boots, moving with maddening slowness. "Who are you referring to, Detective?"

Frost stared. He couldn't believe the Chief had said that. Who else would he possibly be talking about?

"Dart," he said, hearing the edge in his own voice. "The scumbag who introduced an innocent girl to a hellish world she never should have seen. That guy, Chief. Remember him?"

"Forget Dart," Steadman replied, leaning over to tie his bootlace.

Frost felt as if someone had reached out and thumped him on the chest, the impact was that physical.

"What do you mean, forget Dart? How is that—"

"The sheriff didn't send us out here after Dart," Steadman interrupted. "We have a job to do and now that Maddie is safe and Dart is gone, we go back to the business at hand."

The lukewarm sugar-frosted milk threatened to come back up.

"You don't know that! You don't know for certain she's safe, and he's on the run."

Steadman fixed him with a stern look, his brown eyes harder than Frost had ever seen them.

"Yes, I do know it, Detective. And so do you. Don't you?"

Frost swallowed. He knew it—with as much certainty as anyone could, after the precautions they'd taken and the distance they'd covered where no one could have followed.

But that didn't satisfy the rage inside him, the burning need to snap the cuffs on Dart's filthy wrists and pull them maybe a little tighter than need be. That didn't stop the acid drip that boiled his blood every time he thought about what Dart had meant to do to that little girl.

"We are not just walking away from this," he snarled.

"Frost," Steadman said, his voice soft and low, "Dart will not get away with this. He will be caught, and he will be punished, to the full extent of the law. But that's a point for another day. Right now, we've got—"

"Oh, right!" Frost knew his voice was spiraling up in pitch and volume, but he did nothing to stop it. "This is what you meant when you said we'd cross this bridge when we came to it. You meant we'd give up. I didn't figure you for a quitter, Steadman."

The chief sighed and stood from the couch, hands doing the automatic pat, checking badge and holster.

"We've got three dead bodies back at Rico's place," he said.

Frost felt a blank spot in his mind light up as if someone had flipped a switch. He had forgotten about that. How could he have forgotten that three people had been butchered in his jurisdiction, that their murder is what had started him down this path?

"And if the Bellevue detective is correct," Steadman continued, "there's a serial killer in an unprotected neighborhood less than five miles from here. I'm still in charge of this investigation, Frost, and I say we head to Mountain Vista and do our job."

The heat in Frost's belly went from full flame to burning embers. He was not ready to let go of the anger generated by Dart's escape, or the resentment he was feeling toward his boss, but Steadman's pointed reminder was like a bucket of cold water, bringing it down to a simmer.

He set his jaw and remained silent.

The chief stood before him, head cocked sideways, face craggy and inscrutable. Frost felt he was being weighed and measured. He straightened his spine and lifted his chin. Steadman held out a hand.

"Are you with me?" he asked. "Partner?"

Frost wanted to let the chief's hand hang out there, unmet. The thought registered in his mind, and he knew it for the spiteful, defensive piece of nonsense it was. He shook Steadman's hand but didn't meet his eye or say a word. He was still mad as all get-out they weren't going after Dart and wanted that to be clear between them.

Steadman shouldered the shotgun and locked the house as they left. Frost climbed into the passenger seat of the Swenson's old SUV, slamming the door harder than was necessary and feeling a grim little glint of satisfaction at the wince on Steadman's face.

The gloom of ash in the sky brought an early nightfall, but there were still streaks of orange and dark pink painting the backdrop behind the trees. If the road between Maddie's house and Mountain Vista was unobstructed, they might arrive before full dark. Frost slouched back in his seat to enjoy the ride, hoping the chief picked up on his subtle message.

This is all on you.

Large puddles and heaps of debris dotted the road, but nothing they couldn't get around, or through, in the big SUV. Frost felt his chest loosening up a little as they rounded a curve, and he glimpsed an old Ford pickup parked on the shoulder ahead.

It seemed to shudder, and Frost wondered if an earthquake was causing it.

"Hang on!" Steadman shouted, slamming on the brakes and yanking the wheel to the left. The SUV headed straight for the old pickup, headlights bouncing crazily.

A split second before impact, the SUV's rear wheels slewed right and the whole vehicle dipped backwards and sideways, pulling it away from the truck.

Frost looked out his window. Darkness veiled his view, but something was moving out there.

A splash of muddy water slammed against the glass, and he realized he was suspended over the churning inlet, the SUV balanced precariously on the broken road.

Frost froze. Any shift in weight could send them over the edge.

"Easy now," Steadman said, and Frost felt an insane urge to laugh.

"It's a car, Chief, not a wild stallion."

Frost heard the click of Steadman's door handle.

"I was talking to you, not the car."

Frost couldn't believe he was still hanging on to his grudge against the chief, but he just couldn't seem to let it all go.

"Yeah? Well, the same thing applies."

Steadman pushed open the driver's door by slow degrees and they both leaned in that direction. The SUV leveled out slightly, and Frost felt like they might both make it out if they moved quickly enough.

Before he could twitch a muscle, a horrific screech of metal meeting a hard surface tore through the car and it tilted again, sinking lower.

The SUV began to shake.

"Now, Frost!" shouted Steadman. "Take my hand."

The car jolted and dropped another notch toward the frothing waves below. Frost's heart leapt into his throat. There was no way back for the SUV now.

He began to think about his training, how to escape from a submerged vehicle, but panic seemed to erase his thoughts as they came to him.

"Get out, Chief!" he screamed. "I'm going down."

"Grab my hand, partner, or I'm coming with you."

Frost felt something give way beneath him and without conscious thought, he sprang toward Steadman, clutching at the chief's outstretched hand.

A mighty ripple went up his arm, nearly tearing it from its socket, and the SUV dropped away, taking a huge bite of earth with it.

Frost scrabbled desperately, trying to find something to stand on, but his legs dangled over the jagged edge. Only his elbows found purchase as the ground continued to crumble into the hungry maw.

Steadman still had a hard grip on his hand, twisting it at an awkward angle, and spears of pain shot up from his wrist. Frost gritted his teeth and dug his elbows into the rough, pitted surface and pulled, gaining several inches.

Steadman did the rest.

Frost lay panting in the middle of the road with Steadman stretched out beside him. The song made of their labored breathing was accompanied by the crash of water and disintegrating asphalt, like cymbals in a symphony.

Frost stared up into the darkened sky, astonished at how clean he felt, wiped of anger and resentment, as if fear had pushed his reset button.

Chief was right.

Dart was not getting away. They would find him and put him away for life. But now Frost felt the pull of those people up the hill in Mountain Vista—vulnerable, in need of help, a killer in their midst. They were his priority now.

He heaved himself to his feet and offered his hand to Steadman.

"We've got a hike ahead," he said, thinking with regret of the flashlights, gone with the SUV.

"Right," Steadman agreed. "We'd better get started."

CHAPTER 36

An ache born of cold and stiffness radiated from Steadman's hips as he shifted on the thin layer of leaves and needles beneath him.

He cracked open an eye and realized he could make out the dark shapes of trees against a pewter gray sky. He stretched and grunted, glancing at the sleeping form of his companion, not quite ready to wake the man.

The darkness of the night before had been complete. No flashlights, no streetlights, no electricity, and a thickening blanket of ash blocking the moon and stars.

After stumbling up a steep hill into the ridge above the ruined highway and pushing into the deep and brambled forest, both he and Frost concluded it was folly to keep moving under those conditions. There was nothing they could do but hunker down and catch up on more sleep.

It had been a cold, miserable night and Steadman woke with a mood to match. Weak light filtered down between the branches and a bitter taste lingered in his mouth as if he'd chewed pine needles in his sleep.

His thoughts went to Vivi, his wife. He was confident she was well and safe at home, but Nan and Hank seemed impossibly far away and unreachable as if circumstances had removed them to another planet.

He'd struck out there, failing to help Nan's situation, and he'd struck out with capturing Dart. He was not off to a great start on the Rico Ferguson case, either, but that was about to change.

He stretched out a foot and nudged Frost, maybe a little harder than was necessary. He wanted to get going.

The detective rolled over and stared up into the sky, lifting a hand like a sensor above his head.

"The wind is shifting, Chief," he said. "More ash coming our way."

"I'm afraid so," Steadman replied. "It's too bad those filter masks went overboard with the 'go bag'. We'll wish we had those."

"At least you had the presence of mind to throw the Remington clear, Chief. That was some good thinking."

"Sheer instinct, Frost. I didn't give it a single thought."

Frost swiped a palm across his forehead and examined the dirt and grit that came away. He grimaced. "I have a feeling it'll be a while before my next shower."

"Too true, my friend. Let's get moving."

They started on a tough uphill slog, made longer by thickets of blackberry bushes crossing their path, forcing them to backtrack and move in a circuitous route. Twice, they encountered deer, and rustlings in the bushes told of other wildlife sharing their space.

The turmoil caused by the eruption and flooding was disrupting nature and who knew what they might come across in the woods. Bears and mountain lions regularly roamed this area, Steadman knew, and by the time they finally broke through the tree line, emerging onto the main road leading to Mountain Vista, anxiety had reached a steady simmer in his gut.

"I don't know what we'll find when we get there, Frost," he said, thinking about the two-footed variety of trouble he was used to dealing with.

"Where, exactly, are we headed?"

"There's a clubhouse at the center of the neighborhood, by the lake. I'd say that's our best bet."

"Right on, boss."

They reached the neighborhood proper and started passing well-kept houses. On this high ridge above the inlet, the community was untouched by the turbulent flooding below, and an eerie quiet prevailed.

Folks were battened down inside with the drapes drawn, doors and windows sealed. Was all of it due to fallout from the volcano, or did these people know about the killer in their midst?

Tiny swirling particles danced in the sky like demon's confetti, blocking the sun, cutting down on visibility so that everything seemed swathed in fine brown sugar snow. Steadman knew many of the homeowners were summer residents and estimated that half the houses stood empty.

Plenty of places for someone with evil intent to hide.

Another half mile down the road, the clubhouse loomed into view, flanked by the lake on one side, and a fairway and green on the other. Mountain Vista was a golf course community. He and Frost crossed a footbridge over a tiny brook and entered the wraparound veranda in front of the clubhouse.

The structure seemed to be made mostly of glass, a series of windows and sliding doors spanning the wooden veranda. Behind the panes, Steadman saw a man and a woman conversing. The man pulled the woman into his arms, stroking her hair, and Steadman hated to interrupt what looked like a moment of much-needed comfort, but he and Frost had come a long way for an urgent reason.

He lifted his fist and pounded against the glass door.

The couple startled and broke their embrace, their faces turning to the window in surprise. They hurried over and the man unbolted and opened the door.

"Hell's bells boys," he said. "You sure took your time."

Steadman swallowed his irritation and made an effort to keep his voice mild.

"Your Mountain Vista is an island paradise," he said. "You have no conception of the difficulties we encountered getting here."

He held out a hand. "I'm Chief Deputy Randall Steadman, and this is Detective Frost."

The man dipped his head in apology. "I'm sorry. I'm wound a little tight right now. We're just about tapped out. Frank Newcombe," he said, taking Steadman's proffered hand.

"Dispatch got a distress call," Steadman continued, "but the message was garbled. Am I to understand you're dealing with a murder?"

Frank nodded. "And then some," he said, the strain in his voice promising a long story. He opened his mouth to go on, but Steadman held up a hand to stop him.

"I see you're running a generator and you've got things well in hand," he said. "We've been working our way to you since dawn yesterday. Any chance we could discuss this over breakfast and a cup of coffee?"

The woman gasped, her face contrite.

"Of course, I'm so sorry," she said. "Please come into the dining room and I'll make sure we've got a pot on."

She turned, hurrying past a wall of built-in bookshelves and a fireplace with bricks running up to the high, vaulted ceiling. Steadman followed her, with Frost on his heels. They passed a lounge area with couches made into beds, piled with pillows and blankets.

Three people looked up as he walked by, and he nodded to acknowledge them. They silently returned his greeting before going back to what they were doing—reading, napping, fiddling around on a grand piano beside the fireplace.

In the dining room, the three men settled at a table made from a thick slab of varnished wood while the woman hurried off through a swinging door at the back of the room.

"That's Millie, my wife," Frank said. "Sorry I didn't introduce you. I'm a bit rattled."

He ran an unsteady hand over his stubbled face and drew a deep breath like a man preparing for an underwater swim.

"You know the killer the media is calling the Puget Sound Slasher?" he asked, waiting for their acknowledgment before continuing. "We believe our little 'island paradise' is harboring the bastard."

Steadman nodded, keeping his features steady. He needed a lot more information before any of this would make good sense to him.

"We got a message from a Detective Quentin," he told Frank. "Has he been in contact with you?"

"Oh Nate, absolutely. You just missed him, in fact."

"How about a Ms. Forte?"

"Riley? She was here too, until this morning."

Millie arrived with a coffeepot and three mugs. Steadman noticed her red-rimmed eyes, smudges of mascara streaked below them.

"You've got to go after them, Sheriff," she said, filling their cups. "I'm scared to death something awful has happened to Riley."

Steadman let her mistake over his rank pass, wanting to get to the meat of the matter. "What can you tell us about the situation?" he asked, addressing Frank.

"I'll be right back with your breakfast," Millie murmured, slipping away. Frank watched her go, his face twisted with regret.

"Three days ago, the world was spinning just fine on its axis," he said. "Now it's bouncing all to hell. My friends are dying, Chief, and I can't stop it."

"Tell me what I need to know so I can help."

"When Rainier erupted, Millie and I opened our home to friends and neighbors so we could band together and support one another. When Millie went next door to invite Riley, Nate was there with her. He'd come to Mountain Vista following up a lead on the Slasher case."

"What lead?"

Frank shook his head. "He didn't share that information with me, Chief. I'm sorry. What I do know is that he suspected someone in the neighborhood, and when more people started dying, sliced across the throat the same way the Slasher operates, it seemed he was right."

"Who else was killed?" asked Frost.

"It started with Rico Ferguson and two of his staff—"

"Yes, we know about them," Steadman interrupted. "Who else?"

"We moved everyone who wanted to come over here to the clubhouse. There's more room, a well-stocked kitchen, and glass walls so no one can sneak up unnoticed. But the killer attacked one of our neighbors right here, in this building. And he got to Harp and Myrna Mayhew. Harp—"

He stopped speaking as if the next words had lodged in his throat, too difficult to spit out. Finally, he said, "Harp died, but Myrna got away."

Amazement spread through Steadman's chest. And hope. "She escaped from the killer? What did she tell you?" he asked.

"She hasn't been able to tell us anything," Frank answered. "She's unconscious. We've got her here, locked in my office for her own safety. We've got a doctor with her now."

"Holy cannoli," Frost said, his fingers beating out an excited tattoo on the polished tabletop.

Steadman reached out a hand, stilling his partner, wanting to communicate a sense of calm and control to all in the room. Millie brought two plates, piled with omelets and cinnamon rolls and trailing a tantalizing aroma. He and Frost dug in without hesitation, nodding their thanks, their mouths full.

"And now Riley's out there on her own," Millie said. "With a killer on the loose."

"And the detective?" asked Steadman.

"He, and another one of our men, went out to find her," Frank said. "Before the killer does."

Steadman had more questions, but before he could swallow his mouthful of exquisite cinnamon pastry, another woman swept into the room, bringing with her an air of haste and drama. She stared at them, trembling, her eyes huge and black against the pallor of her face.

"Annette," Millie said, "what's wrong? Has something else happened?"

The woman swallowed so hard Steadman could hear it from where he sat. She raised a shaking hand and pointed back the way she'd come.

"Myrna's awake," she said. "And you'll want to hear what she has to say."

CHAPTER 37

FROST LOOKED OUT THROUGH the bank of windows that stretched around the edges of the dining area.

The sky was sullen, like the onset of a troubled dusk or a rainstorm, but it was hours before sunset, and he knew it wasn't rain but ash that fell from the sky and darkened the atmosphere to a gloomy charcoal gray.

He could smell it, too. A sooty smell, slightly sulfurous, touched by the brimstone of hell. Even inside the building the odor pervaded, seeping and insidious.

Outside, the lake stretched between stands of pine and scattered houses, dark and still, undisturbed by the geese he'd seen winging above them during their walk through the neighborhood. A shiver feathered over his shoulder blades, teasing at the hairs on the back of his neck.

The name spoken by the awakening woman had shocked and distressed these people. Frost thought about how he'd feel if he suddenly discovered a trusted member of his community had sliced up a series of unsuspecting folk.

He grimaced and turned his attention back to the table where Steadman was bent over a map of the area, tracing his finger along its surface.

"How about it, boss—are we going on a manhunt now?"

Steadman straightened. A pained look crossed his face, shadowing his eyes, and he half opened his mouth to answer but before he could speak, Frank Newcombe rushed the table, clearly upset and demanding action.

"Two of our people are still out there, Sheriff," he said. "With a killer. What's the plan?"

Steadman stepped around the table and laid a hand on Frost's shoulder.

"We're going to pull together an old-fashioned posse," he told Frank. His fingers tightened over Frost's bicep as he continued. "I'll leave Detective Frost here to cover home base. You and I," he motioned to Frank, "will comb the ridge. Can you gather three or four men to go with us?"

"Give me ten minutes," Frank said before hurrying away.

Heat raced through Frost's veins. He slapped Steadman's hand off his shoulder.

"What the heck, Chief? You're leaving me at home to guard the women and children?"

Steadman's lips tightened. "It's an important job, Frost, and someone's got to do it. How well do you know the ridge above the lake? Ever been up there?"

Frost gave a growl of frustration. "No, I haven't."

"I'm willing to bet these men are more familiar with the territory, Frost, and I'll need the benefit of their experience. But if I take them, it spreads protection pretty thin on the home front. I'm sorry. I truly am, partner. I'd feel a lot better having you beside me on that mountain, but there are innocent people here that need you."

Frost knew the chief was right, but it rankled after being yanked off Dart's trail yesterday. Still, he had to remember he was the junior guy here—very much so. This was his first time out wearing the detective hat and there'd be plenty more times down the road if he didn't screw this one up.

He swallowed his irritation. Had Steadman been sincere when he said he'd feel better having him along, or had he just been pouring oil over troubled waters?

Frost lifted his shoulders in a reluctant shrug. "Okay, boss, you've made your point. I'll hold down the fort while you take the posse out."

"Good man, Frost."

He watched Steadman fold the map and stuff it into a pocket in his uniform jacket.

"That was the best cinnamon roll I ever ate," said the chief, flashing an apologetic grin. "Hanging here, I'll bet you get a crack at another one of those."

"There is that," Frost agreed, not fully mollified but trying to be a good sport.

Frank returned, bringing three men with him.

"Let's get going," he said. "Riley's my favorite neighbor and if anything happens to her, I'll be very pissed indeed."

Frost saw Millie standing in the background, silent tears rolling down her face. Rainier's eruption had sent shock waves rocketing out far and wide. The volcanic effects were bad enough, but the disaster had traumatized so many people in so many ways that went far beyond what anyone could have expected.

And Frost feared there was more to come.

He watched the posse leave through the glass door, their boots making hollow thunking sounds on the wooden veranda. They headed toward the northern shore of the lake, five shapes bobbing in the gloom, filter masks strapped to their faces, flashlights clutched in their fists.

Frost watched until they rounded a twist in the road and disappeared, five men representing justice and the law, pursuing a killer who spurned those very values.

A sharp pang cut through him like a hot knife through butter.

Oh, how he missed his father.

CHAPTER 38

STEADMAN AND HIS POSSE tramped along beside the lake, skirting around it to the steep, forested ridge beyond.

No one spoke, and a palpable dejection hung in the air, thickening it as much as the particles of ash.

Steadman blinked, wishing he had a pair of goggles. Grit stung his eyes, and they teared up to rid themselves of the abrasive material. The filter mask Frank had given him tasted stale and trapped hot breath against his face, magnifying the sound of it into something frightening.

His vision swam as he focused on the tree-lined slope, trying to determine the best way up. The foliage looked to Steadman like something primeval. Shaggy-barked trees, cedar maybe, twined with tall firs and the wispy trunks of birch, all of it festooned with ropy vines and carpets of moss.

Undergrowth lay thick along the ground—ferns and thorny bushes—and the terrain was uneven, soft and crumbling in some places, stony hard in others. The kind of ground that could break an ankle.

A flash of color to the left caught Steadman's attention, and he turned toward the lake. The peaked end of a red kayak poked from beneath a swath of willow branches, almost obscured by their drapery. He brought the group to a halt and pointed, speaking through the thin barrier of the mask.

"Looks like someone came ashore there," he said. "Could that have been Riley or the man we're looking for?"

Frank shrugged. "I don't know why either of them would have been out in a kayak, but I suppose it's possible."

"I doubt anyone would be out for a recreational paddle, things being as they are. Whoever beached and abandoned that boat had a reason."

Steadman scrutinized the ground and surrounding vegetation. They'd been traversing a paved cart path that ran along the far side of the lake, providing a shortcut for residents to reach the golf course.

Traces of dried mud striped the path in front of him and Steadman dropped into a crouch to examine them more closely.

Though faint, he thought he could make out the treads of shoe prints or boot marks and they seemed to point across the path rather than along it. He let his gaze follow their trajectory and saw hints in the steep hillside—broken twigs, a few instances of churned soil—that might indicate someone had chosen this spot to scale the slope.

And why not? The rest of them had to get up there somehow, and this seemed as good an entry point as anywhere else he'd seen.

"I assume you're leading us to an established trail that leads up ridge?" he said to Frank.

"I am. The trailhead's about a quarter mile further along this path."

Steadman shook his head. "I don't want to go that far off track. I think someone went up the hill here, and recently. It may have been one or both of our targets. Let's go."

He pushed into the greenery, using tree trunks and vines to pull himself along. The other men followed, though he heard grumbling and a few choice curse words. The going was steep at first, but leveled out a little as they ascended.

"Do you know this area?" he asked Frank.

"Pretty well," the man responded. "There's an old ranger's hut up the hill a piece."

Steadman nodded. "I've been there a time or two, hiking in from the canal side to make sure no one's turned it into a meth lab. We'll check it out."

The five of them spread into a rough V-shape as they pressed on up the ridge, looking and listening for any signs of their quarry. The air swirled with mist and ash, coating their skin and clothing with a grimy film, and the woods were quiet, the thudding of their boots strangely without resonance, as if the sounds were being sucked into a vacuum before they could leave an impression on the ear.

It felt to Steadman as if they'd entered an alien world, where the laws of physics differed from all he'd known before, and anything could happen.

It was unsettling.

The mass of vegetation thinned as they approached the clearing and Steadman's hand tightened on the Remington's strap. A man sat on the porch step of the old hut, and he had a knife in his hand.

Steadman looked a question at Frank, but got only a mystified shrug. Whoever the man was, Frank didn't know him.

As they drew nearer, Steadman saw the man was using the knife to whittle a Y-shaped bit of branch. He knew what this was. They'd called them "flippers" when he was a kid and he'd carved several himself, back in the day. Cheap entertainment fashioned from deadfall and a pocketful of pebbles.

The man put his project aside as they approached, but Steadman noticed he still held the knife, a KA-BAR. He rose to his feet and walked forward, extending his arm for a handshake.

"I'm so glad to see you guys," he said. "It's getting kind of creepy up here, all on my own."

Steadman took his hand, giving it a firm pump. He inclined his head toward the hut. "That's Forest Service property."

The man's eyes widened, and he bobbed his head, holding up a placating hand.

"Oh, I know. I know. I'll clear out and no harm done."

Steadman looked hard into the young man's face, noting the flush that crept over the sharp cheekbones and into the hollows under the eyes as he continued his defense.

"I was driving to my aunt's house, over in Union, but the roads were washed out. I tried to hike over the ridge, but when I came across this little cabin, I thought no one would blame me for taking a rest."

He dipped his head in apology before adding, "under the circumstances."

The man's face was all innocence—slightly bucked teeth that gave him a goofy smile and sandy blond hair that stood out from his scalp in awkward patches—but there was something about him that perked on Steadman's radar. He let the subject drop and picked up a new one.

"Have you seen anyone else up here? A woman, perhaps?"

"Oh yes, about half an hour ago. I called to her, but she ignored me."

"Which direction was she headed?"

"That a-way," the man said, gesturing up the ridge to the southwest.

"And she was alone?"

He shrugged. "I didn't see anyone else with her."

Steadman pulled his filter mask down, letting it dangle around his neck. He reached for the canteen at his belt, taking down a few swallows while he considered the young man's account. He capped the canteen and wiped his mouth with the back of his hand.

"All right," he said, replacing his mask. "We'll be moving on. Take care you leave that facility the way you found it."

He gave the man a final glance and nodded a farewell before heading to the southwest tree line. Frank and the rest of the makeshift posse followed.

"The man says she went this way and I've got nothing but my gut to tell me otherwise." He ground his teeth and fought down a wave of frustration. "Let's fan out a little," he instructed, "but stay in shouting distance."

Steadman plunged back into the spreading forest, hoping this was not an exercise in futility. His skill at reading people may not have served him well at the poker table, but he was realizing it boiled down to confidence and experience.

He had both, when it came to police work, and they were driving him to a conclusion he couldn't escape.

He didn't know what or why or if it had anything to do with this business, but he did know one thing.

The young man with the whittling knife was hiding something.

CHAPTER 39

FROST RAISED A FIST and gave a gentle rap on the door of Frank's office. Floorboards creaked beneath him as he shifted from foot to foot, waiting for someone to answer his knock, wondering how to make the best use of his time while the chief was off catching bad guys.

The door opened and the hospital smell of rubbing alcohol greeted him. A tired-looking blonde woman with a stethoscope draped over her shoulders peered at him over half-rim glasses, her lips pursed in an expression Frost wasn't sure how to interpret. He gave her his best smile.

"You must be the doctor," he said. "I'm Detective Frost."

She raised a warning finger to her lips and spoke in a voice a mere shade above a whisper. "Doctor Summerton—better known as Doctor Deb. What can I do for you?"

Frost felt like a schoolboy in front of the principal. She exuded that air of authority, and he could do nothing to stop the blush he felt rising on his cheeks except to trust that the poor lighting in the hallway would keep it a secret.

"I was hoping to have a word with your patient," he said. "She'll need to make a full statement later, but I'd like to hear the short version as soon as possible."

"I'm afraid now is not that time, Detective. She's out of the woods, I think, but still has a lot of healing to do—physically and emotionally. Right now, she's sleeping, which is the best thing for her."

He nodded. "I understand. I'll try back later, Doctor Deb. Good to meet you."

Frost retreated down the corridor, floorboards groaning underfoot as he stepped along. The building was old and weathered, though graciously appointed, but he bet it had never been through a trial like this one, housing fugitives from both natural disaster and a killer's knife.

He walked to the lounge area and stopped. Couches decked with pillows and blankets gave it the intimacy of a bedroom and Frost didn't want to intrude on privacy or disturb anyone's rest. He just didn't know where else to go.

A woman rose from one of the couches with a single graceful movement and came to his rescue, pale silvery hair radiating out from her head like the tresses of an undersea mermaid.

"I'm Jess," she said, her voice low and throaty, "and you're a man in uniform." Her languid eyes moved over him, colorless as clear water over a bed of silver pebbles. "My favorite kind."

Uh-oh. The corner of her mouth flickered, but the smile came mainly through her eyes. It was warm, inviting, and surprisingly enticing. Frost felt himself pulled into her vortex, a blood rush warming him despite his efforts to steer clear.

She had to be nearly as old as his mother but fashioned from vastly different material. Before he could move away, she'd claimed his left arm, wrapping it in her cool, smooth hands.

"You're here to serve and protect, am I right?" she murmured, pulling him into a slow stroll toward the glassed-in lobby.

She'd delivered her question in that same seductive voice, but Frost felt an underlying tension in it and knew, despite her bravado, she was frightened. He noticed the bandage on her upper arm and grazed it lightly with his finger.

"What happened there?"

He felt her shiver and guessed it was part real and part for effect. She stopped walking and stood at the bank of windows, staring out with a vacant gaze and clinging to his arm. At last, she spoke.

"The killer tried to make me a sacrifice for his altar." She gave a harsh laugh and started moving again along the narrow, windowed room. "Perhaps he mistook me for a virgin."

Frost pulled her again to a stop and faced her dead on. "You were the one he attacked here in this building?"

She pointed toward the lounge. "Right there, Detective." She gave him a sultry pout. "Ruined my favorite negligee."

A wave of pity hit Frost in the gut. This woman's need to always be provocative, whatever the circumstance or however inappropriate, spoke volumes about the deficiencies in her life. He hoped she could find what she was looking for and knew it wasn't him.

Lieutenant Jamieson's face flashed into his mind, and once more he wondered how she fared through the catastrophe, hoping she was safe, surprising himself by the strength of his worry that she might not be.

Jess drew an audible breath and let it out on a long sigh. "You've got a woman, don't you?" she said, as if reading his mind.

"No," he said, tightening the muscle in his arm, intending to pull it out of her grasp as if that would break the connection she had to his thoughts. But she refused to relinquish her grip on him, instead pulling him along as they resumed their indoor stroll.

"Let me show you around."

Frost suspected that resisting her pull would be more trouble than it was worth, and he did need to see the layout of the building and meet the people he'd been tasked with protecting, so he let her lead him from room to room and introduce him to the temporary residents of the clubhouse.

He met several members of the community who were elderly or disabled and was glad to see this group of neighbors banding together to help those in need during a time of crisis.

Jess introduced him to single folks, couples, and families with small children. In all, about forty people had staked out spots in the building and Frost saw sleeping bags, duffles, and backpacks spread all over the basement floor in a way that would make the fire marshal squirm.

But he wouldn't tattle. They were doing what they could, in the best way they knew how, and Frost found himself choking up a little as he looked around.

Jess had used a mocking tone when she asked if he was there to serve and protect, but despite his protests to the chief, he saw no reason for ridicule in what he did. Steadman had proclaimed it an important job, and he was right.

Frost's granddad had done it, his dad had done it—both serving with honor and giving their lives in that service. It was a proud tradition—an American tradition—and Frost, by virtue of his heritage, was part of it.

Could he make that ultimate sacrifice for folks such as these? Lay down his life in their defense as his dad and granddad had done? He didn't know.

And he hoped fate wasn't planning to press him for an answer.

CHAPTER 40

STEADMAN SQUINTED UP AT the lowering sky.

A veil cloaked the forest, composed of ash and fog, cutting visibility and stinging his eyes, making the trek through the thick undergrowth more challenging
and dangerous the further he pressed on. He heard faint noises from the other
men in the group, but they were distorted and unreliable as indicators of distance
or direction.

The mist separated them from one another, culling them apart like a living
entity, and a jolt of desolation stabbed through Steadman, making him feel as if
he were the last man standing in a deserted world.

Brambles tugged at his pant legs, snagging the fabric, scratching at the skin
beneath. The smell of damp leaves and moss, slimy and moldering underfoot, rose
up from the ground, growing stronger as his boots stirred their layers, releasing
spores into the air to mingle with the ash and fog.

A wave of unease flooded over him.

"Hold up!" he shouted, wanting to pull the posse back together. The low
visibility increased the chances that one of them might get lost or hurt, and their
well-being took precedence over catching a criminal or finding Riley.

"Follow the sound of my voice," he instructed, his words slightly muffled by
the folds of fiber covering his mouth, "and make your way to where I am."

He lifted the mask and spat onto the ground, clearing the sour taste from his tongue. Every five seconds or so he gave another shout until all four men stood before him, dingy and smudged with soot.

The dirty mist swirled around them, agitated by the intermittent breezes that came on as the day lengthened toward evening, creating shifting pockets of clarity that winked and disappeared like a desert mirage.

Frank's eyebrows were raised, a quizzical expression on his face as he approached Steadman and spoke in a hushed tone.

"I heard something in the brush up ahead," he said, pointing out the direction. "It could've been a man, maybe a bear or cougar, but it was definitely bigger than a breadbox."

Steadman smiled. "I had an uncle who used that phrase a lot. I haven't heard it in years."

"So I'm an old-timer," said Frank, "but my hearing is still good. What do you say, Chief?"

"Lead on, old man. Let's check it out."

The five men pushed forward, Frank leading with Steadman right behind. The going was steep and clogged with vines and thorny undergrowth. Eerie silence suffused the ash-laden air, punctuated only by panting and grunts from the posse as they scrambled up the hill.

At length, the ground leveled out again and the faint markings of a long-neglected trail opened up to the right.

"That's where I was headed before you called us back," Frank said, nodding toward the narrow footpath. "Something was moving ahead of me. I couldn't see it—only heard movement through the brush."

Steadman dipped his head in acknowledgment and took the point position, leading the way forward along the path. He stepped carefully, ears straining to catch any noises coming from up ahead, whether man-made or environmental, but the sounds of their own footsteps wiped out anything he may have heard.

He stopped abruptly and held up a hand, halting the men.

Furtive rustling continued from up ahead for a second or two before ceasing. The five of them stood frozen and Steadman stared into each of their faces, noting degrees of eagerness and apprehension.

Giving a decisive nod, he charged down the path, moving just under a run, careful to lift his feet free of the entangling vines. He rounded a bend in the trail and caught a flash of dark blue moving among the trees.

Their quarry was human.

Steadman put on a burst of speed and the man ahead plunged off the path, disappearing into the leafy embrace of giant ferns and bushes. In seconds, Steadman reached his jumping-off point, branches still quivering where the man had passed, and turned to pursue.

Before he even broke through the tree line, a deafening boom rang out, followed by a cry of pain from behind him.

"Get down!" he shouted, knowing his warning came too late for somebody on his team.

One of his men had been shot.

CHAPTER 41

FROST SETTLED BACK IN the dining room chair, enjoying that extra cinnamon roll Steadman had predicted would come his way.

Jess had smuggled it for him from the kitchen, and she sat across from him now, watching him eat with a cat-like expression, cool and mysterious. The fragrant, sugar-laced pastry melted in his mouth, causing him to drool a little. He used a napkin to cover the lower half of his face but knew it wouldn't hide the blush that crept up to his hairline.

"I love a man who appreciates the pleasures in life," she said, raising one slim eyebrow.

Frost swallowed and wiped his lips, deciding to ignore her comment. He shifted focus and refrained from licking his fingers as he said, "Tell me about the attack. As many details as you can remember."

Her face changed, a shadow moving across it, darkening her remarkable eyes from clear pools to murky depths. She shuddered.

"It happened Sunday night, after a long and terrible day. Harp and Myrna were attacked that morning, and all hell broke loose after that. We spent all day searching for Myrna, hoping we'd find her alive, but she hadn't turned up. Most of the men went out after dark to continue the search, and those of us remaining kept the doors locked up tight."

189

She stared at him, her eyes wide and bewildered. "I don't know how he could've got in. It makes no sense at all."

Frost crumpled the paper napkin and tossed it on the plate.

"I'm sorry, Jess. I know you probably don't want to talk about it, but it would help me get a clearer picture of what's going on. And it might even help you feel better, letting it out, coming to grips with it."

Her look was doubtful, but she shrugged and continued. "Riley and I had just finished having tea in the kitchen, and I was exhausted. She wanted to linger over her cup, so I left her and went to the lounge to bed down for the night. As I came through from the dining area, he rushed me, barreling out of the shadows and swinging a knife. I screamed."

She bit her lip and looked away, hugging herself.

"He sliced my arm and raised the knife for another go, but Riley came running and he went for her instead."

"Was she hurt?"

"No. He knocked her down and ran off through the lobby and out the front door."

"What was he wearing?"

"A black hoodie, pulled down over his face."

She let her hands drop to the tabletop, curling them into fists. "What does it matter now? We know who the murderer is. Myrna told us."

Frost gave a grunt of frustration. "I know, but my boss is out tracking the guy, and I'd like to feel like I'm doing something useful, too."

She changed again, going all soft and sensual. "You are doing something useful, Detective," she said in her husky voice. "You're protecting me."

Frost felt the heat come up in his face again and cursed his red-headed DNA. He stood, gathering his dirty plate and glass, and headed for the kitchen. She followed.

"There's something else you can do, if you want," she told him.

"What's that?" he asked, then cringed. He was almost afraid to hear her answer, but she surprised him.

"I can take you to examine Harp's body."

He hesitated, not sure how he felt about the opportunity. He had little experience with dead bodies, and he didn't want to admit how green he was to Jess.

On the other hand, if he let her take him there, his ineptitude was unlikely to escape her notice. Especially since the kit he'd been trained to use was somewhere at the bottom of the inlet.

"Didn't the Bellevue detective process the scene and gather evidence?"

"I doubt it. Things were crazy around here." She grimaced. "We had to move Harp into the Newcombe's garage to keep the coyotes off him. Beyond that, I don't know how much Nate was able to do."

He rinsed the traces of milk from his glass and placed it in the sink. "I should stay here."

"I get what you're saying, but it's only two doors down and as you saw, there are others here who can hold down the fort for an hour or so."

Should he take the initiative and maybe earn Steadman's approbation? Or step outside his orders and risk raising Steadman's ire?

Folks here would be okay without him for the few minutes it would take to check out the body and make some notes. After all, the killer was up on the ridge, miles away by now.

But what if he wasn't?

What's the right thing to do, here? Given the circumstances, what would his father have done?

He turned to Jess. "Let me go downstairs and talk to some of those men I met earlier, see if any of them strike me as a good lookout. If I find someone I'm comfortable with, then we'll go."

She gave him a sad smile without a trace of flirtation.

"I'll be waiting."

CHAPTER 42

THE RUSH OF BLOOD through his dilated veins was an audible thing to Steadman, the pulse pounding in his eardrums.

The fleeing man was armed and willing to use his weapon against those in pursuit. He couldn't have been able to see and take aim, but his random shot through the wall of vegetation had hit a target.

Steadman heard low moaning from one of the men behind him.

A desperate thrashing twenty yards ahead told Steadman the quarry was on the move again, heading away from their position. The late afternoon sun, blocked by the tall pines and screened by ash, did little to illuminate the scene.

Steadman caught a few brief glimpses of the man's dark blue jacket before he evaporated into the sooty mist, the sound of his exit fading fast. The lingering odor of burnt gunpowder filled the air.

Steadman turned his head and shouted to his men.

"Who got hit and how bad?"

"It's me," one of them shouted back, strain apparent in his voice, and Steadman for the life of him couldn't remember the man's name. Frank's introductions had been hurried, and in his distraction over the details of the situation, the names had gone right through Steadman's head without leaving much of an impression.

He felt bad about that as he made his way back to the injured man and saw him sprawled out on mossy stones and pine needles, blood seeping from a pair of jagged holes in the thigh of his denim jeans.

Aware that the man they were pursuing was busy putting distance between them, Steadman stripped off his uniform shirt and removed the T-shirt he wore underneath. He folded it and tied it around the wound, making it as tight as he was able. Shrugging back into uniform, he turned to the others.

"Everyone else okay?" he asked.

He took in their nods and their pale faces. Anger gripped him as he addressed Frank.

"You and I," he growled, "are going after this prick. You two," he waved his hand toward the men standing beside their injured friend, "need to get him back to the clubhouse. Looks like the pellets missed the artery, but the shot's still in there. He'll need a doctor, and soon. Go quick."

He turned back to Frank. "You ready?"

Frank's face was pasty, the hollows under the cheekbones bringing out the planes of his skull, but his eyes burned blue fire.

"You bet, Chief."

Steadman gave a curt nod and hustled off the path and into the rising brush, trusting Frank to follow.

Gray on gray drifted in his shortened line of vision, twilight mixing with ash in a surreal layer that distorted sight and sound, disturbing and disorienting. He plunged ahead with a sense of unreality, feeling like anything could happen—a wormhole in the universe could open up, a spider the size of Godzilla could scuttle down from the towering pines—and it wouldn't surprise him.

Everything in the swirl of mist felt that much different from the world he was used to.

The going was uphill again and as he worked harder to suck in breath, the mask stuck to his lips, bitter and tasting of wood pulp. He pressed on, almost like swimming as he used his arms to swipe low-hanging vines and branches out of the way.

He hoped it wasn't just his imagination that he detected signs of someone ahead. Little sounds, spindly limbs still swaying in the wake of passage. He glanced back to make sure Frank was still with him and saw the sole remaining member of his posse trailing about twenty yards behind.

And then from ahead, though it was hard to pinpoint the exact direction, Steadman heard an exclamation followed by a thunk, as if the man had tripped and fallen.

He put on a burst of speed, wanting to capitalize on the opportunity. The commotion grew, augmented by the sounds of dislodged stones skittering downhill, and Steadman slowed slightly, realizing the peril that lay in front of him, not wanting to descend in the same precipitous manner.

He broke from the tree line and saw the land drop away before him, the approach covered in a quivering sea of green. Spreading ferns, interlacing leaves that looked like clover, and plants with curling stems and tiny, delicate purple flowers converged to form a thick camouflage over the ground, disguising pitfalls and providing lots of potential for broken legs and headlong spills down the sharp ravine.

Steadman barely paused.

"Watch your step!" he shouted over his shoulder to Frank before rushing to the edge and looking down into the shadowed crevice. Through the shifting, patchy sheets of fog and ash, he saw the man in the blue jacket sprawled in a tangled heap on the floor of the ravine.

He'd lost his hold on the shotgun, and it had stopped its fall three or four yards short of the man's position, partially buried in the muck that stretched along the bottom of the gully.

The man was face-down in mud but appeared unharmed. He got his legs beneath him and half rose, reaching his hand toward the shotgun.

"Don't touch it!" Steadman commanded, his own gun trained down on the man.

Frank reached his side, and they stood together.

"Step away from the weapon and make your way up the side of the ravine. My men and I are waiting for you, so get moving."

The man stayed in a crouch, his head down, face obscured by a filter mask, but he raised his open hands out to the side and took three or four steps as if obeying Steadman's instructions.

Suddenly, he broke in a zigzag, scooped up the shotgun, and ran away down the center of the ravine.

Steadman fired.

The shots went wide and then fell short as the man moved out of range. Steadman stepped off the edge of the gully and started the slide to the bottom, one hand gripping the Remington, the other held out for balance.

Somehow, he stayed on his feet as the earth shifted and fell away beneath him and he reached the bottom with only a scraped palm to testify to the difficulty of the feat.

Visibility here was even worse than above, but squinting into the mist, Steadman caught sight of the navy blue jacket scrambling up the opposite bank of the ravine, making for the far side.

Steadman heard Frank descending the steep slope behind him as he took off running down the gully floor, straining hard to reach the man who was now nearing the top of the ravine. Mud sucked at the soles of his boots, slowing his progress, and he watched his quarry gain the opposite side and disappear into the foliage.

He swore.

Another boom echoed in the confines of the ravine, followed by a blood-curdling scream of agony. The acoustic baffles created by ash and the walls of the crevice made it impossible for Steadman to tell where it was coming from, but he turned to see Frank's body bouncing and sliding down the rugged slope.

"Frank!" he shouted.

"I'm not shot," Frank yelled back.

There was a pause and Steadman heard a series of grunts, though he couldn't tell if it was pain or disgust that prompted them.

"I lost my footing and fell," Frank continued. "And that scream didn't come from me, Chief. He's wounded. Don't worry about me. Go get him!"

Steadman ran down the ravine, the hair on the back of his neck prickling as he realized the vulnerability of his position, his enemy gone to high ground. It would be like shooting fish in a barrel, but there was nothing else he could do.

He ran on.

When he reached the point where the other man had made his ascent, evidenced by darker patches of churned earth, Steadman gripped a protruding root and hefted himself up, clawing for purchase.

As his head cleared the top of the crevice, Steadman expected to have it blown off, but he scrambled up the rest of the way, unmolested.

He gave himself ten seconds to catch his breath before plunging into the thick vegetation. Two steps into the tree line, he stopped. At his feet lay a Mossberg shotgun, its barrel shredded like a stick of string cheese.

That explained the blood-curdling scream.

Steadman recalled the gun lying half-buried in slime at the bottom of the ravine, and the episodes in his life when he'd witnessed mishaps due to mud-blocked barrels. Here was another one for the books, and all the more justification for vigilant gun maintenance.

The surrounding gloom was now so thick that he had to stoop down to see it, but there was blood. A plentiful amount of it. The man was wounded and without his gun.

In addition, he'd left a blood trail.

Steadman fished a flashlight from his jacket pocket and shone it on the ground, picking up the nickel-sized scarlet splashes like Hansel and Gretel breadcrumbs.

He followed the drops, aware that he might come upon the injured man at any moment but elated at the possibility of bringing him into custody.

He was so focused on what was ahead that he almost missed the warning sign from behind.

Steadman caught the flash of movement as the man leaped out from the cover of a wide-trunked birch. He whirled aside, but felt a stab of pain, piercing and sharp, high on his chest as he managed to shake the man free.

Looking down, he saw the slice across his shirt, already turning bright with blood. A chill ran through him.

He'd just been slashed by the Puget Sound Slasher.

CHAPTER 43

FROST'S CURIOSITY VIED WITH a few dregs of doubt as he climbed the creaky stairs from the basement of the clubhouse.

A faint odor of paint hung in the air and he noticed the walls looked like they'd recently received a fresh coat of cream-colored semi-gloss. He emerged from the gloom of the stairway into the upper floor where the light was only slightly more vibrant.

He'd spoken with two fellows downstairs who'd agreed to walk a patrol during his absence, keeping an eye on things. Jess caught sight of him and rose from the sofa in the lounge, coming toward him, her hair like strands of silver filament, almost glowing in the darkened room.

Together, they walked to the glassed-in lobby and Jess released the lock and opened the door leading out onto the veranda.

Frost took a step out onto the weathered wood and stopped, frozen in his tracks. The shifting sheets of dirty haze made visibility difficult, but he swore he saw movement thirty or forty yards off to the right.

He squinted, trying to sharpen the acuity of his vision, and saw it again.

"Good gracious," Jess exclaimed. "Someone's hurt."

They clattered down the steps and ran to meet the approaching party, two men carrying a third between them. The injured man wore a bloodied make-shift bandage around one leg.

"Get Doctor Deb," one of them shouted. "He's been shot."

Frost felt a jolt of frustration and alarm. He should have been the one up there, not this civilian.

Relieved to see the man looked as if he'd live, Frost motioned to Jess, and she hurried off to alert the doctor. He would have helped carry the wounded man, but the posse members had a rhythm going and Frost decided he'd be more use opening doors and clearing the way.

"What happened?" he asked as he ushered them into the dining area where they hoisted the bleeding man onto a table just as the doctor arrived, carrying a medical bag.

"We tracked the guy up the ridge, but when we got close, he opened fire. It never occurred to me he might have a gun. A sharp blade is his weapon of choice."

That settled it. The killer was up on the ridge, making for the other side and a viable escape route. Not lurking down here, waiting for a chance to strike on the home front.

Frost was going up there, orders or not. He considered the two men before him and chose the one who looked like he still had some steam left in him.

"What's your name, sir?"

"Sandy Dawson," the man answered.

"Sandy, are you willing to take me back up there, show me where this happened, help me find the chief?"

The man's gaze wandered to the stairwell and Frost guessed he was thinking about the family down there waiting for his safe return. His lips hardened into a grim line, and he brought his eyes back to meet Frost's with a resolute snap.

"Yes, I am. Give me a minute to use the bathroom and get a drink of water and we'll be on our way."

Frost did the same, and after rounding up a working flashlight and a filter mask, he found the lookouts he'd lined up and informed them about the situation.

He made sure the injured man was in good hands with Doctor Deb and met Sandy at the front door. The sky beyond the glass was an ominous charcoal color, heavy with soot and peril, offering teasing glimpses and then covering them up.

Frost's scalp prickled as he stared into the miasma.

Sandy stood beside him, looking as if he was preparing to step into the gates of hell, but he gave a decisive nod as if reaffirming his commitment to the mission. He also carried a flashlight and had a canteen strapped to his belt.

Frost assumed he'd share.

He returned the nod, adding what he hoped was a confident smile.

Opening the door, Frost stepped outside and into the mist.

CHAPTER 44

STEADMAN SAGGED AGAINST A rough-barked pine, blood seeping warm between his fingers as he pressed a palm against the wound in his chest.

Pain speared through him, sending streaks of agony racing along his legs, weakening his knees so that when he collapsed, sliding down the trunk of the tree to rest on the prickling needles with the Remington lodged beneath him, it wasn't all pretense.

But it wasn't all genuine feebleness, either.

He stared at the Slasher, the man who'd done this to him, crouched six feet away, cradling his own bleeding injury—a damaged left hand—and clutching a blade in his good fist.

A knit beanie covered the top of his head, and his face was half-hidden behind the filter mask he wore so that Steadman couldn't see his expression. But his body language suggested he was winding up for another attack.

In the time it would take Steadman to roll off the shotgun, level it, and get his finger on the trigger, the Slasher would have him sliced to ribbons.

Steadman was up against a vicious opponent, and he recalled Rafferty's training at the poker table.

Third level thinking.

Convince your opponent you have a weak hand, encourage him to become overconfident, and he's liable to bet where he shouldn't.

Steadman's wound had produced enough blood to soak the front of his shirt, but he felt it gumming up already, the bleeding slowing, and he suspected the cut was more superficial than serious. He'd whirled aside at the last moment and the knife, when it hit, had connected with something solid, deflecting the worst of the blow.

But there was a chance the attacker had perceived it as a fatal strike.

Steadman moaned low in his throat, letting a few seconds of it escape into the ashen air before clamping down his lips to stop it. He rolled to his side and pulled his legs up into a fetal position. He didn't want to ruin his performance with too many dramatics, so he left it at that, allowing his eyes to fall almost closed, watching the man with the knife through slitted lids.

The Slasher approached slowly, warily, pausing between each step to see if his target stirred, but Steadman kept still, waiting. He concentrated on his breathing, letting it come in shallow, ragged gasps.

He'd watched a man die once, and it hadn't been like this. More like a quiet letting go, the eyes meeting his with resignation backed by fear, the face going waxy almost instantly as he gave up the ghost.

But the man with the knife knew Steadman wasn't dead.

He was coming to finish the job and Steadman figured a man down, bleeding and fighting for breath, wouldn't look like much of a threat. He remembered that the Slasher's preferred method was to tase his victims before slicing their throats.

He wasn't used to them striking back.

The man was three feet away now. Steadman resisted the urge to move, to scramble out of reach of that knife. He had to bring the man one step closer, within the effective range for what he had planned.

He let his eyes flutter open and cried out, holding up a hand imploringly, cringing under advance, his leg cocked and waiting.

The Slasher darted forward, his arm raised to deliver the blow. Steadman released his leg, kicking out with all the force he could muster, aiming for the hand holding the blade, but landing low.

His foot connected, instead, with the man's chest, sending him staggering backward, his arm knocked over his head by the shock of impact. He lost his grip on the knife and it went sailing, disappearing into the undergrowth.

Steadman rolled off the shotgun, bringing it up level with the Slasher's chest, working the pump action.

The man froze.

"Hold it," Steadman said. "Keep your hands where I can see them and turn around."

The Slasher did as Steadman commanded, holding his hands out to his sides as he'd done at the bottom of the ravine.

Remembering how that had gone, Steadman watched him close. Now, however, the left hand was bloody, two of the fingers so mangled they'd probably have to come off.

"Drop to your knees, sir," he said, "and slowly onto your stomach, hands stretched out to your sides, palms to the sky."

The man complied.

"All right, I want you to put your left hand behind your back, and then your right hand."

The man didn't move.

"Do it!"

"It hurts."

The man's voice came out as a whine that set Steadman's teeth on edge. He stared down at the shredded hand, still bleeding, and knew the handcuffs wouldn't work. Not only could they qualify as cruel and unusual punishment, but they wouldn't be secure. With a hand like that, broken and malleable, the subject could wriggle out with only the price of pain to pay for it.

"Don't move. You understand me?"

"Yes."

Steadman sighed. He'd already lost his T-shirt, and he wasn't giving this guy his skivvies. He fished in his back pocket and came up with a handkerchief. Vivi sometimes tucked one in there before he left for work.

It was her firm belief that a man should always have a handkerchief to offer a lady in distress. It galled him to use it on this dirtbag, but he'd better do what he could to stop the bleeding.

Placing the shotgun where he could reach it and the prone man couldn't, Steadman knelt and bandaged the hand, tying the handkerchief tight, a bit shamed by the grim satisfaction he got from the groans of pain emitted by the brutal killer.

Finished, he rolled the man onto his side.

"Knees together," he said, frisking for weapons. As he switched the man to his other side to complete the search, the Slasher began writhing, crying out in pain.

"You can't touch me like this," he said. "You're violating my rights."

"Shut up. Your rights have not been violated, unlike those of the people you killed. I could touch you a whole lot harder than this. Truth is, I'd like to shove your teeth down the back of your throat, so count yourself lucky and keep your damn mouth shut."

"You've got the wrong guy, sheriff. I didn't kill anybody."

Steadman snorted but didn't bother answering. He gripped the man by the upper arm and pulled him to his feet.

"March," he commanded, prodding with the barrel of the shotgun.

The killer started walking, stumbling a little on the uneven ground, continuing to protest his innocence.

"Really, sheriff, there's been a mistake. I only shot at you because I was afraid for my life."

"I'm not the sheriff. I'm the Chief Deputy in charge of homicide, so you and I will be spending some time together. Only, you'll be minus a few fingers and locked in a cage, so I wager it'll be more fun for me than it will for you."

The man kept the rolling tirade going as they retraced their steps to the ravine, alternating between indignant rage and wheedling persuasion.

Steadman worried how he'd get the man to the opposite side without him falling and breaking his neck and then decided if that happened, it would be a boon to taxpayers and a mercy to the families of the victims who wouldn't have to put up with years of appeals.

"Stop there," he told his prisoner. Keeping the gun trained on the man, he walked to the edge and peered over, catching sight of Frank, a dark shape dimly perceived through the falling dusk and shifting ash.

"We got him, Frank," he shouted. "We're coming down now."

Frank hadn't moved since Steadman left him to pursue the fleeing man, and he didn't answer Steadman's enthusiastic announcement. Dread, like a lead weight, sank in Steadman's gut.

"Frank?"

A tense moment passed, then a shaky voice rose out of the crevice. "I'm here."

"What's wrong, Frank? You told me you were okay." Steadman couldn't keep a note of accusation from creeping into his words.

"No, I didn't," Frank replied. "I said I wasn't shot. I never claimed my leg ain't broke."

"Oh hell, Frank. Hold on—I'm coming."

Steadman motioned with the barrel of the shotgun. "All right, down you go."

The eyes above the filthy mask grew big, whites showing around the irises. "I only got one good hand. I'll never make it down that steep slope without taking a tumble."

Steadman shrugged.

"Do your best. You can step off under your own power, or I can give you a nudge. You decide."

Hostility radiated off the man like a Death Valley heat wave as he lowered himself into the crevice and began a desperate scrabble to the bottom. Steadman followed, also one-handed, like he'd done it the last time, because he was unwilling to let go of the Remington.

He arrived at the bottom without once losing his balance. If they ever made this kind of thing into an Olympic event, he'd be a contender.

The prisoner made it about halfway down while staying upright, finishing the descent on his belly, picking up a snout full of dust. Steadman gave him a moment to catch his breath before escorting him, at gunpoint, to Frank's side.

Steadman looked up to the top of the ravine's opposite wall and shook his head.

"We'll need help getting you gimps out of here," he said, turning his gaze back to Frank. Frank was staring at the killer, his mouth hanging open, amazement etched clear in the lines of his face.

"I don't know who you went and caught, Chief, but that's not the fellow we set out after."

"What!" Steadman demanded.

The prisoner waved his hands in the air. "That's what I've been trying to tell you. I'm not the guy."

Astonished and disconcerted, Steadman renewed his grip on the shotgun. He narrowed his eyes, considering the stranger and the turn of events.

"If you're not a fugitive from the law, why'd you stab me and shoot one of my men. Innocent people don't behave like that. Who are you?"

The man clamped his lips shut, refusing to answer.

Steadman looked more closely at him, pulling off the remaining shreds of the filter mask so he could see the whole face, an uneasy suspicion stealing over him, sending an icy shudder down his spine.

He unzipped the man's jacket, ignoring his protests, and yanked open the checkered shirt beneath, sending buttons flying.

A purple scorpion tattoo glared out at him, its stinger raised among the sparse chest hairs.

Dart!

Before Steadman could put words to the questions that spiraled through his brain, a shout sounded from above and he looked up to see Frost peering at him from the rim.

"Ho, partner! I thought you could use some help."

CHAPTER 45

DART ROSEDALE SWALLOWED WHAT tasted like a mouthful of acid.

His stomach was kicking it up, cranking the heartburn a notch higher with every turn in this nightmare of a day. And now, here was another notch—two more men arriving to help drive the nails into his coffin.

Pain and betrayal wrenched through him, twisting and tangling around every nerve. Things never should have turned out like this.

Rage against his father roared through his gut, vying with the heartburn and the fires of hell that inflamed his battered hand. His old man should have stayed to help, should have taught his son, his own flesh and blood, the tricks to staying ahead of the law. This was his fault.

And Maddie's.

If she'd only stayed put instead of running all over hill and dale, this never would have happened. It wasn't fair. He still didn't know how she'd managed to escape, ruining all his plans and careful preparations.

If he could get his hands on her now, he'd drain the life out of those magnificent blue eyes, watch them close forever.

Even the volcano god had let him down. He thought she'd smiled on him, opening the way for fantasy to become real, wreaking havoc as a camouflage for his own activities. But it hadn't turned out that way, and now that he thought about it, it seemed she too had been working against him.

But there was one stroke of fortune left to him, and maybe that would be enough.

The sheriff's attention was on the new arrivals at the rim of the crevice, and handy Harold was still tucked down in his boot. Dart had made sure to squirm and whine during the frisk, hoping his complaints and constant movement would allow Harold to escape notice.

And it had worked.

The man with a broken leg wouldn't be a problem. Dart only needed to take down the sheriff and make his escape along the ravine before the other two could reach him. It was a longshot, but it was all he had left.

In one swift movement, he pulled the knife from his boot, flicked it open, and charged at the sheriff's turned back, arm raised to deliver the killing blow.

CHAPTER 46

AMAZEMENT TINGLED THROUGH STEADMAN as he stared up at Frost.

The surprises were coming thick and fast. He was still wrapping his head around the idea that Dart Rosedale was the man he'd taken into custody, and he couldn't be more glad to see his deputy, his partner, arriving on the scene to share in the moment.

He took in a breath, preparing to shout up a response, but the look of horror that dropped over Frost's face in that moment—eyes going wide, mouth opening with the beginnings of a scream—telegraphed an urgent warning.

Steadman swung around, the Remington raised, but before he could level it and fire, he felt it buck to the side, driven by a kick from Dart's solid boot.

He saw the wicked-looking blade in Dart's hand move toward him and was grateful the kick had thrown his attacker off-balance enough for him to leap atop Dart, throwing him to the ground.

The gun clattered to the rocky soil as the two men rolled, locked together, the narrow, pointed knife straining between them, thirsty for blood.

Steadman had the advantage of two good hands and a bit of combat training, but desperation and disregard for human life lent strength to Dart's efforts.

He leaned forward, teeth bared, and tried to take a bite out of Steadman's nose, using the moment of confusion to gain the upper position, leveraging the knife downward. Steadman felt the tip of it nick a spot near his Adam's apple.

He gritted his teeth and pushed at Dart, trying to put more distance between the knife and his neck, but Dart held fast, gaining small increments. With lightning swiftness, Steadman freed his own right hand and curled his fingers around the stumps of Dart's damaged left hand, squeezing with all his might.

Dart loosed a shriek that raised prickles on Steadman's scalp. Without compunction, he pushed Dart off him and rolled over the Remington, taking it with him to a distance about four feet away.

Still lying on his back, he lifted the shotgun and aimed it at Dart's rising figure.

Shouts filled the air. Frank, from his place in the dirt, joined his voice to Frost's frenzied yells as they drew rapidly closer. In the chaos, clouds of dust and ash danced in the air, distorting and obscuring, but through it all, Steadman saw Dart's knife hand rise, the wrist cock back with a practiced flick.

In the instant before the fist moved forward to release the deadly blade, Steadman pulled the trigger, the recoil slapping against his gut.

Dart took the blast at point blank range, crumpling to his knees before falling face forward onto the muddy floor of the ravine, the knife falling from his nerveless fingers. Steadman stood over him, watching for the rise and fall of respiration, waiting to feel something and wondering what it would be.

Relief, mostly, when it came. Tinged with anger and regret that the whole sorry incident had happened in the first place.

He crouched down, feeling for a pulse, and finding none. Steadman looked at the knife, the long, sharpened blade, and thought about Maddie. A wave of gratitude engulfed him, and pride for her strength and ingenuity. That girl's courage had vanquished evil, and he was happy to be a part of that.

The scrambling sounds of Frost's descent snapped him out of that reverie, and he stood to greet his partner.

"I was itching for him to give me a reason," he said, and added, "Thanks for the heads up. The SOB would've sunk that blade into me if you hadn't sent a warning."

"I didn't get a chance to," Frost replied.

"You sure did. I didn't need a four-day seminar to read the meaning in your face, partner."

Steadman turned to the man standing beside Frost. "Thanks for bringing him."

"Happy to help," Sandy said. "What do we do now?"

"Between the three of us, we need to get Frank back to the doctor. He broke his leg."

"Hey," Frank grumbled, "you make it sound like I did it on purpose. That shotgun blast and the scream that came after scared the holy crap out of me. I lost my footing, and down I went. Heard it snap as I fell."

Frost grimaced. "What do we do with him?" he asked, nodding toward Dart's body.

"He's not going anywhere," Steadman replied. "We'll have to come back for him."

"Coyotes will get him," Frank warned.

Steadman lifted his mask and took a drink from his canteen.

"Couldn't happen to a more deserving fellow," he said. "Let's get you to a doctor, Frank."

CHAPTER 47

THE DOORBELL RANG, RESONATING a cheery tone through the house as Maddie raced to answer it, sliding to a stop in her stockinged feet, the dogs frolicking beside her, as anxious as she to greet their guests.

She pulled the door wide and threw her arms around the chief, so happy to see him she could almost burst. Crushing him in the fiercest hug she could muster, her cheek pressed painfully against his badge and buttons, she smiled across at Detective Frost.

"Don't go anywhere," she warned him. "You're next."

She heard the click of her mother's heels on the hardwood floor of the hallway.

"Don't make them stand on the porch, Maddie—let them in. Lunch is on the table."

Maddie released her hold on the chief and kept her promise to his partner, folding him in a tight embrace before stepping back and beckoning them inside. There was no way she could explain the bond she felt with these men. They'd been together for only a few short hours, but in that time, they'd become family to her. They'd shared an experience no one else could really understand, and the intensity of it had forged a connection in Maddie's heart she knew would always be there.

Grabbing hold of the chief's hand, she pulled him down the hall to the kitchen where she'd helped her mother lay out a meal of fresh fruit and crab salad sandwiches, with brownies for dessert. She'd made the brownies herself and was pretty proud of that fact.

The chief had called a few days ago and talked to her father, giving him the news that Dart was dead, and getting an invitation to lunch. As Maddie offered to take jackets, hanging them on pegs next to the back door, she watched her mother hug the men as tightly as she had done before turning to the refrigerator for a pitcher of lemonade, dabbing at her eyes with a paper napkin.

"Daddy!"

Her father came in from the garage to shake hands, and they all settled down around the kitchen table. Maddie noticed how the sunlight poured in a golden stream over the bare wood grain of the table, released from the dingy hold of ash.

Rainier had finished fuming, as her father put it, and the wind had shifted, driving the dregs of ash to the east. Life was returning to normal, but Maddie felt sad for all the families who'd lost people in the eruption.

And a guilty relief that her family wasn't one of them.

Her mother said grace, and Maddie took a bite of crab salad. "You're not allergic to shellfish, are you?" she asked.

Munching away, the men assured her they were not. She watched the chief swallow and wipe his mouth with a napkin.

"Best way this could have ended," he said, putting a voice to what they were all thinking about. "Maddie won't be called upon to take the witness stand, and it'll save the time, trouble, and expense of a trial."

"The bastard got what he deserved," said her father.

"Isaac," her mother said softly, giving him a warning glare about the curse word, but Maddie thought he could have said something a lot worse and still be short of the mark.

"I'm sorry I forgot to tell you about Harold," she told the chief.

He looked at her, his eyes dark and solemn, and she noticed the muscles in his jaw tighten.

"I don't want you ever to worry about that, Maddie. None of this was in the least bit your fault. Harold was Dart's downfall. Pulling that knife was his fatal mistake, and I can't say I'm sorry it happened the way it did."

Maddie pictured Dart lying face down in the dirt, the way her father had described it when he got off the phone with the chief. His own choices put him there, he'd assured her, and Maddie knew he was worried about how she'd take it.

She was glad he was gone.

Gone for good, except for the memories.

She shuddered.

"He was always whistling this creepy song," she said, "And sometimes he'd put words to it and sing."

She remembered the tune and voiced the words for them the way she'd heard him sing it. "Oh, my darling, oh my darling, oh my darling Madeleine."

She put down her sandwich and looked at the chief, a feeling of triumph swelling in her chest.

"But Dart got it wrong. My name's not Madeleine. It's Madison. That song wasn't about me, and it never will be!"

CHAPTER 48

FROST LOOKED BACK AT Maddie's family, gathered together on the porch to wave them goodbye, the smile on Maddie's face reaching nearly to her ears, the mother's eyes suspiciously shiny. Maddie's father had one arm looped around his family, the other raised in a salute that shouted thank you as loud as anything he could have said.

These were good people, the building blocks of a strong society, and he'd been a part of keeping them that way. He appreciated his paycheck as much as the next man, but no amount of money could match the feeling of pride and gratitude that swelled in his chest as he lifted a hand to return the farewell salute.

"Strange how it all turned out," he said to Steadman as the chief guided the car down the long driveway, engine whining a little as they tackled the steep incline.

"We set out to reach a crime scene, then went in pursuit of Dart, then stopped to go after the first guy, and ended up bagging Dart, after all. Crazy," he said, shaking his head. "I'm so glad Dart is gone. Saves me years of nightmares and wondering what he's up to."

The chief grunted what sounded like agreement, but didn't comment. After a moment, Frost ventured a question that had been bouncing around the back of his head.

"What happened with the Slasher case, Chief? I never heard how they caught the guy."

"I don't know the details," Steadman answered, shifting gears. "You can read the file if you're interested."

Frost was surprised by the clipped tone of the words. He noticed the chief's white-knuckled grip on the steering wheel as he turned out of the driveway and started down the narrow, winding road that led to Highway 3.

The main thoroughfare was still under repair. It would take months before it was restored to full capacity, but a patch job made it navigable for the time being.

Two minutes passed, and the silence that hung in the air between them was not altogether comfortable. Frost wondered if the chief would get around to speaking about whatever was weighing on his mind. The feeling of satisfaction he'd started to enjoy after Dart's demise was dissipating, leaving him with an unsettled feeling, as if something was missing.

Another moment passed and Frost just had to break the tension.

"Did I do something wrong, Chief?" he asked.

Steadman looked startled, the grim frown on his face melting into something like chagrin.

"No, not at all," he said. "I'm just preoccupied. Got a family issue on my mind." After a pause, he added, "I want to thank you, Frost."

The chief's voice was low, his gaze focused straight ahead on the road before him. "You're a good partner," he continued, "a handy man to have around in a rough patch."

Frost sensed there was a lot more behind the words than their surface implied, but the chief didn't seem inclined to elaborate.

They drove another couple of minutes in silence. Frost didn't want to stick his nose in where it didn't belong, but if there was something he could do to help, he was willing to toss in with the chief.

"I'm guessing your family situation would qualify as a rough patch," he ventured. "I'm still here, Chief, if there's anything I can do."

He watched Steadman's face, but the man continued to stare forward, the muscles in his jaw bunching as he ground his teeth. A beat or two passed before he spoke.

"I'm grateful you offered, Frost, but the mess I'm in…"

He shook his head, a harsh sigh breaking free from between his lips as he raked a hand through his hair, giving it a yank. "It's not something I'd invite you into. It's nasty and dangerous."

Frost thought about that, let it percolate through the gray cells, but the process didn't change his gut response. He still felt the same.

"My granddad died saving a man and his baby daughter from drowning," he told Steadman. "I lost my dad when his peace-keeping mission was blown apart. I love and miss them both, every day, and I'd be a sorry son indeed if I didn't go on as they raised me to be. They taught me what matters. That living is a gift and a blessing, but there are some things worth dying for."

Frost clamped his teeth together and swallowed hard.

"We spent four days of rough and dangerous work keeping that family together," he continued, gesturing down the road toward the house they'd just left, "and I don't regret a single moment of it. What makes your family any less worthy of fighting for?"

He'd spoken with some heat, he realized, as he watched the chief's face go through a series of expressions that finally ended with a grudging smile.

"When you put it like that," said Steadman, "how can I refuse your help? But I'll grant you the right to change your mind after you hear what's going on. Any solution to the problem will be risky and bound to skirt the edge of the law."

Frost straightened in his seat, a mix of curiosity and apprehension settling over him. "I'm listening," he said.

As Steadman navigated the clog of traffic on the reduced highway, he told how his brother-in-law had been duped and manipulated into colluding with a band of criminals and losing to them at the poker table.

He told how Hank had ended up owing them a lot of money, and how they'd savagely beaten him to demonstrate their complete control over him and coerce him into selling everything he owned to pay the debt.

"Why didn't you call in the local cops?" Frost asked. "It may be out of your jurisdiction, but surely the Portland Bureau could've looked into it."

"These thugs made it very clear to my sister that if she did that, the only evidence of crimes committed would point to her husband, and they followed up with a suggestion that talking to the police would incur a fatal accident. I did some digging and discovered at least three 'accidental' deaths that can likely be laid at their door."

Frost whistled through his teeth. "That's tough, boss."

Steadman nodded, his lips pressed together in a grim line. "And there's more. They told Nan they've got cops in high places on the payroll."

The chief flexed his hands on the steering wheel, mashing it under his fists.

"After a bit of discreet research," he continued, "I believe that claim. I don't think going to the police is a viable option."

"Then what is?" Frost asked.

"Well, Nan came up with a plan. She thought I could get into one of their high-stakes poker games and win enough money to clear the slate for Hank."

"Ah, that's why you holed up with Garth Rafferty for those two weeks you told me about."

"That's why," Steadman agreed. "Rafferty schooled me hard on the ins and outs of Texas Hold'em. But it was a hare-brained plan from the start. It'll give you some idea about the level of my desperation that I even gave it a try."

"It didn't work?"

Steadman snorted out a bitter laugh.

"Nan sold mom's jewelry with the notion that I could go into the casino with a few thousand and come out with enough for the buy-in at their illegal high-stakes game. It didn't turn out that way. I lost bad, and just when the tide was turning my way—*poof*—up in smoke."

"You mean that literally, don't you? That's when Rainier exploded?"

"The very moment," Steadman confirmed. "Utter chaos reigned in that casino and at the end of the day, this is all I had to show for it."

Steadman took something round and dark blue from his breast pocket and tossed it over. Frost caught it, holding it flat on his palm as he read the casino logo on the ten dollar chip.

"Turn it over," Steadman said.

Frost flipped the chip and ran his finger over the deeply scarred plastic surface, sending Steadman a questioning look.

"Turns out," said Steadman, "that's all I needed."

He paused and patted a hand over his breast pocket. "That chip saved my life. It deflected Dart's knife and allowed me to get the upper hand when I needed it most."

Frost examined the chip with a little more respect.

"But there's more to it than that," the chief continued.

Frost waited for him to go on, but the silence stretched for several minutes, both men staring out at the passing pavement, before he spoke again.

"That chip, the whole thing with Dart—they helped me to realize that Nan was right about one thing."

"What's that?"

"She said we need to beat them at their own game. Only thing is, she thought that meant poker."

"But it doesn't," Frost guessed.

"No. Their game is intimidation, Frost. And manipulation. They may have learned it at the gaming table, but they carry it into all their business operations, and I suspect they're into a lot more than just illegal gambling."

"So, do you have a new plan?"

"I'm starting to form one," Steadman said, the corner of his mouth lifting in a sardonic grimace. "Only thing is, we'd need a gorgeous femme fatale to carry it out."

Frost hesitated, but figured he might as well volunteer what he was thinking. "I know a good candidate for the job," he said.

CHAPTER 49

STEADMAN LOWERED HIMSELF INTO the familiar chair, listening to the creak, feeling it wobble a little to the left as it always did. He was back in Garth's basement, back at the poker table, but this time he was here to prepare for a different game.

And this time, he thought he knew how to play.

He looked across the table at his friend, Garth. Before the volcano blew, Rafferty hadn't wanted to get involved. He was willing enough to mentor Steadman, put him through the paces of poker at the big boy's table, but then he drew the line, preferring to steer clear of the details.

Now, the situation was different.

Rafferty's brother lived in Puyallup with a wife and three teenage daughters. They, along with their faithful German Shepherd, a bowl full of goldfish, and the whole damn neighborhood, had been obliterated by a raging wall of mud from Rainier's western flank.

Steadman didn't know how much of Garth's newfound zeal stemmed from survivor's guilt, how much was prompted by grief, and how much came from a manic need to strike out.

He figured all these things and more weighed into the equation, but Rafferty was now ready to take on an army. He had a lifetime's worth of knowledge and experience, and Steadman was glad to have his support, if a little leary about where it might lead.

Garth chewed his habitual toothpick with even more vigor than usual, and Steadman reflected that it might require a small forest's worth of wood slivers to get them through this maneuver. Frost leaned sideways in the chair next to Rafferty, and Steadman felt a surge of gratitude toward his stalwart partner, realizing how glad he was to have the young man along.

He noticed Frost had arranged his hair in a careless-looking tousle, one lock falling artfully across his forehead. The faint scent of a citrus-based aftershave emanated from the young detective's direction, and Steadman knew all this was for the benefit of their fourth team member, due to arrive any moment.

"You want I should switch chairs, Frost?" he asked, waggling his eyebrows. "Let her sit next to you?"

The detective's face went pink. "Please tell me you're not going to be like that, Chief," Frost pleaded.

"Here," said Rafferty, "borrow one of my toothpicks. You've got a little something. Just there." He pointed to Frost's front teeth.

The doorbell rang.

Frost grabbed a toothpick and scraped frantically at his teeth while Rafferty went to open the door for Lieutenant Jamieson.

"Relax, Frost," Steadman said, taking pity on his nervous partner. "Garth was just messing with you." He couldn't help adding his own playful taunt. "Besides, you look beautiful."

Frost narrowed his eyes, glowering, as Rafferty returned with Jamieson.

"All right," Steadman said, clasping his hands together and giving them a shake to emphasize his words. "We're ready to begin."

The lieutenant gave a nod in his direction as she slid into the empty chair at the table.

"First," Steadman began, "I want to say thank you for being here, for agreeing to help. My sister and I are in a fix—one we can't get out of without a hefty dose of assistance. I know I mentioned this before, but I want to make sure we're all clear on this—there's a lot of risk involved. If any of you wants to back out, now's the time to do it, and no hard feelings."

He looked around the table, but no one even blinked. Just three faces returning his gaze, waiting for him to go on.

"Okay," he continued, "here's the brief. The real movers here are a father and son team. Colombians by the name of Lizardo—Abe and Eddie Lizardo. They've got a line-up of henchmen, but those are the two who really need reckoning with. They go down, the rest will crumble."

Jamieson piped up. "You said they run illegal poker out of a suite at the Hilton?"

Steadman nodded. "They do, but I'm guessing that's a sideline, maybe they wash a little money that way. What I think they're really into is cocaine."

Rafferty waved his toothpick in the air. "Cocaine *is* making a comeback in America. Prescription painkillers are losing their cachet."

"Colombia's been producing bumper crops of illegal coca and the boom is spilling into the American marketplace. I put out some feelers and the word I get back is that the Lizardos are moving merchandise in the Portland area."

"Why can't we get the Feds involved? Get some help that way?" Frost asked.

"We can, and we probably should. But I want to get my brother-in-law out of it first. His name is Hank, by the way, and my sister is Nan."

Steadman cleared his throat, taking a few seconds to gather his thoughts.

"These thugs have Hank in a vise. Back in the days before Hank had a clue what was going on, they had him run a series of minor and meaningless errands which they videotaped and which will act as damning evidence, along with some other items they've thrown together, in case Hank tries to turn them in."

"Chief," Jamieson said, "I'm sorry to ask this, but we're putting a lot on the line, here. Is there any chance Hank is guilty of what their evidence indicates?"

"I understand your concern, Lieutenant, but no way. Hank is a white hat, all the way. Naive enough to get squeezed, played, and manipulated into the position he's in, but he'd never be a willing participant in a dirty operation like this."

"How are you suggesting we deal with this, Chief?" Frost asked.

"I'll tell you—my main concern is retaliation against my family. What I'd like to do is put the Lizardos out of commission without blowback on Hank. It can't look like he had anything to do with it. Also, I'd love to cripple their operation enough to send them packing. Across the border, if possible."

"What does that mean, in practical terms?" Jamieson asked.

Steadman knew what he was thinking was crazy, but his gut told him it could work.

"I want to find their warehouse and destroy their stock," he said. "Even though their operation is relatively small and family-operated, the Lizardos have got to be in deep, and the sudden loss of merchandise will leave them empty-handed in front of some powerful and dangerous people. If we do this right, they won't know who hit them—a ruthless competitor or some arm of the law. I'm hoping they'll find it in their best interest to simply disappear."

"Any ideas about how we can track down where they're keeping the cocaine?" asked Frost.

"Over the last couple of days, Garth and I have spent some time talking with my brother-in-law. He played against these men at the poker table and was able to give us an idea of their behavior. We need to exploit their weakness." Steadman turned to Rafferty. "Garth, you can explain it better than I can."

Rafferty removed the toothpick and tossed it into an empty ashtray where it skittered with a tiny *ping* against the glass. "The game of poker," he said, "is steeped in machismo. There's a lot more than money at stake."

He slapped a palm down on the table, glaring around at his listeners. "Pride," he said, his voice a low growl. "To admit your opponent might be stronger than you—smarter or better than you—is to admit a terrible weakness, something a poker-minded man will go to great lengths to avoid."

Steadman pitched in, adding to Garth's explanation. "Both the Lizardos are prone to pride," he said, "but Junior is our ticket. He's itchy, wanting to bite off more than the old man will give him. What we need here, is a little recon. We need to find a weak link, a loose thread we can pick at to unravel the whole thing."

"I'll install a few well-placed listening devices," Rafferty announced. "The first of which will go inside Eddie's fancy convertible which he conveniently leaves open to the elements. As long as it's not raining, I'll get that up and transmitting tomorrow."

"And Jamieson," Steadman said, turning to the lieutenant, "I'd like to stake you for a couple of drinks at the nightclub Eddie frequents. See if you can strike up an acquaintance, open an avenue for how we can best proceed."

"Aye, aye, cap'n," she said, giving him a little salute. "Is there anything special you'd like me to wear? Like a wire?"

"Why, yes." Steadman smiled, appreciating her wit and willing spirit. "Our tech specialist will set you up," he said, nodding toward Rafferty.

"What about me?" Frost asked.

"You and me, partner," Steadman answered, "will man the listening post in the van, making sure Jamieson stays safe. If anything starts sliding south, have your shining armor ready. You up for that?"

Steadman noticed the tips of Frost's ears turn a charming shade of scarlet, but the younger man rallied with a grin and quick response.

"I'll be standing by," he said, bowing toward the girl, "sword and shield at your disposal, my lady."

Rafferty leaned forward, clapping a large hand down on Steadman's shoulder, gripping it hard. "Are you ready, my friend?" he asked. "You're throwing in the big blind, you know."

Steadman swallowed, a sudden tightness in his chest making it difficult. "I'm throwing in everything I've got. The stakes have never been higher."

Rafferty nodded. "You're ready, then. A man, once blind, has opened his eyes." He raised his toothpick as if making a toast. "You'll see us through to the end, Steadman."

"Hear, hear," shouted Frost, and Jamieson beamed a smile at him.

Steadman fervently hoped they'd all live to toast another day.

CHAPTER 50

IT WAS WARM IN the van.

Frost peeled off the linen suit jacket, relishing the feel of air moving through his thin shirt sleeves, wishing he could free his face in the same way. The whole left side of his head itched under the heavy makeup Jamieson had painstakingly applied. She'd be less than pleased with him if he messed it up.

Steadman insisted they each come incognito, leaving their ID at home and using hallmark features that would have people looking in the wrong direction, if it came down to that.

Frost had a cubic zirconium stud glued to one earlobe and a gnarly network of burn scars across his left cheek. Jamieson, the costume designer on their team, had completed his makeover with a linen suit and well-styled hair, achieving an urbane appearance that marked him as a higher class of thug, a rung or two above street level.

He looked across at Steadman and had to admit the man looked impressive. His craggy features, normally clean-shaven, now sported a precisely trimmed goatee and mustache, his thick hair finger-styled into a mass of waves atop his head.

The Brioni suit he wore—a lucky find at Goodwill—had been altered and now looked like a custom-tailored job. The Rolex on his wrist was the genuine article, borrowed from Rafferty who told them not to ask where it came from.

Rafferty manned the bank of buttons, sliders, and screens that comprised their command center. He'd succeeded in bugging the younger Lizardo's swank convertible, a red Mercedes, and planted a GPS tracker for good measure.

Rafferty had somehow concealed a wire beneath the figure-hugging cocktail dress Jamieson wore like a boss. Frost didn't want to even think about the mechanics of that process, and just kept reminding himself that Rafferty was a professional.

In the wee hours of the morning, they'd positioned cameras in the parking lot and across the street, but had no visual on the inside. Once she stepped into the interior of the club, Jamieson would be audio only.

The squeal of plastic on styrofoam had Frost clenching his teeth as Rafferty removed the lid from his cup of coffee, releasing the aroma of French roast into the enclosed space. He wrinkled his nose. Not being a coffee drinker, he had little appreciation for the scent, but he watched as Rafferty drew in a deep breath of the rising vapor, a rapturous smile breaking across his face.

"Heaven in a cup," he murmured.

"And gone in a gulp," Frost responded. "I go for a more eternity-based heaven."

"Give a man his vices, Detective. I'm a gambler who likes coffee and I trust the good Lord won't send me to hell for it."

Frost had to smile. "You may be right," he began, but immediately forgot the smart rejoinder he'd been about to make.

Jamieson was on the move.

Frost tapped the screen, and the men fell silent, watching her grainy black-and-white figure move across to the front entrance. She stopped and dug through her little evening bag for a tube of lipstick.

"Can you hear me now?" she asked, her face turned downward as she pawed through the purse.

"We hear you, Jamieson," Rafferty replied, "but it'll be a mess once you get inside. We'll pick up what we can, but if there's anything special we should be hearing, make sure it's aimed toward the cleavage."

"That shouldn't be a problem," Steadman said. "Not with that dress."

A rush surged through Frost, as if a flock of tiny butterflies had been released into his bloodstream, and he suddenly didn't want her going into that club.

He pressed a button and spoke into the mike. "You don't have to do this," he said. "I can go in there. We can find another way."

"Relax, Frost," she responded. "I got this. Besides, I don't think you're Eddie's type."

She snapped the lipstick closed and dropped it into the purse. "Here I go."

Steadman had parked the van on a side street, a block down from the night-club Eddie Lizardo frequented. On the monitor, Frost watched as the doorman admitted her and Jamieson disappeared inside as if swallowed by an enormous beast.

He fought the stab of apprehension that seared through him at the loss of visual contact and wiped his sweaty palms on a napkin from Rafferty's coffeehouse.

A burst of noise screeched into the van and Rafferty adjusted the controls, bringing it down to a tolerable level. The pulse of a bass beat underlaid the transmission, accompanied by chatter and shrieks of laughter.

Frost imagined Jamieson moving through the crowded rooms, drawing the eyes of every man she passed. He hadn't the slightest doubt she'd be able to attract Eddie's attention.

The cacophony continued for almost twenty minutes with nothing standing out. They knew Eddie was in there. His car was in its usual spot in the parking lot, close under the eye of the valet.

Just as Frost was beginning to both hope and fear that nothing would happen, Jamieson's voice cut through the chaos.

"I'm in his sights," she said, "and he's making his approach."

A few seconds later, Frost heard a male voice with a slight accent come through on the wire.

"Hello there," it said. "Sorry to bother you, but I need your name and phone number. For insurance purposes."

Jamieson responded with just the right amount of concern and flirtation. "What do you mean?"

"I mean, you blinded me with your beauty. I'll have to make a claim."

She laughed, throaty and delighted. "Does that ever work for you?"

An answering masculine laugh. "You'd be surprised."

Her voice dropped to a honeyed, seductive tone. "I am surprised. It seems to be working on me."

"Buy you a drink?"

"I wouldn't mind."

"What's your name, sweetheart?"

"Anita."

"Beautiful name, Anita. I'm Eddie."

The banter continued for a few minutes more, reminding Frost why he never went looking for women in a bar. Mindless meat markets.

Steadman might have been thinking the same thing because he suddenly said, "That's enough. I'm going in."

He pulled off his headset and opened the door of the van. Frost moved to go with him.

"No, stay here Frost. I'm going to shake things up a bit, see if I can start the ball rolling down the right track. Keep listening. You'll know if you're needed."

The door slammed shut and Frost watched the chief run the block, disappearing between parked cars until the monitor picked him up. He entered the club, and Frost strained to hear what was happening. He caught a few more smarmy lines in exchange and then Jamieson's voice, changed in tone.

"Oh no," she said, and then, "it was nice meeting you, Eddie."

"Don't go," Eddie said, a whine in his voice. A pause followed and then Eddie spoke again, in a harder tone. "Is that guy a problem for you? Let me take care of him."

Jamieson, with a note of urgency. "Stay out of it."

"No, really—"

"Please, Eddie. Forget you ever met me."

"Not going to happen, sweetheart."

And then the chief's voice, harsh with anger. "Anita! I'd like a word."

A confusion of noise came across the wire, punctuated by a clunk that might have been a bar chair hitting the floor. Frost heard Eddie exclaim, "What the hell?"

Then Jamieson screamed.

CHAPTER 51

STEADMAN PUSHED THROUGH THE crush of people, a thump of bass notes resonating through his skull in a way that would give him a headache if he stayed long. He hoped that wouldn't be an issue.

A haze hung in the air, made up of perfume, stale cigarettes, and perspiration. It competed against the strong smell of alcohol, the combined odors swirling through the air in nauseating eddies.

He tried to steer clear of the dancers and had to pull a few fancy moves himself to keep from getting an elbow to the face. A bleached blonde in a hot pink halter top stepped on his foot, nearly spearing his big toe with her stiletto heel.

He caught sight of Jamieson at the bar, the younger Lizardo at her side. He recognized the moment she spotted him too because her face changed, an expression of deep annoyance passing over it.

He saw her murmur something to Eddie and turn away. Before she could take a step, Eddie had grabbed her arm, casting his gaze around until he met Steadman's eye.

Jamieson was improvising, and her instincts were good. Here was something to not only hook Eddie's interest, but give him a chance to play the hero. Steadman understood she'd cast *him* in the role of the jerk.

He stormed toward her, trying to remember what she was calling herself, and got it in the split second before he reached the bar.

"Anita!" he shouted, packing his voice with fury. "I'd like a word."

He glared at Eddie and yanked Jamieson's arm, pulling her away from the bar. She managed to catch her foot on the barstool, and it fell over, hitting the floor with a clang. Jamieson screamed in rage and swung her hand to slap him, but he caught her wrist and held it fast, maneuvering her into a corner.

Eddie started to follow, but both he and Jamieson motioned him away, indicating their desire to speak privately. He glowered, but kept his distance.

The noise in the club made it possible for them to talk without being overheard, but Steadman was careful to maintain his angry demeanor, staging an argument and making sure a word or two escaped occasionally for Eddie's benefit.

"You told me you'd deliver the package today. I showed up as agreed, but where were you?"

"It's not my fault, Manny. My supplier stood me up."

"So you treat me the same way?" Steadman curled his face into a sneer. "Not very professional of you, Anita. We had a deal. What are you willing to do to keep your side of the bargain?"

Jamieson shrugged and folded her arms across her breasts, her jaw jutting out in a defiant gesture. "I'll have to find another wholesaler. Give me a week."

"A week!" Steadman shouted, shaking his fist. "Two days, Anita. Not a minute more."

He gripped her upper arms, nearly pulling her off her feet, and raised his voice to a heavy growl. "Mark my words or dig your grave."

He released her, and she executed a convincing little stumble as he strode across the dance floor to the exit. Letting himself out, he stopped to pull in a few breaths of untainted air and wondered what Eddie had made of the incident.

He almost wished he were a smoker, because this would be the perfect moment to light up reflectively and wait for something to happen. Instead, he gazed at the stars.

When he heard the door to the club open behind him, he started walking across the parking lot without looking back. He ignored the shouted demand and the clatter of footsteps, but the clout across his head got his attention.

He turned, slow on the pivot to allow Eddie another shot at him, but the man didn't take it.

Steadman pulled himself up to full height, pleased to note he was at least three inches taller than Eddie. "I assume you've mistaken me for somebody else."

"No mistake," Eddie sneered. "I'm talking to you."

"And this is me, *not* talking to you," Steadman said, turning to continue his strides across the parking lot.

"What do you want with Anita?" Eddie shouted.

Steadman flapped a dismissive hand over his head and kept walking.

"Hey!" Eddie grabbed Steadman's arm and swung him around in an about-face. "I asked you a question. What's your beef with Anita?"

"Drop it, pissant," Steadman hissed. "It doesn't concern you."

"It concerns me plenty. I want you to leave her alone."

Steadman took a step forward. "I don't give a flying leap what you want."

He swung a fist up fast and hard into Junior's gut, sending the man staggering backward, a look of pure fury suffusing his face.

Steadman knew he'd knocked the breath out of him, and that suited him just fine. He wanted the last word.

"Get lost," he said, "and if you're smart, you'll stay that way."

He left Eddie bent forward in a prolonged gasp and took his own advice, getting lost among the cars until he could work his way back to the command post, unseen.

CHAPTER 52

JAMIESON'S SCREAM, HUMMING AT high volume through the wire, sent Frost into full-blown protection mode. He'd been halfway out the door of the van before Rafferty caught him by the back of his jacket and hauled him back in.

"Hold on, lover boy," Rafferty said. "Don't go blowing her cover."

"But she needs us," Frost insisted, scrabbling once again at the door handle.

"No, I don't think so."

Rafferty pulled the toothpick from between his teeth and surveyed the splintered end. "That scream sounded like anger, not fear, and I'm guessing it was pure theater. Get your ears on and listen, kid."

Frost took a deep breath and replaced the headphones he'd thrown to the floor. His heart was rushing blood through his eardrums so he could hardly hear, but after a few seconds, he realized Rafferty was correct.

He listened to the argument between Steadman and Jamieson and began to get an inkling about what they were up to. He heard the chief's gruff parting line, and a moment later the monitor picked him up exiting the club.

"Why's he just standing there?" Frost asked.

"Wait and see," Rafferty replied.

236

Frost felt cold. The sweat that had sprung up on his brow at Jamieson's scream had cooled into a clammy film. He swiped at it with a jacket sleeve and watched Steadman stare up into the sky.

The door to the club opened and Frost watched the scene play out like a silent movie, marveling at the chief's restraint. By all rights, he should have pounded Eddie Lizardo into the blacktop pavement for what he'd done to his family.

Instead, he let the punk knock him across the head and limited himself to one answering slug, playing the part to perfection.

"Yes!" Rafferty said, pumping his fist in the air for victory. "The fish is on the hook."

"How do you know?"

"This is a game not far different from poker. The chief just put the creep on tilt. He's got to save face now, and he won't be using all his brain cells to make decisions."

The door of the van rolled open, and Steadman climbed inside, his mouth curled in a tiny grin of satisfaction. Rafferty clapped a big hand over the chief's shoulder and gave him a squeeze.

"I taught you well, grasshopper."

Steadman gave a respectful bow, palms together like a kid at the dojo.

"Grasshopper?" Frost questioned.

Rafferty tossed him a smirk. "Before your time, kid. Now, pay attention. I don't know what happens next, but it'll be good."

"I got him pegged as loose-aggressive," Steadman said. "You agree?"

"Hell yes," Rafferty replied. "He's a maniac."

Frost rolled his eyes. "Can you guys just speak English? That's more poker talk, am I right?"

"That you are," Rafferty said, the toothpick jumping up and down with every word he spoke. "I'll give you this for free, kid. The loose-aggressive player is tough to read. They use their chips as weapons and apply constant pressure on their opponents. They like to bluff, and they're good at it."

"You called him a maniac. Is that good or bad? For us, I mean?"

"Well," said Rafferty, pulling out the toothpick for an inspection. "It's a bit of both. It makes him unpredictable, but it also means he'll overplay his hand. You can always come out ahead in the long run with a maniac."

Steadman snorted. "It's the short run I'm worried about," he said.

"Amen," Rafferty agreed, replacing the toothpick. "But you got him riled. He's acting on emotion now. He'll do whatever he thinks is necessary to save our damsel in distress and restore the dent in his masculinity."

Frost felt like a school of minnows swam in his stomach. He was queasy with nerves. Had his father ever felt like this, torn between the desire to retreat and the compulsion to press on?

The backdrop of noise through the headphones was like a nightmarish soundtrack, accenting the feeling of unreality that shimmered over him like fog in the night.

And then Jamieson's voice sharpened, cutting through the fog like a lighthouse beam.

"Forget it, Eddie," she said. "Trust me, you don't want to know."

"But I do, sweetheart. I do want to know, and I'll bet I can help."

The background noise was quieter now, and Frost figured they'd moved out onto one of the club's patios. Jamieson's voice changed too, taking on a softer, more vulnerable quality, and Frost suddenly knew this wasn't her first crack at undercover work.

"Manny and I had a business arrangement," she said, "and I screwed up. He's coming after me if I don't get this fixed. I have two days."

"Okay then, sweetheart. Let's fix it. What do you need?"

"Come on, Eddie. We just met. I don't know you, and I don't trust you."

"Ah, but you can. I promise."

The pause lasted long enough for Frost to suspect a kiss had passed between them. The muscles in his neck were so tight they felt as if they might snap. He forced himself to relax. Jamieson was a pro, and she had things well in hand.

"Fill me in," the junior Lizardo said. "I know people in this town. Chances are, I can solve your problem."

"In exchange for what, Eddie?"

"Tell me what you're into, and I'm sure we can make a mutually beneficial arrangement."

The pause was longer this time.

Frost pressed his fists against his thighs and concentrated on breathing. When Jamieson spoke again, her words carried overtones of both resignation and hope.

"I brokered a deal," she said. "I had it all set up and my supplier left me hanging. Now I've got two days to find a new guy."

"You say deal. What kind of merchandise are we talking about?"

"Pineapples," Jamieson responded, a note of anger back in her voice. "You know, forget it, Eddie."

"Wait up, sweetheart. You still don't trust me, but you should. You need to. I can set you up fast, but you have to trust me."

"Coke, Eddie." She fired the words at him. "I'm talking blow. Can you handle it?"

"Oh baby, are you talking to the right man! I knew we were made for each other."

Frost suffered through another disturbing break in the discussion and then Eddie said, "I got you covered, babe."

"I need something in two days."

"I can hook you up now. Right now."

His voice was oily smooth and full of seduction. It made Frost sick to hear it and he swallowed the bitter taste that rose in his throat.

"The fish is wriggling on the line," Rafferty said, blue light from the monitor reflecting off his rapt expression.

"Now all she's got to do is set the hook," Steadman agreed.

Frost hoped she'd make it hurt. He tuned back into what Jamieson was saying.

"...You're putting me on."

"Not at all. Call your guy. Let's do this."

"Come on, Eddie. What are the chances? You're blowing smoke, trying to impress me. I'd have to see the stuff to believe it."

"Sure. We can do that," Eddie replied. "But I'll have to put a blindfold on you."

"What happened to all your big talk about trust?"

"I trust you. It's not an issue of trust. Let's call it company policy. Let me show you what I've got."

"Do you make all your customers wear a blindfold?"

"No, but none of my customers are as demanding as you. Or as beautiful. You'll be the first one I ever took home to papa."

"Ah, Eddie," Jamieson cooed, "that's sweet. I'll agree to the blindfold, but I draw the line at whips and chains."

"No problem. I was saving those anyway for that jerk you brokered the deal with."

"You mean Manny?"

"Yeah, Manny. He never should have treated you like that, sweetheart. I've got a thing or two to say to the guy next time we meet."

CHAPTER 53

STEADMAN DROVE THE VAN, weaving between the sporadic late-night traffic, staying well back to avoid notice as he followed Rafferty's directions.

The air inside the vehicle smelled stale, the humidity of it clinging to his skin like oil. He longed to open a window but wanted to make sure he could hear every word of Jamieson's exchange with Eddie, and he was afraid the breeze might interfere.

His stomach coiled in a tight knot, and he gritted his teeth, then caught himself at it and tried to relax. The plan was working.

Jamieson knew how to conduct her end of it and get out. He and the others were prepared to execute their part. It was all going according to schedule.

He loosened his death grip on the steering wheel and concentrated on staying under the speed limit.

Jamieson's voice piped up over the wire and Steadman perked his ears to hear the conversation from the bugged convertible, knowing she was speaking as much to them as she was to the man beside her.

"You're quite adept at tying on a blindfold, Eddie. I can't see a thing. Where'd you get it, anyway? Carry one in your back pocket?"

"Come now, sweetheart. Allow me to maintain my air of mystique. If I divulge all my little secrets, how will I keep you coming back?"

"Personal charm, Eddie. You've got plenty of that."

Steadman grimaced at the thug's self-satisfied laugh but had to hand it to Jamieson—she knew what she was doing.

Rafferty instructed him to make a left turn at the next light. He activated his turn signal, wondering how close they were to their destination. Blocks of warehouses sprouted on either side of the van, a virtual maze of commerce, some active, others defunct and deserted.

"Pull over," Rafferty said. "The dot on the screen has stopped moving and we don't want to get too close."

"Where are they?" Frost asked.

"Looks like a row of abandoned warehouses," Rafferty answered.

Jamieson came back over the wire. "Are we there yet?" she said, pitching her voice high, like a child's.

"We have arrived," Eddie told her. "Uh-uh, no peeking. Just take my hand and I'll walk you in. Don't worry—I'll be the perfect gentleman."

"Ha!" Frost snorted. Even in the van's darkened interior, Steadman saw the angry flush that stained his partner's face.

They listened as the junior Lizardo apparently led Jamieson from the car. The sudden sound of a metal door rolling up on rusty hinges burst into the transmission, making Steadman jump.

He wondered if the jerk had engineered it that way to get a reaction out of the blinded Jamieson, hoping she'd jump into his arms like a date at a scary movie.

They listened as the noisy door came down again and half a minute passed in silence before Eddie spoke. "Here we are. Let the scales fall from your eyes."

"Wow," Jamieson said. "Oh—just wow, Eddie. You *weren't* kidding. What—? How—?" she spluttered, showing the proper degree of awe. And then, "I hope you've got tight security on this place."

"We've got cameras, a sophisticated alarm system, and two guards who walk the property. I could have introduced you to Tonio, but you were wearing a blindfold and it seemed a little awkward, so I left him to his appointed rounds."

"I have to say, I'm impressed, Eddie."

"Not bad for a family business, huh? Me and pops."

"And he won't mind that you brought me here?"

Steadman imagined the thug bridling under Jamieson's innocent, well-crafted question.

"Of course not. I'm a full partner. I can conduct business as I see fit."

"In that case, I'll give Manny a call."

More talk interspersed with moments of silence passed between them before Steadman heard the metal door go up again.

"Oops!" said Eddie. "Almost forgot the blindfold. Sorry, sweetheart, but it's got to go back on."

"Whatever you say. You're running this show, Eddie."

The sound of the convertible starting and peeling out with a showboating squeal served as Steadman's cue. "All right," he said, "get your heads down. They're about to pass."

The car drove by, the sound of its motor dissipating into the night. Steadman started the van and drove the two blocks to the warehouse, letting the vehicle roll to a stop where Tonio wouldn't find it out of place. Rafferty appeared between the two front bucket seats and handed both he and Frost a pair of binoculars before raising his own.

"Well, what do you think?" Rafferty asked. "We ready to go with this?"

Steadman surveyed the block of shabby, decrepit warehouses, glimpsing a passing form that must have been Tonio. He thought about what they planned to do.

Lowering the binoculars, he said, "No. It doesn't feel right. We burn this place down, someone could get hurt, and it opens up an arson case. Besides, it would cripple the family business, but might not be enough to shut them down for good. I think we can do more."

He paused, his thoughts going to Nan and Hank, picturing their faces, so dear to him.

And Thad's.

"I think we can do better," he finished.

"So, what are you saying, boss? What do we do now?" Frost asked.

Steadman lifted the glasses and took another look, paying closer attention to the metal door and the surrounding buildings.

"Give me a minute," he said. "I'm working on Plan B."

CHAPTER 54

FROST STRETCHED OUT ON the couch.

It was a little too short to accommodate his entire length, so he let his feet hang over the edge, flexing and relaxing his toes in a lazy rhythm. The hideous orange and yellow plaid fabric of the couch was rough and scratchy against the backs of his bare arms as he lay slightly propped so he could watch Jamieson working in the kitchen.

The sight of her stirring something in a pan while the soft autumn light from the window over the sink outlined her appealing figure felt a lot like a dream to him. But the cheap hotel with kitchenette they'd rented was less than idyllic.

Peeling linoleum stretched side by side with a thin, obnoxious carpet, forming the shabby floor, scraped and scarred by the passing feet of a thousand former guests. Heat escaped the baseboard ducts only to die an early death in the chill of the room and the stale ghosts of too many bygone cigarettes scented the rust-colored curtains in a way that made Frost wrinkle his nose every third breath or so.

And yet, beauty stood before him, swaying in front of the stove, a soft, tuneful humming floating back to him from her exquisite lips. How could he complain?

He watched her move, emptying a bowlful of flour into the pan, her triceps tightening as she beat the mixture. The smell of it wafted into the air, hitting him like a brick.

"What are you cooking?" he cried, before he thought better of it. "It smells awful."

She turned from the stove, lifting the pan and switching off the burner, a huge smile spreading over her face.

"Doesn't it though? Time to get up, Frost—it's just about ready."

Frost rolled off the couch and approached the pan like a wary dog, coming at it sideways, trying to avoid full visual contact. Jamieson laid a towel on the counter and placed the pan on top.

"My mama used to make this all the time when we were kids," she said. "It's a favorite recipe."

Frost didn't know what to say. The last thing he wanted to do was offend her, but the next-to-last thing he wanted to do was eat whatever was in that pan.

"Spoons are in the drawer next to the sink," Jamieson said. "Grab one and get over here."

Spoon in hand, he at last came face to face with the mixture and saw that it looked as bad as it smelled, a pasty, colorless, dough-like lump.

"Do we have any sugar?" he asked. "Maybe a bit of butter?"

She scowled. "No, that would ruin it. It's perfect just like Mama made it."

She paused, her eyebrows going up, a look of astonishment crossing her lovely features before they crinkled and she dissolved into helpless laughter.

Frost watched her double over, clutching her stomach, tears pouring from her mink-brown eyes, and felt like a fool. Clearly he'd done something to send her into such a fit but he couldn't make the connection and didn't know how to respond.

At last, she pulled herself upright and pressed her lips together, stifling further merriment, her eyes still brimming wet. She opened her mouth but ended up clamping down on another burst of laughter, and yet another, before she was able to utter a coherent sentence.

"Good gracious, Frost—you thought we were going to eat it, didn't you?"

Relief overcame his embarrassment. He let out a pent-up breath and grinned. "We're not?"

She clapped a hand over her lips and shook her head.

"Heavens, no! Mama made sure the stuff tasted awful, so we'd keep it out of our mouths. It's play dough, Frost."

Sudden comprehension dawned, and he remembered Steadman turning Jamieson aside to discuss certain details while he and Rafferty had addressed other parts of the plan. Now it made sense.

He understood what they'd be doing with the play dough, but he had another question, something that'd been plaguing him since the day they met.

"What now, Frost?" Jamieson asked. "You're looking at me funny."

He had to know. "I assume your name's not Anita," he said. "What *is* your real name, Jamieson? Your given name. If you don't mind my asking."

Her eyelids dropped shut, sweeping her lashes across her cheeks in a way that made his stomach flutter. And then her eyes were on him, open and sincere, the corners of her mouth turned up in a tiny, gentle smile.

"It's nice to meet you, Detective Frost," she said, holding out a hand for him to shake. "My name is Lily."

He took her hand, his fingers curling around hers in a perfect fit. "Delighted to meet you, Lily. I'm Cory."

They stood like that, hand in hand, the smell of slightly scorched flour lingering between them, and Frost found himself reluctant to let go.

Before he could act on any other ideas he might have had, the cheap wooden door to the room burst open and Chief and Rafferty spilled inside, their arms laden with bags from the local big-box hardware store.

"Well," Steadman said, eyeing the two of them, "don't just stand there. Help us with these bags. We've got a bomb to make."

CHAPTER 55

ONCE MORE, STEADMAN WAS behind the wheel of the van, steering toward the warehouse district and certain danger. His gut clenched into a tight knot as he thought about the letter he'd written to Vivi that afternoon.

In case things didn't go well.

The faint smell of motor oil and hot electrical equipment hung in the atmosphere, and he adjusted the vent, letting the cool night air flow over him, calming and bracing all at once. He sucked on a peppermint. Jamieson had claimed it might settle his roiling stomach, but so far all it had done was freshen his breath.

At least there was that.

He drove slowly, careful to obey every traffic convention, giving no cause for anyone to notice the van, hoping to set up a pattern of successful execution for the evening's program. He went over the plan again in his mind, trying to account for every contingency that reared its ugly head, wanting to assure himself all the pieces were in place, or soon would be.

He'd made a lot of arrangements earlier that day, setting a lot of balls in motion. Now it was time to see how it all played out.

They'd done a nice job on the bomb, adding a slight tint to Jamieson's play dough and molding it into bars, encasing them in shrink-wrap which they'd tightened with a blow dryer to a passable facsimile of C4 explosive.

He'd removed the guts of a large flashlight and used the battery compartment, complete with four D cells and a simple kitchen timer to fashion the bomb's "control center."

After attaching wires of various lengths and colors, the thing looked damn scary and since bombs came in all kinds of configurations, chances were good the Lizardos would move fast to act in their own interests when they saw it, saving questions for later.

Rafferty continued to monitor Eddie's convertible, but nothing of note occurred beyond an argument between father and son regarding payment for a shipment they'd just received. The father's manner was domineering, making it clear he considered his son more a subordinate than an equal partner in their illicit family business.

Steadman wondered if Junior had even scraped up the nerve to speak with his father about the deal he was cooking up with Anita. If not, pops would soon get a double slap in the face.

Steadman looked in the rearview. Rafferty, his face radiating blue light, toothpick clamped between his teeth, was bent with rapt attention over the bank of equipment, lost in a haze of intelligence-gathering furor.

The widower, now bereaved of his only brother, had needed something to lose himself in. Steadman only hoped he'd somehow find meaning and solace in this whole crazy process. It would make him feel a hell of a lot better to claim some constructive benefit out of this venture for his friend and mentor.

His gaze moved to Jamieson. She was extraordinarily lovely, but it was her verve and shrewdness that amazed him most about her.

The list of her talents was long and varied and he couldn't ask for a lieutenant more suited to the challenges of the situation. She'd handled every curveball pitched their way with courage and aplomb, and he was more grateful than he could say that she'd jumped on his tentative invitation to take part in this scheme.

And in the seat next to him, Frost—his partner.

Hardly more than a month ago, the detective had been green as a willow in spring, and Steadman had harbored a few doubts about his usefulness in difficult circumstances. Those doubts were gone, washed away like the chewed-up road that had almost swallowed his brand-new partner.

He remembered the ache of fear that had suffused him as the doomed SUV groaned and bucked, threatening to cradle Frost to a watery grave.

He remembered the look in Frost's eyes, scared but shot through with sparks of courage and—ultimately—determination as he lunged forward and caught hold of Steadman's hand.

He remembered sprawling back on the broken road, breathless after the near-death experience, staring up into the sky at a scattering of distant stars and listening to the panting breath of his partner.

We're alive.

That's what he'd been thinking, reveling in the knowledge. We're alive, and whole. In time, we'll get up and keep on moving.

They'd survived everything Mt. Rainier had dished out, and the ash was blowing off, allowing Steadman clear vision, giving him hope.

He had his team with him now. As he drove into the night, toward real and certain danger, he sent up a prayer, reaching for and finding his faith. When this night was over, God willing, each member of his team would be alive and whole, able to get up and keep on moving.

He dipped his head in a little bow and whispered.

Amen.

Chapter 56

The engine was still hot.

Frost heard it tick as it cooled down, tiny noises in the still of the night, yet the ticking ratcheted up the tension he was feeling, making him more aware of his breathing and the tightness in his chest. He struggled to keep a rein on his nerves.

Fitting the headphones over his ears, he adjusted the equipment like he'd seen Rafferty do, so that the phone call would be recorded and all parties could hear it from their various positions. He and Lily were alone in the van, waiting for the go-ahead signal from Steadman.

Lily sat motionless, her eyes closed. She looked serene, almost asleep, but Frost knew better. She was preparing herself for the role she was about to play, probably running the scenario through her head, making it real.

He longed to reach out a hand, touch her velvet cheek, so smooth in the light of a streetlamp, but restrained the impulse. Now was not the time to explore the parameters of their budding relationship.

She leaned forward, opening her eyes and pulling the pins from her hair, letting it cascade down over her shoulders in dark, glossy waves, releasing the floral scent of shampoo.

Frost breathed it in, an exotic smell that evoked images of jungle flowers. She smiled at him but said nothing, tossing the hairpins into her open purse and curling her feet beneath her, waiting.

The text message came through on Frost's phone. "It's time," he said.

Lily took a deep breath and shook herself. Frost saw her hands were trembling slightly as she dialed the number into her cell phone and held it to her ear.

"Eddie," she said as the call was picked up. "Eddie, is that you?"

Her voice quavered, sounding small and lost, like nothing Frost had ever heard coming out of her mouth.

"It's me, sweetheart. What's wrong?"

Lily put a sob into her next words, and they came out broken, sounding very convincing to Frost's ears. "They got to me, Eddie. I'm sorry. I didn't know what else to do."

"What are you talking about, Anita? Who got to you?"

"Manny's guys. After I left you last night, they jumped me. They know about your family business, Eddie. I think they were using me to get to you. That explains why my original supplier never turned up. There wasn't one. We've been played."

"How could they get to me, Anita? What did you tell them?"

She sobbed harder now, letting fear color her words.

"They beat me up, Eddie. They broke my arm."

A pause while she fought to get control of her rising hysteria. "I had to make them stop, Eddie. They might've killed me."

"What did you tell them," Eddie repeated, his own voice heating with anger.

"They wanted to know where you stockpiled the coke."

"So you told them about the warehouse, is that it?" A raging growl came through over the phone. "There are hundreds of warehouses in the Portland area, Anita. Did you tell them anything that would lead them to mine?"

Lily's sobs subsided into sniffles, and she let the tension build before answering. "I told them about the broken Sinclair sign."

"What?"

"When we were leaving, Eddie. You forgot to put the blindfold back on when you opened the door to leave. I saw the green dinosaur on that high pole, sticking up above the buildings, an old advertisement, and I recognized it as Sinclair. I told them that."

A slew of curses sizzled through the connection and Lily waited until their volume was at a manageable level before she broke in. "You need to get over there, Eddie. You and your dad. Get there before they do."

"Ya think?" Eddie said, and the phone went dead.

Lily held up her hand for a high five and Frost met her palm square, loving the smile that had replaced her sobs.

They both turned to the monitor screen at Frost's position, watching the dot that represented Eddie's convertible. Less than sixty seconds passed before a chime sounded, indicating a change in status.

Frost messaged Steadman's phone.

"Target is on the move."

CHAPTER 57

STEADMAN'S CALF MUSCLE TWITCHED as he crouched beside Rafferty, his eyes trained on Tonio.

Shifting his weight, he eased up on his cramped position, keeping his head down behind a wall of rusty fuel barrels. He hoped the change would stave off a full-fledged charlie horse and cursed his aging muscles. Their increasing unpredictability grieved him, making him feel like an old man before his time.

Adding to his discomfort, was the little roll of flesh that squeezed out from beneath his light-weight Kevlar vest. He didn't use to have that little love handle. He sighed, choosing to ignore the itch and irritation, and concentrated instead on staying in the moment.

His left hand rested against the flaking, iron oxide surface, helping to maintain his balance, while his right hand gripped the Glock, keeping it ready for immediate action. He wasn't a hundred percent sure what his cue would be, but when it came, he intended to meet it full on, all systems go.

The smell of recycled oil was strong here, behind the barrels, and Steadman saw a sheen of it floating like pond scum on a large puddle between where they crouched and Tonio's position. The guard leaned against the peeling paint of the warehouse wall, smoking a cigarette, a dark outline of shadow on shadow, his head making an occasional sweep up and down the alleyway.

A ring tone, faint and familiar, floated on the cool night air. They watched Tonio crush out his cigarette, smashing it under his boot, before lifting the phone to his ear.

"Yeah?" he said.

Steadman looked at Rafferty, meeting his eye, and they nodded to each other. This was it.

"No, Jefe, I'm outside now. I have seen nothing—"

Steadman stepped out from behind the barrel, gun raised, and hurried to Tonio's side, stopping the man mid-sentence. The surprised expression on the guard's face almost made Steadman laugh, but he choked it back, not wanting to let his nerves get the upper hand.

He motioned with the gun and the man wordlessly handed the phone to Rafferty.

"Still there, Jefe?" Rafferty said. "Don't bother to come running. By the time you get here, the merch will be gone."

Rafferty ended the call and slipped the phone into his pocket. He pulled out a zip tie and made a twirling motion with his finger, indicating that Tonio should turn around. The man knew the drill, and in seconds the guard's hands were secured behind his back. Rafferty drew his own weapon and used it to persuade Tonio to join him.

"Let's take a walk, buddy."

Steadman watched Rafferty nudge the guard down the alleyway, taking him out of the picture. He retrieved the package from behind the barrels and made his way to the main entrance where the rusty metal door awaited his ministrations. He placed the phony bomb, connecting wires, making it look good.

Surveying his handiwork, he used a rock to knock out one small pane from a window in the warehouse wall. He ran a long red wire from the bomb through the smashed window, giving the impression there were more explosives inside.

That done, he made a quick phone call. "Everyone in place?" he asked Frost.

"Aye, aye, cap'n," Frost replied. "Ready when you are."

"I don't know if this is something I'll ever be ready for, Frost, but there's no going back now." He paused, swallowing the lump in his throat before it could properly form. "Thank you, partner."

"If this isn't in my job description, Chief, it ought to be. A lot of good will come from this if we can pull it off."

"That's a pretty big 'if,'" Steadman said. He cleared his throat. "Look, Frost, I left a letter for Vivi in the glove compartment of the van. Can you—"

"Let me stop you right there, Chief. Whatever needs to happen with that letter, you can do it yourself." Frost waited one short beat and then changed the subject. "How long do you suppose it will take the Lizardos to show?"

Steadman considered. "It shouldn't be long. I'd love to hear the discussion taking place in the convertible right now. I'll bet Lizardo Senior is going ballistic."

"Sure to be," Frost said. "Heads up, Chief. I hear those squealy wheels."

"Okay, we're on."

Steadman hit the end button and pocketed the phone, retreating into the shadows to await the Lizardos' arrival. Within seconds, the convertible rounded the corner and skidded to a stop, top down, the smell of burnt rubber emanating from beneath, and Steadman saw Abe Lizardo behind the wheel.

Daddy had taken the T-bird away, reclaiming power previously meted out to the son.

The passenger door flew open and junior ran to the warehouse entrance, staring down in dismay at the multi-wired device, numbers ticking down on the timer.

"It's a bomb!" he cried.

Before he could back away, Steadman stepped forward, holding a small remote control above his head, finger pressed against the button.

"Freeze right there," he said. "I've got a dead man's switch. My finger comes off this button, and the bomb detonates."

Eddie stopped moving, caught like a child in a game of "Red Light, Green Light," his hands held stiffly at his sides, one of them holding a gun. Steadman neared the driver's side and addressed himself to the man in the car.

"You got here just in time for the fireworks, Lizardo. This is turning out better than I planned."

"I don't know who you are," Abe Lizardo said, his face a mask of fury, "but you're in a world of hurt. I called the police, and they'll arrive any second."

"The police? I'll excuse your ignorance, Lizardo, since you're a foreigner, but in America the police don't come to protect cocaine importers from rival dealers. You're on your own here."

Lizardo laughed, as if enjoying banter at a party. "You're in for a surprise, stranger. The American police do indeed protect me. They have been protecting me now for quite some time, and they'll protect me again, tonight. They will perform their duty and they will shoot you. The good citizens of Portland will learn about it on the morning news. Another robbery foiled in the warehouse district."

Steadman waved the remote control in his hand. "Is it a robbery they'll hear about, Lizardo, or a raging inferno? I lift my finger and it all goes sky high, including your son. Including you and me, unless we move far enough and fast enough."

Lizardo's face twisted in a grimace of annoyance, but Steadman saw fear flickering in his eyes.

"Perhaps we can come to some kind of arrangement," Lizardo offered. "There's a lot of good product in that warehouse, amigo. Burn it up and no one profits. Deactivate the detonator, and we can work something out."

Steadman laughed, shaking his head. "See, here's something funny, Lizardo. I came here tonight to rip you off. I took out your guard, but when I couldn't get past your security system, I decided to blow your operation to bits, cripple the competition. Portland was my town once, and it'll be my town again."

Sirens sounded in the distance, growing louder, the wails echoing eerily in the concrete canyon formed by the maze of warehouses.

"The bomb is counting down!" Eddie shouted. "We have less than four minutes."

The police arrived, two unmarked SUV's carrying six men. The dirty cops. They stopped at a distance, spilling out onto the pavement, shielded by the car doors, their guns trained on Steadman. The one in charge, a deputy chief in the Portland Police Bureau, raised a bullhorn to his lips.

"Stay where you are and keep your hands where I can see them," he said, the words loud and authoritative.

"Don't shoot!" screamed Eddie. "He's holding a dead man's switch. The bomb's set to go off in three minutes."

"How much merchandise is in the warehouse?" asked the officer with the bullhorn.

"We took in a big shipment two days ago," Abe Lizardo shouted, anger and panic causing his voice to climb in pitch and volume. "The place is packed. There're millions of dollars in there waiting to go up in smoke. Can't you do something?"

"What do you want me to do, Abe? Shoot the man holding the detonator?"

"No! There must be some way to stop the bomb from going off. Your men are trained in these matters. What is the procedure for such a situation?"

"Well, let's see. We have a couple of options, Abe. We could call in a hostage negotiator."

"Do I have one on my payroll?"

"No, Abe. You do not. We might try the bomb squad."

Abe Lizardo made an impatient gesture with his hand. "I do not appreciate your sarcasm," he shouted.

"One minute!" shrieked Eddie, his eyes bulging from their sockets.

The senior Lizardo raked a hand through his greasy hair, oaths and curses flying from his lips.

"Yes, yes! Shoot him," he screamed. "Why not? In less than sixty seconds it won't matter, anyway. Shoot him and let's get out of here."

"Father!" Eddie cried, aghast. His face, lit by the street lamp, was spread with raw pain, glowing with the sweat of panic. "What about me?"

Abe Lizardo looked at his son, his harsh features carved from a cold, hard substance. "You brought this on yourself," he said. Turning to the officer with the bullhorn, he pronounced the death sentence.

"Shoot the man."

Abe Lizardo's foot went down on the gas pedal and the car fishtailed, the tires seeking purchase on the oily pavement. Steadman dropped the remote and dove into the tiny back seat of the convertible as an explosion of guns went off, bullets ripping into the upholstered headrest in front of his face, pinging off metal, gouging through fiberglass. The car shot forward, carrying him away from the firing squad.

As they gained speed, Steadman groped for the Glock, rising slightly so he could point it at Lizardo's head. Before he could speak a word, a bullet hit him in the back, stunning him breathless, sending a shock wave of pain to every nerve ending in his body.

And that's when he noticed the back of Lizardo's head. It was bathed in blood, bits of skin and tissue sticking to strands of hair like lice. As he watched, the driver pitched forward, face to the steering wheel, foot pressed firmly down on the accelerator.

Clearly dead.

Steadman dropped to the floor of the back seat and braced himself, a split second before the car slammed full speed against a brick wall.

CHAPTER 58

His ears were ringing.

That was the first thing Steadman became aware of. The second thing was that something beneath him was digging painfully into his thigh. He tried to move, and that's when the third thing made itself known.

He was trapped.

Sirens wailed in the distance. Their distorted screaming woke the pain center in his brain and streaks of agony shot to his extremities. A strong odor of gasoline laced the air, nauseating him and making him wonder if the next thing on the agenda was an explosion.

He swallowed hard and started praying.

"Chief!"

It was Frost's voice and Steadman felt a surge of gratitude knowing his partner was right there.

"Chief, can you hear me?"

"I hear you, Frost. Can you get me out of here?"

"The ambulance is just arriving now, but it looks like they'll need the jaws of life to pull you out of this mess."

"Or a can opener."

"The fact that you're joking about this tells me you'll be all right, boss. Just hang on. Help is coming."

"Frost," Steadman said, a tiny leap of fear in his chest. "Rafferty and Jamieson—are they okay?"

"More than okay, boss. They're having a great time sorting this out. First, they had to convince the cops—the good guys—that the bomb is a fake. Then they had to explain how so many reporters and camera crews were already on site. The crooked cops tried to sell their own version of the story, but when Gina Jenkins from Channel 3 showed the footage her team captured prior to the shooting, they knew it was over and clammed up. They're not saying another word until their lawyers show up."

"And then they'll try to lay as much of it off on Lizardo as they can," Steadman said. "After all, it looks like he's in no shape to speak up in his own defense."

"Or anyone else's," Frost agreed.

The blat of a helicopter arriving caught Steadman's attention. "Is that a press chopper?" he asked.

"No. Medical helicopter. Nothing but the best for you, Chief."

Steadman swallowed. His throat burned, and it hurt to speak, but there was so much more he wanted to know.

"What happened to Junior?" he croaked.

"He's in custody. He was so happy not to be blown to bits that he succumbed without a fight. Now, though, the daze is wearing off, and he's getting mouthy. He went off like a volcano when Lily blew him a kiss."

Steadman chuckled, but it turned into a cough that hurt his ribs. "Wish I could have seen that," he told Frost.

"It was a thing of beauty, I assure you. Here come the paramedics, Chief. Hang tough."

Steadman wanted to hang tough. He wanted to see the jaws of life pry open his tin can prison. He wanted to see Frost's face when they lifted him out. He wanted to enjoy his helicopter ride above the city.

Instead, he blacked out.

CHAPTER 59

STEADMAN PRESSED THE BUTTON on the remote control, raising his bed into a sitting position.

His lips twisted into a smile at the irony. The last time he'd held his finger against a remote control button it had landed him here, in this hospital bed.

He'd been well and whole, then. Now he had six broken bones, a ruptured spleen, and an assortment of other injuries. He and Hank could be bookends on the shelf of battered lives the Lizardos left behind, but at least their injuries would heal.

Many others had suffered wounds they might never recover from. Drug addiction, police corruption, families torn apart by the ripple effect.

But he, Frost, Rafferty, and Jamieson had heaved a hell of a big rock into the Lizardo pond, sending out new ripples. He liked to think those ripples would override and wipe out some of the harm already done. Once he got out of here, he'd do what he could to make sure that happened.

The institutional odor of hospital food wafted in the air, letting him know lunchtime had arrived and a tray loaded with blase fare was on its way. An enormous arrangement of bronze and yellow mums, still looking fresh after four days, rested on the table beside the bed, and next to the mums sat Nan and Hank. He smiled at their worried faces.

"It's not as bad as it looks, right Hank?"

Hank swallowed, a flush coming up in his cheeks. He had a fair idea how bad it was, and he gripped his wife's hand. "Rand, I'll never be able to thank you enough—"

"Bah," Steadman interrupted. "You did me, and the city of Portland, a favor. Without your involvement, the Lizardos would still be running cocaine up and down the coast. And I—" he broke off, not knowing how to put into words what the whole experience had done for him. "Trust me, Hank. I'm the better for it."

"Or you will be," Nan insisted, "once those ribs mend."

"Amen," Steadman replied, trying to wriggle into a more comfortable position and facing the fact it couldn't be done. Nan rose and leaned over him, pressing her lips to his forehead. When she drew back, her eyes were wet.

"Bless you, little brother."

She clasped his hand and Steadman thought she might have intended to say more, but he knew his sister. She hated getting maudlin. Pressing her lips together, she gave his hand a squeeze before settling back beside her husband.

The door opened, letting in the scent of mystery meat and boiled carrots, along with three new arrivals.

"Dibs on your jello, Steadman," Rafferty said. "I hope you get cherry."

"If it's cherry, you'll have to fight me for it," Steadman replied.

He smiled at his friends, noting the huge box of chocolates Jamieson carried under her arm. "Is that for me, guys? Break it open now so I can ruin my appetite before lunch."

The beautiful girl laughed and hefted the box so Frost could break the seal and remove the cellophane wrapping. She set it on Steadman's lap and everyone leaned over it, perusing the possibilities.

"The square ones are usually caramels," Frost said. "They're the best."

"I've always been partial to squares, myself," said Jamieson, giving Frost a look from beneath her lashes.

Frost blushed, the corners of his mouth twitching in a suppressed smile, making Steadman wonder just how much had passed between the two of them over the last four days.

He had to get out of this bed.

He looked around at the ring of friends circling him, chewing their way through his box of sweets. He thought about what they'd been through together, how much they'd risked for each other, the level of trust they'd invested in one another.

A swell of pride and affection pulsed in his chest, pressing against his broken ribs. There was only one thing that could make this moment any more meaningful to him. He rested back against the pillows, savoring a coconut cream and thinking if she timed it just right, Vivi could walk in that door and complete the picture, adding the missing touch.

But things rarely turn out the way you imagine, and life doesn't usually offer up pitless cherries and perfect endings. Murphy's law is more the norm, and that's okay because it keeps things interesting. You don't always get—

The door handle swiveled, and the solid wood slab moved inward. Steadman waited, holding his breath, to see what was on the other side—Vivi, or lunch. At the sight of his wife's blonde head, Steadman broke into a joyous grin. Vivi stepped forward, his dream fulfilled, and she carried a bucket of fried chicken.

Sometimes, you get the bonus plan.

AUTHOR'S NOTES

Why a paraquel?

Shortly after I began writing , the first book in this setting, I realized I had too many characters with something to say. I felt bad cutting their stories out, but leaving them in would have overburdened the book and taken focus off of Riley's story.

After I finished writing Nocturne, Steadman continued to speak to me, whispering his story into my ear at night when I was trying to sleep or during a conversation with someone when I should have been paying more attention. He demanded to be heard.

This book is the result.

I'm fascinated by point of view—the idea of seeing the events from a different perspective. I had a lot of fun writing this, and I fervently hope you enjoyed reading it.

And if you read *Nocturne* first, I hope you got a kick out of reading the crossover scenes and seeing how these two books dovetail together.

If you haven't read , I hope you are now inspired and excited to get your hands on the book and read the story behind Riley Forte, Nate Quentin, and the serial killer known as the Puget Sound Slasher.

Mt. Rainier

When I sat down to write , the thriller novel from which this story arose, I knew that I needed a particular kind of setting. If you're interested in how I arrived at my decision, I go into some detail on this in the Notes section of that book. Here, I will suffice it to say that the eruption of Mt. Rainier seemed just the ticket for my characters and the situation surrounding their story.

Once I decided on a volcanic disaster to provide the setting I needed, I watched a TV documentary on the History Channel to gather information and get some idea of the scope I was dealing with. It was called Mega Disasters, Season 1, Episode 4, American Volcano.

This was absolutely terrifying to watch, and fascinating at the same time. The scenario it presented of Rainier's potential for damage made my incredible idea seem quite plausible. This is where I first learned about the altered rock on the western flank, weakened by centuries of sluicing in sulfuric acid.

This is where I first learned about lahars, how fast and ferocious they are and the devastation they cause.

I also read *In The Path of Destruction,* by Richard Waitt. The book is a pretty comprehensive coverage of the Mount St. Helens eruption. This is where I first learned of David Johnston and his heroic efforts to warn the public and save lives.

Until I read this book, I had no idea of the political machinations working behind such an event. It made for interesting reading and I was tempted to use more of it in the novel, but didn't want to pull readers in the wrong direction, placing too much focus on a side story, albeit a fascinating one. Riley is the heart of the book.

I visited some fun and informative websites. The United States Geological Survey (USGS) has pages of information about the .

Also, check out the interactive site at USGS, about . It puts you in the role of the geologist who must monitor the volcano and issue warnings to the public based on your observations.

Another good site to visit is .

Mt. Rainier *will* erupt with devastating consequences. It's only a question of how soon.

Everyone who lives in the shadow of an active volcano should be aware of the hazards and prepare for a possible eruption. Visit the sites I mentioned above for more information about volcanic eruptions and spend some time preparing your family for emergencies of any kind.

I've included a few good places to go for information:

The Red Cross   http://www.redcross.org/get-help/prepare-for-emergenci es/be-red-cross-ready

The Epicenter   https://theepicenter.com/blog/preparing-for-emergency/

FEMA   https://www.fema.gov/blog/2015-04-29/everyone-must-be-prep ared-emergencies

USGS Volcano Hazards Program   https://volcanoes.usgs.gov/observatorie s/cvo/prepare.html

The Survival Mom   https://thesurvivalmom.com/

SurvivalBlog   https://survivalblog.com/

And, specific to Mason County, Washington, a couple of emergency management divisions got together and created a guide to cover the hazards most likely to hit the area, with details how to protect your family, home, and neighborhood. You can find the guide at https://mil.wa.gov/asset/5ba420af53ebf

Liberties with Location

While both *Steadman's Blind* and *Nocturne In Ashes* are set in Mason County, Washington, it is a fictional version of the county. I took many liberties with the layout to meet the needs of my story and while residents and visitors will recognize some of the landmarks, they will also realize what I wrote in the books doesn't necessarily match the landscape.

That's one of the perks of writing fiction!

I'll also take this opportunity to reiterate that all the characters, incidents, and dialogue in the book were drawn from my imagination and are not to be construed as real. Any resemblance to actual events or persons, living or dead, is fictionalized or coincidental.

The Chief Redfish Tie-in

Readers who are familiar with my short story, , might have recognized its main character, George Henry, during a brief appearance in Steadman's thoughts as he steered the boat around Squaxin Island.

George, better known as Chief Redfish is an honorary sheriff's deputy in a nearby jurisdiction. He and Steadman have met and perhaps, at some point, they'll work together on a particularly intriguing case that needs solving, somewhere near the Hood Canal.

This goes out to you!

If you're still reading, I'll consider you a bona-fide fan! Thank you so much for your interest in my books and I hope to provide you with more of the kinds of stories you crave.

If you haven't yet joined my readers' group, I hope you'll do so by now. You'll get updates and bonuses, some of which are exclusive and can only be had by joining the group.

Many, many thanks!

Thank you for reading *Steadman's Blind.*

I hope you enjoyed the story, and I invite you to read more Joslyn Chase books. Visit my book page at ParaquelPress.com for more suspense-packed stories, or scan the QR code.

Thanks again, and if you liked *Steadman's Blind,* please consider leaving a review to help other readers find and enjoy it too.

Also, don't forget to sign up and join the growing group of readers who've discovered the thrill of Chase! You'll get *No Rest: 14 Tales of Chilling Suspense,* as well as VIP access to updates and bonuses.

Visit joslynchase.com to get started or simply scan the QR code below.

Get The Ebook

MORE BOOKS BY JOSLYN CHASE

DON'T MISS THE EXPLOSIVE
JOSLYN CHASE THRILLER
NOCTURNE IN ASHES
Available at your favorite bookseller
in eBook and paperback

MORE BOOKS BY JOSLYN CHASE
Steadman's Blind
The Tower
No Rest
What Leads A Man To Murder

For a complete listing, visit Joslyn's Book Page at joslynchase.com

SAMPLE FROM NOCTURNE IN ASHES

PROLOGUE

THE SUMMER HE TURNED thirteen, he took his first life. His first human life.

He'd killed scores of animals. His mother had taught him that.

"We're living off the fat of the land and sometimes that calls for killing," He watched her work over their latest kill, her long hair tangled and dangling, her arms bloodied to the elbow in the belly of the deer.

He'd learned to heed that call.

He gathered what he needed, sharpened the blade, laid everything ready to hand, the small pile of sticks and stones, the strip of cotton fabric. A three-quarter moon peered down through the trees, smoothing a layer of silver over the crisped and browning leaves and waving grasses, gilding the rippled lake. The last of the summer warmth came now in brief snatches, like the kiss of a capricious child. Autumn approached, and with it the familiar melancholy, the stirring ache of loss, after so many years, still sharp.

He felt the mantle heavy upon him, mourned the lonely course he was compelled to follow. So few understood his work. No one alive could appreciate his sacrifice. Was it necessary, what he did? Must he continue?

As he had that first time, in his thirteenth year, he asked the questions. As every time since, he has asked the questions. So many times. And every time, her voice comes back to him in a whisper. Yes.

And so he plods on. He has seen the fruit of his works, his gift to the world. And yet the hunger, the need grows stronger. Always, more is required.

The killer let his gaze and his thoughts wander to the clump of bushes to his right. No sound or movement drew his attention, but he strained his eyes through the blackness and wondered if the slight shape he discerned was real or a product of his hyped-up imagination. He remained still, regulating his breathing and the beat of his heart.

The scrape of metal against metal reached his ears, raising him from his seat against the smooth bark of an aspen. He watched through the low branches, his eyes focusing across the small clearing. The sound was repeated, made by the door of an RV scraping across the ill-fitting steps which extended from it. A figure emerged and lurched down the steps, weaving and muttering as he staggered between the tall birch and pines. Into the silence of the night came the splash of an over-burdened bladder being released, and it was under cover of this noise that the killer moved.

The man in the trees zipped up and dug into the pocket of his grungy, low-slung jeans. He came up with a twist of paper, lighting it, puffing on it while he gazed up at the distant moon. Spread over his bare chest and biceps, a parade of inked figures swayed slightly with the gentle movements of hand to mouth. Cricket song resumed. The night's gentle pulse beat out.

The killer waited, letting the man finish his smoke. He listened as the man sang and repeated an unfamiliar phrase. He sang, revised, and tried again. The man was a songwriter, a guitarist and talented musician. Two nights ago, the killer sat in the twentieth row, enjoying the man and his band in concert. A Tuesday night, in a half-filled auditorium. Rolling Stone had featured an interview with the man in one of last year's issues, but the great band's comeback tour was falling short of expectation.

The man flicked the butt onto the urine-dampened earth and blew one last lungful into the velvet air. The killer nodded, gripping the knife, and stepped forward.

The man stopped singing.

CHAPTER ONE

RILEY STOOD NAKED on the dressing room floor. She fingered the smooth black silkiness of the gown she would wear to cover herself on stage, knowing the very essence of herself would remain exposed, uncoverable by any length of silk. It was what she always felt before a performance and the knowledge exhilarated and terrified her.

She slipped a robe over lace-trimmed undergarments, knotting the cord at her waist, and walked to the battered upright, sitting down on the bench, touching naked fingers to naked keys. In Beethoven, there was no room to hide. Perhaps with Rachmaninoff and Debussy there can be some small degree of dissembling, but the spare lines of the Classical masters demanded the utmost precision and she had always been known for accuracy. Execution, interpretation, emotion—all are exposed under the stage gels at the piano.

For twenty-three months she had rehearsed and prepared, pouring herself into the work. She was ready. Certainly, she was ready.

There was a knock at the door and Helen entered, a sheaf of printed programs in one hand and a spray of roses in the other.

"They're lovely, aren't they?" she said.

"Which? The flowers or the programs?" Riley asked, inspecting the thick, ivory-colored cards that spelled out the evening's fare. This concrete evidence that she was about to go under the spotlight kicked off a rush of epinephrine, bringing the heady mixture of anticipation and dread. Why do I put myself through this? flashed through her mind, followed by the thought, what else is there? Her very soul was made of music. Sharing it was all she knew.

Helen placed the flowers on a corner table, pushing and pulling at the blooms, arranging them to her satisfaction. She was a tiny woman, plump in a way that rounded her features and made her look like a wise, old child. She came to Riley at the piano, dropping beside her on the bench, and squeezed an arm around her.

"You're gonna do great, kid. Jim would be so proud."

Riley nodded. She had no doubts on that score.

Helen patted her leg and switched to business. "Miller Cantwell is in the crowd tonight and I think a rep from Universal. Also Frank Coston and Gabrielle Wilson, so keep your smile pasted on whatever you do. Now get dressed and warm up your fingers. It's time to knock 'em dead."

She waved and left the room, and in that interval before the door shut behind her, Riley heard the bustle of backstage, the faint chatter of the hall filling with people. Her hands were like ice against her skin as she pulled the silk gown over her hips and drew up the zipper on the low-cut back. She took the pins from her long, auburn hair and let it fall loose, filling in the space left bare by the fabric. Running scales at the piano, she numbed out, shook herself, and numbed out again. She tried to remember the initial notes of Chopin's Fantasie Impromptu which opened the program, but came up blank. A jolt of panic speared through her chest and she felt the urge to pull out the sheet music, study, cram, but she knew from experience that the notations would only turn to blurred Chinese characters before her face. Heaven help me, what have I done?

She closed her eyes, exhaling into her hands to warm them, and brought her breathing into a slow, steady rhythm. Her grandfather, Zach Riley, for whom she was named, had been a jazz pianist doing USO shows during WWII. She fastened her thoughts on him playing doggedly through raids and bombings. She thought of the orchestra members on The Titanic who went down with the ship as they played through, lending courage to others. This was the heritage she claimed. She could do this.

She had to do this.

Applause flooded over her as she stood center stage and bowed her acknowledgment to a houseful of half-seen faces. Turning toward the piano, she took the first steps on what was always the longest walk, the distance stretching out and holding all the possibilities of triumph and disaster.

Her back was straight, chin lifted, as she seated herself, arranged her skirts, flexed her fingers, and began.

She struck the first chord, letting it resonate, floating up, drawing the expectant audience, and then the Chopin flowed out, her hands agile and dancing on the keyboard. Her heart pounded, pumping out adrenalin, speeding the tempo, and she pulled back just slightly, a gentle tap on the brake as her fingers raced. The music enveloped her like a flurry of golden butterflies, filling her with a rush of pure excitement. She executed a perfect, rippling chromatic scale, spanning the keyboard and building to a series of crashing chords.

A slight stumble as she crescendoed down the piano, one finger sliding off the slick surface of a polished key. None but the most distinguishing of ears would catch it, but it threw her concentration and she struggled to maintain the rhythm and balance of the piece as she transitioned into the central melody.

Drawing strength from the gentle, lyrical notes, Riley regained her equilibrium, preparing to face the second round of chromatics and thundering chords. She felt a blip of panic as she approached the section, fighting to control the impulse to flee that always hit her when she lost focus. She clenched her jaw, then released it, zeroing her attention on the keyboard choreography.

Her hands flowed up the keys like a wave on the beach and moved back down again, hitting the chords with determination. She navigated the passage without mishap, returning to the tranquility of the melodic line. As the last gentle notes faded, applause surrounded her, and she felt her face grow pink with pleasure and relief. A good opening.

She sat at the bench, breathing in, breathing out, nodding her thanks to the audience. Lifting her hands to the keyboard, ignoring their palsied tremble, she straightened her spine and began the Tchaikovsky Barcarolle. She watched her fingers, almost with wonder, as they produced the tones of heart-rending sadness, feeling the music pulse within her, building through the impassioned midsection before coming back to the opening theme.

The gondola rocked, moonlight rippled, the midway storm raged and she conquered it. Riley was inside the music, constructing the image, living it, swaying and bobbing on the Venetian waters of the picture she played. As the last melancholy notes drifted and diminished, applause burst over Riley and it felt like sunshine.

This was her first concert in over two years and she had designed a short program, without intermission. She floated through the Bach Prelude and Fugue, the Haydn Sonata, and the Scarlatti. Only the Gershwin Preludes now and then the Beethoven.

She tried to push the thought from her mind. It was always at this point, when it seemed she was home free with a near flawless performance, that she tensed up and mistakes loomed like rocks on the shoreline. She focused, instead, on Jim, as she always had. He was her fortress, her rock, her support. He was her family, the father of her child. He was her anchor.

He was gone.

Jim was dead and Tanner, their son, gone with him. But she had practiced through this, prepared for it, playing through the pieces while holding this thought, this harsh fact, in her head. She'd learned to draw strength from it, to make her work a sort of tribute, to hold them with her in the music. But tonight, it wasn't working.

The fall was coming. She felt its approach as the tension in her neck and arms increased. Her mind fumbled, small tremors at first and then increasing in intensity like the buildup to an earthquake. The flight impulse threatened again, and she wrestled it, fighting to keep herself at the piano even while her mind was already fleeing out the door, down the staircase, into the night.

She was furious with herself, felt hot tears on her face and ignored them. She skittered along to the end of the last Gershwin piece, hardly hearing or acknowledging the applause as it rose and petered out.

It was time to finish the program.

Her stomach roiled and the silence stretched and grew, punctuated with short coughs and the rustling of paper. Riley took a deep breath and positioned her shaking hands for the opening chords. They hung there, frozen above the keys for an agonizing eternity.

The blood rushed in her ears and a moan tore from her throat as she jumped up, tipping the piano bench. The swirl of her skirt caught in the adjuster knob and she heard it tear as she ripped free and fled the burning spotlight. The bench fell with an echoing thud, punctuated by the staccato clattering of her heels as she ran from the stage, leaving the shreds of her comeback performance drifting like the tatters of her silk dress.

CHAPTER TWO

"I'M NOT A groupie, I'm his wife."

Detective Nate Quentin eyed the woman who claimed she was married to Coby Waters, bygone rock star and notorious bachelor. He pressed his palm against the air as if activating a giant pause button.

"Phoebe?" He tossed his voice to the fingerprint tech but his gaze never left the witness. "What do you know, Feebs?"

"Married, huh?" The small black woman looked up from where she crouched, rolled her eyes, and considered. "No. I didn't hear anything about a wedding."

Nate folded his hands on the table in front of him, waiting for a response. The woman seated across the scarred board that doubled as eating surface and spare bed in the spacious RV sent a searing look in Phoebe's direction. The bones in her shoulders rose like hackles under the spaghetti-string tank top and a flush spread from her breast up and over her cheekbones. She seemed to be gearing up for an explosion but then the huff went out of her. She shrugged.

"Three and a half weeks ago, in Vegas. We kept it quiet." She paused, the pink-tinted cheeks turning sepia. "We didn't even make it to one month."

Nate leaned back against the bench seat, glancing at his partner, Rick Jimenez, who hovered over the kitchen sink with a notepad, taking down the details.

"I'm sorry," Nate said, holding her gaze. "I am. Will you tell us what happened?"

"I already told. Twice. It's not a moment I want to live over again."

Nate leaned forward. "Mrs. Waters, those other times you told it, that's for the record, well and good. But we," he gestured at Rick and back to himself, "we are the ones who are going to find the guy who did this. You need to be real clear on that and tell us everything."

"Okay, yeah. I get it." She fumbled through a shoulder-bag on the bench beside her, pulled out a pack of menthols and lit up. Nate watched her eyes turn inward as she accessed the part of her brain that housed the terrible memory. She took a long drag.

"We got drunk, you know. We were sleeping it off." Puff and pause. "I woke up feeling like—" She shuddered and blew out a cloud, waving it away. "I brushed my teeth, got in the shower. Pretty soon, Coby comes hammerin' on the door."

"What time was this?" Rick interrupted.

She stared at him. "How do I know? It was the middle of the night. I got no reason to look at a clock that time of day. I had the door locked, you know, and I tell him to find a bush." She hugged herself, blowing out another mouthful of smoke. "I sent him to his death."

Nate shook his head. "Don't shoulder that weight, Mrs. Waters. It's not your fault."

She gave him a bleak look and crushed out the cigarette, wrapping her arms tighter. "I put my wet hair up in a towel and went back to bed. Never saw Coby again until—" Her hands clenched down on her own flesh, talon-like. "I woke up in broad daylight and came out here to the kitchen to put on the coffee. I looked at the clock," she threw Rick a glare, "and it was eleven forty-seven a.m."

Rick's gaze was impassive. "When did you go looking for your husband?"

"After two cups of coffee and three slices of toast. With jam. Let's make it a quarter past noon. I began to wonder what he was up to, so I went looking. Started off in the wrong direction, walked down caravan way." She flung her arm eastward to indicate the sprawl of buses, trucks, and vans that hosted the remainder of the band's entourage.

"I asked around. No one'd seen Coby. I got to talking with some of the girls, never dreaming anything was wrong, and then that chihuahua started sounding off. We thought he might have got himself hurt. You know, stuck in a trap, sprayed by a raccoon, something like that. But he'd found Coby and raised the alarm."

She fell silent. Her eyes raked the tabletop as if searching for something to cover the awful scene inside her mind.

"He was cut bad, right across the neck, and it seemed every last drop of blood in him must have found its way out. The ground was soaked with it. Damn dog was standing in it, yapping his head off. Danny led me away, then, and I didn't see no more."

Nate let a respectful silence pass and then asked, "Why is your trailer separated from the others?"

Her washed-out blue eyes met his with reproach. "It's not a trailer. It's a motorhome. Coby'd kick your butt." She caught her breath and swallowed hard. "He liked to be apart from the crowd. It's a status thing, you know. Heaven knows he got precious little respect any more from the band, but he took what he could get."

"Downed Illusion used to be a pretty big deal and I understand this tour was meant as a comeback. Can you think of any reason someone might have for harming your husband? Were there any disputes among band members, for instance?"

She stared. "You think someone here could have done this?" Her mouth fell open a little as she considered, then snapped shut with her emphatic head shake. "No way. Their arguments were small-time stuff. A punch in the face, maybe. Never this."

Nate's cell phone buzzed with his ex-wife's ringtone. "Thank you, Mrs. Waters. That's all for now." He walked down the rickety metal steps and pressed TALK.

"What's up, Marilyn? I'm at a crime scene so make it quick."

"Quick as I can, but it does involve our daughter's welfare. Forgive me if I take up too much of your time."

"Come on, that's not what I meant."

"Yeah, I know. Sorry. I've got a lot on my plate, too. Can you take Sammi next weekend? I want to head out of town for a few days. I need a break."

"Oh? Who's going with you? You don't like traveling alone."

There was a pause. "Brad is taking me to Vancouver."

"Geez, Marilyn. That guy? He gives me a bad vibe and I don't want him around Sammi."

"Sammi will be with you, I'm hoping."

"For the weekend, sure, but what then?"

"You're being ridiculous. Brad is a nice guy. The first guy I've really liked since I liked you. And does this mean you'll take Sammi?"

Nate sighed. "I would love to have Sammi spend next weekend with me."

"Wonderful! I'll let you go. Bye."

Rick joined him and they sat at a picnic table in the twilight. Lunch and dinner time had come and gone, hours ago and unheeded, and they fell like wolves upon the coffee and sandwiches being passed around.

"Are you thinking it's the same guy they're after in Seattle? We got a serial case?"

Nate chased down a bite with a swig of coffee, wiped his mouth with a paper napkin, and nodded. "That's what I'm thinking. We need to get up to speed on those files. Looks like we've joined the team. Congratulations. First case out and you drew the short straw."

"Hey, I'm happy with it. Go big or go home, right?"

"Sure, but if you foul this up, you'll never be able to wash the stink out of your career. It doesn't even have to be you that falls short. We don't put this guy down, and fast, we're all gonna catch hell, but first case makes or breaks."

"Okay, pressure's on. Let me tell you what I got from the Specials. Hansen found a place in the trees where the guy must have waited. Except, get this, there are two spots. So, did he switch from one to the other, or were there two guys? Hansen's still working it out."

"We'll check the other cases, but I don't remember hearing anything about a second suspect."

"Also, there was a scattering of sticks and stones which might have been arranged like the cairn-type structures found at the other sites. It may have been knocked apart in the struggle, disturbed by animals, who knows? The makings were there, but unorganized."

Nate drummed his fingers on the table to accompany his thought process. "Okay," he said. "Continue."

Rick checked his notes. "Stevens went into the lake, turned up a plastic raincoat weighted with rocks. Shows traces of blood, no fingerprints. Guy wore gloves and probably galoshes. Heck, he'd have to be completely encased to escape that bloodbath. If he likes the water, there's plenty of holes around here where he could've dumped the gear and weapon, but nothing else has turned up."

Nate watched a couple of grid-searchers sign their findings into the evidence log. Karen Boggs glanced up, caught his eye, and walked over. She carried something carefully in her gloved hands. Nate hoped it was something good.

"Hi, boss," she said. "This was outside the perimeter, about a mile from camp, but I snagged it anyway. Figured it wouldn't hurt. Wanna take a look?"

Nate cleared a spot on the table and she opened the large paper bag and used it like a tablecloth, placing the item in question gently on top. It was a dark blue zip-front jacket, sized for a man. One hundred percent polyester, with a tiny red figure playing polo stitched to the left breast. Nate lifted the cuff of the right sleeve, angled it so Rick could see the smears of blood. In the pocket, he found a wrinkled score card with Mountain Vista Golf Course printed at the top and an eighteen-hole score of 93 penciled in at the bottom.

"Not bad." Nate liked to golf but hadn't had time for a round in over three years.

"If you say so." Rick was not a golfer.

"Relevant to our crime?"

"Hmm. Found a mile away, in a direction traveled only by foot. The blood on the sleeve seems too small an amount and in the wrong place if our guy was wearing gloves and a raincoat." Rick tilted his head back and forth. "Ehhh...I'm leaning toward no."

Nate ran a gloved finger down the length of the jacket. "On the other hand, it looks recently dumped and blood is blood. My experience, and my gut, tell me it's important."

"Yeah? Okay," Rick said doubtfully. "Where's Mountain Vista?"

"Hell if I know, but be ready to head out there tomorrow morning."

CHAPTER THREE

TOPPER WORKED IN the dark. Ordinarily, he wouldn't go near the crater of an active volcano at night. Such an expedition, even in full daylight with a helicopter waiting, is fraught with risk. But there was nothing ordinary about these unfolding events and Topper's amazement outweighed his fears. He was riding the edge of this thing. Like David had.

Early in the summer, Mt. Rainier had woken like a fussy baby after a long nap, gassy and petulant. She'd spit up and burped, raged and bawled, and then fallen back into an uneasy sleep. For two months she'd snored away, uttering only an occasional harmless grumble, and Seattle let out its tense-held breath and went about its business.

Topper's business was volcanoes and his harvest of data suggested that Seattle's nonchalance was unwarranted. Geoscientists primarily monitor three predictive factors for volcanic eruption—thrust faults, earthquakes, and tiltmeter readings. When the three factors register critical levels, a warning is issued to the public and safety measures activated.

Last February, Mount Mayon in the Philippines had drawn the gaze of the world. Her thrust fault measurements and tiltmeter readings took drastic turns, but seismic activity remained low and stable. Two out of three tipped the scales, officials issued alerts, and media hyped the story. Cities and communities were evacuated. Citizens put their lives and livelihoods on hold, perched in temporary housing, and watched the mountain puff serene on the placid landscape. Ten days and millions of pesos later, they returned to their homes and commenced recovery efforts from the damage not caused by the volcano.

Such occurrences are the land mines of leadership, and the political and economic fallout is harsh. Scientists may be willing to lay it on the line, but the political figures who hold the reins are more skittish, put in a position where they must weigh the potential for lost lives against the potential for lost dollars. And where the bottom line is lost votes.

At Rainier's first sign of unrest, scientists had deployed an army of "spiders" and other devices able to monitor the mountain's activities remotely and their readings were followed with great concern. But as the weeks passed, public interest waned and only the scientists remained keenly aware of the volcano's activity while Rainier wrapped herself in a blanket of cloud and went back to sleep.

Topper clambered nearer the crater, his snowshoes making a rhythmic shushing sound. The light from his headlamp opened a little vista in the dark, pushing back the shadows which pressed in from all directions. Mt. Rainier appeared to be pulling a Mayon move, but he believed the end of this story would be far more dramatic than the instance in the Philippines.

The west flank of Rainier was primed to blow. For centuries, sulphuric acid had been mixing with rain and snow, seeping through the rock, altering it into a clay-like substance, unstable and susceptible to landslides. The Osceola mudslide, 5600 years ago, had blown away the east side of the mountain, displacing the altered rock and making the west side the weak spot in the next major eruption.

He collected samples of ash and snow, pressing the tube from a solution-filled gas sampling bottle into the vent, taking care to avoid a steam burn. He should have waited until daylight, but he was determined to make his case. His gut told him that Mt. Rainier was poised to erupt and time was short.

He imagined he felt the hair at the back of his neck singe and crackle. He started down the mountain, headed for the panel of tiltmeters and beyond that, the four-mile hike to the snowcat. At the tiltmeters, he paused to log in the readings. The figures were astonishing and he made a note to check the calibration. He stowed the samples and the logbook in his backpack and climbed into the tracked vehicle, maneuvering it forward over the rough terrain, navigable in the dark only because he knew these trails so well.

He worked his way down the mountain until he reached the ranger station, where he parked the snowcat and transferred himself and his collections to his Jeep Wrangler. He started down the road into the lower range of the mountain. As he came into cell phone tower range, his mobile blipped. He pulled it out of his pocket and squinted one eye at the screen, keeping the other eye on the road which became smoother as he neared civilization. Four text messages and three missed calls.

He stopped the Jeep and scrolled through the texts. All were from Candace.

Call me.

Call me, it's important.

Urgent you call now.

Call now or die.

His heartbeat surged as his phone blipped again.

If you value your paycheck, pick up the phone.

Candace was his USGS supervisor at the Seismology lab at The University of Washington, Seattle campus. She was calling from the lab and with this degree of urgency, he bet they'd hit the Trifecta. Thrust faults, check. Tiltmeters, check. If Rainier's seismic activity was on the rise, that could bring attention in all the right places.

Before he could punch the speed dial, Candace's jazzy ringtone blared in the Jeep's interior. He pressed answer and heard the excitement in her voice.

"Get down here now. You gotta see this."

CHAPTER FOUR

THE RISE AND swell of voices in the corridor seemed to Riley like the hum of angry bees. She'd fled to the dressing room, locked the door, and ignored the persistent demands for entry. Her stomach churned and rolled under an enveloping wave of buffeting, suffusing misery. She dreaded looking into any human face and longed for the unreserved championing of a dog. In human eyes, she would encounter disdain, resignation, or worst of all, pity. And before she could face that, she needed to identify her own feelings, understand the mechanism underlying her disaster. The wraith of some destructive force teased at the edges of her mind, refusing to come into focus. She could only return to the conclusion which she, and the world at large, had accepted for the last two years. That Jim and Tanner—beloved husband, treasured son—had been taken from her and that the hole they left is a maw which continues to consume her.

The pain was like stepping on broken glass under a threadbare rug. Riley sensed something sly and furtive, unwilling to be seen and dealt with, an unknown monster crouching in the shadows of her mind.

A banging louder and above the other pounding came at the door now and the theater manager's voice rose above the ruckus in the hallway.

"Mrs. Forte. There's an urgent matter we need to discuss."

He set up a clatter on the thick wooden door and Riley's mind scooped her away, took her back to fourteen years old, when she was a pale, skinny girl in a green one-piece swimsuit. She'd begged her parents to let her go with friends on a rafting trip down the Snake River in Idaho. Such a rare thing. The life of a budding concert pianist yields few such occasions and she remembered how peculiar it felt for her to do things, and eat things, and say things that ordinary teenagers did and ate and said, as if she was dabbling with another species. She'd started the four-day trip with a surge of homesickness, wishing she hadn't come, feeling amputated from her piano. A day and a half later she'd become entranced with these creatures and their strange ways, wishing she could always live among them, like Ariel wishing for legs. A heady passion enveloped her. She was on a bender, drinking in all they had to offer.

She was burned bright red by then, her fair skin beginning to blister at the shoulders from sunburn, no matter how much sunblock she applied. She'd topped her green suit with a tee-shirt as the group had pulled their rafts up onto a sandbank where some of the boys began to scale the rocks, pulling themselves like monkeys up the steep face of a cliff.

"What are they doing?" Riley felt a shiver of apprehension, but her enquiry was met with a sprinkling of assurances.

"We all do it."

"It's fun."

"You'll love it."

"Come on!"

There was an alternate way up which most of the girls took, though it was still a rigorous haul up the rock face and Riley was filled with misgiving. She was vulnerable to injury here, her hands could be damaged. She was literally pushed and pulled to the top amid laughter and chatter, which fell like an alien language on her ears. When she reached the crown of the rocks, she was horrified to see that the boys were jumping off into the river far below and her horror intensified as she realized she was expected to follow.

When her turn came, she stood at the edge of the cliff and stared down into the circle of water, ringed by the boys and girls who had jumped before her. Their thrashing arms and legs had stirred it into a murky pool, opaque and distant. Unthinkably distant. There was no going back. It would be more difficult and dangerous to try climbing down the steep rock than it would be to jump. Yet, jumping seemed an impossible option.

A boy and two girls pushed past her, throwing themselves over the edge, and then Riley was the last one on the clifftop and still she stood, frozen. The cries of encouragement acquired a tinge of impatience, and then outright disgust. They rose up to her like pounding on a door, like persistent knocking, battering her eardrums and her soul. She pushed away the fear and jumped.

Riley threw open the dressing room door and the crowd surged to meet her, to suck her down like murky water. She couldn't breathe, felt the darkness close in. Her eyes searched the bobbing heads in front of her, focused in on one face as it moved through the murk until it reached her.

Teren drew her back into the dressing room and closed the door with a firm snap. The human wave lapped against it, but muted and murmuring now, and over the sound of it rose Helen's voice. Tiny Helen, turning back the tide. She would handle the press and the fans, deal with the manager.

"Thank heaven for good agents," Teren said, hugging her. "Sorry I got here late. I left my conference early, but my flight was delayed. I rushed straight from the airport, quick as I could get here, but I came in just as you were...finishing up."

Riley dropped onto the sofa, too weary to answer. Teren sat beside her, took her hand and squeezed it. The door opened and Miller Cantwell admitted himself. His recording company had sponsored this event and even Helen knew better than to bar him entrance.

"Riley," he shook his head, blowing out an exasperated breath. "What was that?"

Riley rubbed a hand over her face. "I apologize, Miller. I just blanked. I couldn't remember how the Beethoven begins. I just...couldn't do it."

Miller sighed, stuck his hands in his pockets. "I just got the word from Henry. We're pulling our support. I'm sorry, Riley. We really thought you were ready."

Helen entered the room, slamming the door behind her. "Don't be hasty, Miller. The situation is salvageable." She sent him a look that crackled with challenge and took up a position behind Riley, rubbing her shoulders, like a trainer on a prize fighter. "Let's consider. Some attendees wanted their money back. Four or five. That's it. If that's a fair representation of audience satisfaction, it's hardly catastrophic. As for the press, Frank Coston will write a sympathetic story and garner support, make Riley the underdog. Curious concert-goers will queue up for tickets, just to see what she'll do. That novelty will carry us through this crisis and soon Riley will be in top form. You'll see."

She waved down Miller's protest. "Yes, I know. Gabrielle Wilson will shred her to pieces in that rag she writes for. So what? I think the bump in publicity from this will come out in our favor. Riley's a champ." She gave Riley's shoulders a squeeze.

Miller walked to the door, placing a hand on the doorknob.

"For what it's worth, I agree. You're a jewel, Riley." He paused and Riley watched his shoulders slump under his expensive suit. "I'm sorry. The remaining performances are canceled."

He went out the door and Helen swept off after him, her voice raised and cajoling.

Riley sat hunched on the sofa, steeped in misery, wanting the comfort of her own bed and a box of tissues, unable to believe it had ended like this. Concert pianists do not flee the stage. She cowered there, in the crook of Teren's arm, until the voices in the hallway diminished under a pervading silence.

Teren patted her knee and stood up. "I took a shuttle to the airport, so I don't have a car. Can I hitch a ride home?"

Riley felt dull and weighted. She watched him assess her tired droop and felt a rush of gratitude that he'd come. He pulled her to her feet.

"Give me your keys. I'll drive."

CHAPTER FIVE

THE KILLER STRIPPED off his clothes, folding each item into a neat square, stacking them into a tower, with his shoes forming the foundation as a barrier against the dew-dampened earth. The chill of the early morning gripped him, raising gooseflesh as the watery, lemon-yellow sunlight filtered down through the sparse leaves and pine needles, slowing the flow of his blood to a sluggish stream. He raised the bloody strip, letting it flutter in the light breeze. This is the way she'd taught him. By blood and by fire.

He bent to the pile of sticks and stones and began arranging them, each of the three different types of wood laid in a distinctive pattern, the rocks like cornerstones, kindling on top. A small burlap sack yielded a nest of oakum, which he placed close at hand and from a tin box, he removed a cut of char cloth and folded it in half. A gust of wind slewed through the little clearing, making the leaves dance in a flurry of orange and gold, raising an eerie whistle in the thinning branches. The killer shivered and picked up the flint stone.

He'd found this stone in the run-off from the Nisqually and imagined it had spewed from Rainier in some long-ago eruption. It was smooth as glass, except for the sharp edge where it had shattered from the heat or from tossing down the riverbed, and it felt slightly greasy when he rubbed it. He placed the folded char cloth on top of the stone and took up a thin strip of steel, curling it around the knuckles of his right hand. He swung the steel down at a thirty degree angle against the sharp edge of the stone. Again and again he struck steel against stone, working to peel away a tiny sliver, waiting for the spark to catch and ignite the char cloth.

The steel was unresponsive. In the distance, a dog barked. The inhabitants of the earth were waking, moving, swelling every finger and every vein of her. The killer struck harder, working faster. A cold sweat now coated his naked body, chilling him further, gathering in his creases like a distillation of fear. The dog barked again, nearer this time, and accompanied by the faint droning of human voices.

He threw himself face-down on the leaf-strewn earth, digging his hands and toes into the soil, feeling for the pulse. He pressed his moistened nose into the dirt, drew in shallow breaths through his mouth, and prayed. His mind went away, drawn down into the bowels, the warm, sheltering channels of the earth, the primitive instinct for deep cover enveloping him in her protective womb.

When he returned to himself, the filtered sunlight fell with more heat on his bare skin and the woods were as silent as woods can ever be. He scrambled to his feet and took up the flint and steel. It sparked right away, as he knew it would. He transferred the burning char cloth to the oakum and blew gently as smoke curled up from the nest of delicate fibers, catching and growing. He watched the tongue of flame lick and devour, felt his own arousal, the echoing fire within himself.

Soon the altar fire was burning in earnest. The killer held up the banner of blood and began.

IF YOU LIKED THIS SAMPLE,
YOU'LL LOVE THE REST OF THE BOOK.
GET IT NOW AT YOUR FAVORITE BOOKSELLER!

ACKNOWLEDGEMENTS

For Terry, my biggest fan and constant support.

I am grateful to everyone who has cheered me on during the writing of this book. A hearty round of thanks goes out to my readers' group for coming along on my writing adventure. Their support has been a big help and encouragement, and I thank all the faithful and helpful readers on my blog at joslynchase.com and at The Write Practice.

I appreciate the help and guidance I received from so many people. Among them are Chief Ryan Spurling, Chief Deputy of the North Mason Sheriff's Department, Alice Sudlow, editor at The Write Practice and Short Fiction Break, horror writer Sarah Gribble, romance writer Michelle Dalton, my mentors Dean Wesley Smith and Kristine Kathryn Rusch.

Any and all errors and inaccuracies are purely my own and should not be laid at the feet of any of the experts I consulted.

I owe a debt of gratitude to the many readers at The Write Practice who followed the story's progress, offering feedback and moral support.

A special thank you for my crack team of advance readers: Terry Giles, Dulcie Larsen, Priscilla Fleischer, Andrew Stewart, and Carolyn King.

Credit for naming Rico Ferguson's designer jeans company, Scherzo, goes to Carolyn King.

And I'm sending out a massive dose of appreciation to the awesome members of my launch team.

Most of all, I thank my family for putting up with a messy house and slap-dash dinners while giving me the time to make this happen, and for their continuing love and encouragement.

ABOUT THE AUTHOR

Joslyn Chase is a prize-winning author of mysteries and thrillers. Any day where she can send readers to the edge of their seats, chewing their fingernails to the nub and prickling with suspense, is a good day in her book.

Joslyn's story, "Cold Hands, Warm Heart," was chosen by Amor Towles as one of the *Best Mystery Stories of the Year 2023.* Her short stories have appeared in *Alfred Hitchcock's Mystery Magazine, Fiction River Magazine, Mystery, Crime, and Mayhem, Mystery Magazine,* and *Pulphouse Fiction,* among others.

Known for her fast-paced suspense fiction, Joslyn's books are full of surprising twists and delectable turns. You will find her riveting novels most anywhere books are sold.

Her love for travel has led Joslyn to ride camels through the Nubian desert, fend off monkeys on the Rock of Gibraltar, and hike the Bavarian Alps. But she still believes that sometimes the best adventures come in getting the words on the page and in the thrill of reading a great story.

Join the growing group of readers who've discovered the thrill of Chase! Sign up for Joslyn's readers' group and get VIP access to great bonuses—like your free copy of *No Rest: 14 Tales of Chilling Suspense*—as well as updates and first crack at new releases.

Visit joslynchase.com to get started now!

amazon.com/stores/Joslyn-Chase/author/B071S46SHG

bookbub.com/authors/joslyn-chase

goodreads.com/author/show/16850235.Joslyn_Chase

facebook.com/StoryChase

linkedin.com/in/joslynchase/

pinterest.com/joslynchase/

youtube.com/@joslynchase5955/videos

Made in the USA
Las Vegas, NV
16 January 2024

84473842R00184